"What's so funny... keep a smile from his face, enjoying the sound of her laughter.

"You are." She smiled. "With your formality. Although Grandfather used to tell me stories of Grandmother calling him Reverend, even when they were alone."

"And what did he call her?"

"Ducky dearest."

He could just imagine the dowager's response. He grinned at Clarissa. "Hmm…it has possibilities."

The warmth in Samuel's heart shot a grim warning, reminding him that romantic love was not for him. Sure, the dark-haired beauty before him was his wife, but only because she needed to hold on to this home, and he needed to keep his pastorate. He couldn't treat her as if they had a real marriage, a real relationship.

She laughed again. "Let's leave Grandfather's terms of endearment in the past. At home, you may call me Clarissa."

"And please call me Samuel."

Clarissa smiled, settling this issue, if nothing else. Although the arrangement seemed too casual, too intimate, for a wife who would never truly be his wife.

Christina Miller has always lived in the past. Her passion for history began with her grandmother's stories of 1920s rural southern Indiana. When Christina began to write fiction, she believed God was calling her to write what she knew: history. A Bethany College of Missions graduate, pastor's wife and worship leader, Christina lives on the family's farm with her husband of twenty-nine years and Sugar, their talking dog.

Books by Christina Miller

Love Inspired Historical

Counterfeit Courtship
An Inconvenient Marriage

CHRISTINA MILLER

An Inconvenient Marriage

HARLEQUIN® LOVE INSPIRED® HISTORICAL

Recycling programs for this product may not exist in your area.

ISBN-13: 978-1-335-36957-4

An Inconvenient Marriage

This edition published by arrangement with Love Inspired Books.

www.Harlequin.com

Printed in U.S.A.

It is of the Lord's mercies that we are not consumed, because his compassions fail not. They are new every morning: great is thy faithfulness.

—*Lamentations* 3:22–23

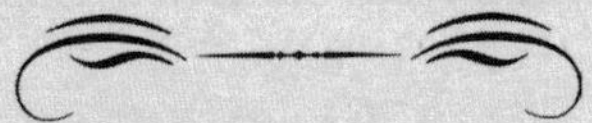

To my grandmothers:

Sweet grandma Ruby Linstrot, whose stories
of long ago made me love the past.

Spunky grandma Violet Kahle, my fun and sassy
inspiration for Grandmother Euphemia.

With thanks to…

The staff at Monmouth,
the setting I chose for Camellia Pointe.
Special thanks to Roosevelt, who served us his
refreshing nonalcoholic mint juleps during our stay.

Steve Laube, my fabulous agent,
for his wise counsel and ever-available listening ear.

Dina Davis, my smart, sweet, talented,
hardworking editor and dear friend.

Jan, my preacher husband,
who cheerfully does life with this writer girl.

Jesus, giver of gifts and fulfiller of dreams.

Chapter One

Natchez, Mississippi
February, 1866

The cry piercing the damp winter air chilled the Reverend Samuel Montgomery's bones even more than the wind blowing up from the Mississippi. He hadn't heard a sound like that since Chickamauga—a cross between a rebel yell and the shriek of an anguished soul.

He raced up the muddy brick walk and toward the ghastly sound, dropping his Bible in his haste. As always, when he'd heard similar screams of agony on the battlefield or in an army hospital, he breathed a hasty prayer for the suffering one. What could have ignited a sound like the strident voice calling through the stucco walls?

"Help me…"

Nearing the white-columned structure, Samuel reached into his frock coat pocket and checked his vial of anointing oil and his portable communion set, issued by the Confederate Army's Chaplain Corps.

His mind sped as fast as his booted feet while he prepared himself to anoint the sick or administer the Lord's

Supper to the dying. Judging from the hair-raising voice, he might be called upon to deliver either sacrament—or both—this windy winter day.

And they were the last tasks he would have expected to perform as he took his first steps into his new church, Christ Church of Natchez.

Samuel crashed through the doorway and crossed the vestibule at a run, the sweet tones of an unfamiliar song grating against his nerves. He snatched off his hat and pitched it toward the nearest corner. As he burst into the chilly, high-ceilinged sanctuary, voices and organ strains blended into a maddening refrain from the choir gathered near the pulpit.

Did none of them understand someone was in trouble? Barreling down the sloped center aisle, he scanned the massive room, from pulpit to vestibule, from balcony to white-paneled box pew doors. No one lay suffering on the carpet. No one sat propped in a pew, gasping for air…

"Help me—"

"Stop the music!" Samuel shouted over the choir and waved his arms to get their attention. "Someone here is ill, or injured or—"

"Who? Someone with you?" In the sudden silence, a dark-haired woman turned from leading the musicians and rushed toward him, her deep green skirts rustling. Perhaps she could help him discover the person in need.

Although stunning with her ivory skin and delicate features, she looked but a mere five or so years older than his Emma—twenty years of age at most.

He turned from her and crossed to the pulpit, then glanced upward. "It was someone inside. I heard it from out on the lawn. Perhaps we should search the balconies."

Her light, fast footfalls followed close behind. "Wait a moment—let's think this through. What did you hear? Was it a man or a woman?"

The compassion in her voice would have moved him under different circumstances. He turned to look into gold-flecked green eyes, sparkling in the light of the overhead gasolier. Those soft, gentle eyes could easily have diverted him from his task—if they belonged to a more mature lady. If he would ever again allow a woman to distract him. And if some poor soul didn't need his help. "A woman is in trouble, and we don't have time to stand around and chat about it. Did you not hear the cries for help? She screamed in agony and—"

The twitters from the sopranos and altos interrupted his words, along with his train of thought.

Had he imagined the sounds? Surely not, but he'd heard of men suffering such maladies after experiencing the terrors of war.

"Father, please..."

His daughter's whisper jarred him back to the present. He turned to Emma, who held his hat and muddy Bible. To his shame, he'd forgotten she was there. Her reddened cheeks cut through him, slicing yet another piece from his heart. Seemed he spent more time embarrassing his fourteen-year-old than he did in any other occupation these days. His daughter stood at a distance, more than arm's length, as she had since he'd fetched her from her Kentucky boarding school two weeks ago.

Until she turned, head bowed, and dashed back toward the vestibule.

Where was she going? Why would she bolt this way in the midst of an emergency?

"Now will you slow down and think?" The woman in green hesitated only a moment and then followed Samuel's daughter down the aisle. Reaching her, she rested her hand on Emma's shoulder and spoke into her ear. Emma immediately broke into a bright smile.

How had the lady won his daughter's affections so quickly when Samuel could hardly coax a word from her?

"That was no scream."

The words broke into his haggard mind like a swarm of cicadas, interrupting his thoughts. He spun toward the sound. That was it—the voice he'd heard earlier. Shrill, piercing, yet with an unmistakable plantation accent—this was the woman in trouble. Samuel searched the choir for eyes pinched with pain, lips drawn in agony.

Instead he saw a feisty-looking antique of a lady, her hazel eyes snapping and her wrinkled lips pursed. "What you heard was my solo, sir."

Solo? The screeching he'd heard had been—singing? "I beg your pardon, ma'am…"

His face must have been as red as Emma's. To insult a woman of her age—it was unthinkable. To do so to a parishioner—intolerable. And in front of other church members—unforgivable.

How had this happened? He'd shepherded hundreds of men during the war, prayed with the sick, comforted the dying. He'd cared for them with the love of a father. But now, in the first moments of his first day at Christ Church, he was failing.

Just as he was failing Emma.

As he scrambled to think of a suitable apology, a man in a stylish suit and ruffled white shirt stepped into the sanctuary. "Chaplain Montgomery."

"Colonel Talbot." He hastened toward his former commander and clasped his hand. If only Samuel had not committed such a blunder, he could have enjoyed reuniting with this friend he'd not seen since Lee's surrender. Instead he leaned in close to whisper. "I fear I've inadvertently insulted a lady in the choir."

"You? I doubt you'd know how."

"Trust me, I did. I know I heard a woman cry for help, but she said she was singing." Samuel chanced a glance at the lady, who stood dignified as a dowager among the sopranos who attempted to hide their smiles behind their hands or sheet music.

The colonel looked in the direction Samuel indicated and then back again. "The lady in black?"

He nodded. "The one who looks like she wants to cane me."

Colonel Talbot covered his mouth with his hand and rubbed his chin, but not before Samuel caught a glimpse of a grin on his face. Even if he hadn't, the man's laughing eyes would have given him away.

"This is not funny, Colonel."

He cleared his throat. "You're right, of course. She used to be a brilliant soprano, but her singing days passed when she left middle age, and no one has the nerve to tell her."

"But I distinctly heard her call for help." *Shriek for help* would have been more accurate, but Samuel held his tongue.

The colonel slowly lowered his hand as if unsure he wouldn't yet give way to an outburst of laughter. "It's a new hymn called 'Help Me Be More Like Jesus.' Since she penned it, we could hardly give the solo to anyone else."

"Hardly." So Samuel had insulted not only the dowager's voice but her composition, as well. This was worse than he'd first thought. "Who is she?"

"Missus Reverend Hezekiah Adams. The founding minister's widow."

No. The woman who'd called him to pastor here. Samuel let out a low groan. Missus Adams was, indeed, a dowager—of the church. He pulled his handkerchief from his pocket and dabbed his brow. "I've gotten myself into a bind. Only you know how much Emma and I need to stay in Natchez—and why."

As they strode toward the choir—and the dowager, the lady in green silently dismissed the singers from the back of the sanctuary, and they trickled out. Emma wiped her little finger under her eyes, no doubt trying to whisk away her tears.

Tears that Samuel had inadvertently caused.

No matter what it would take, he had to keep this pastorate, for Emma's sake. That meant he must win over Missus Adams before she could ship him and Emma back upriver to Vicksburg. Otherwise he could never bring long-overdue happiness to their lives. Happiness they had never yet experienced as a family.

God had led him here, to Natchez, to Christ Church. To a place of new hope, new beginnings. Of this Samuel was sure. Now he had only to convince the dowager.

And by God's grace, he intended to do just that.

Never in Clarissa Adams's nearly twenty-one years had she seen such a commotion in church. Things wouldn't calm down anytime soon, either, judging from the fire blazing in Grandmother Euphemia's eyes.

Nor had she ever seen anyone insult her grandmother, even unintentionally, and escape the dear woman's finely honed sarcasm.

What other new and unexpected thing might happen this day?

"My father's not always like this." The girl set the bowler hat on the nearest pew, drew a handkerchief from her sleeve and dabbed at the mud on the Bible.

With a low laugh, Clarissa leaned in close. "I imagine sometimes he's even worse."

The auburn-haired girl let out a giggle, then she covered her mouth with her hand and lowered her head.

The poor girl. Her distress made Clarissa unsure who she felt more sorry for—her, Grandmother or the dark-haired father.

Studying the girl, Clarissa recognized a subtle air about her, an air she'd herself had at that age. The girl's natural vulnerability and lightheartedness of youth barely peeked through a veneer of stone.

What tragic event had caused such hardness?

Clarissa glanced at the red-rimmed eyes and tear-stained cheeks. The few moments she had wept couldn't account for her appearance. Something or someone had made her cry earlier, that much was certain. Surely the handsome man with the kind eyes hadn't injured his daughter in some way, had he? It seemed unlikely, but Clarissa turned wary eyes to him. Strange men arrived in postwar Natchez every day, seeking a pretty cotton heiress and an easy fortune—or so they thought. They weren't to be trusted.

But who were this father and daughter? And why had they burst in at the end of choir rehearsal?

Clarissa glanced at the cameo timepiece pinned to her shirtwaist. Ten minutes to one. She had little time to find out before meeting her attorney as he'd requested in his terse note of this morning. "I'm sure he didn't mean any harm. Fathers don't realize how they sometimes embarrass their daughters."

"Does your father understand you?"

The pointed edge in the girl's tone brought back memories of Clarissa's own family heartbreak, of the fear that had turned her words sharp as Father boarded a riverboat—alone—for the Yazoo Delta that long-ago February day. Memories of the cold wind blowing up to the bluff as Clarissa waved to a parent who didn't look for her in the crowd. "I think Papa would empathize with me now, if he were here." Instead of a hundred and twenty miles up the Mississippi River.

"My mother went to heaven four years ago. I keep wishing Papa would find a new wife and finally be happy." The girl cast a wistful gaze at her father. "Maybe he'll meet someone here in Natchez. Do you know of a lady he might like?"

"Well, my grandmother is unmarried..." Clarissa pointed toward Grandmother Euphemia in her black widow's weeds.

The girl's giggle made Clarissa smile. Well she knew how a good laugh could make any heartache easier to bear, and equally well she knew the pain of losing a parent. However, although the girl clearly needed a mother, that was a poor reason to wed. Marriages of convenience rarely ended in happiness. "I'm glad you came to town. Please call me Clarissa."

"I'm Emma Montgomery."

Montgomery? Clarissa's gaze fixed on the black-suited man who now approached Grandmother Euphemia, his back straight as a Citadel cadet's. She should have realized this was the Reverend Samuel Montgomery.

She tried and failed to pull her attention from him, although she could feel Grandmother's disapproving glare. This was the famed Fighting Chaplain, the war hero who'd saved his entire platoon from the Yankees? The one who'd traveled the South after the War for Southern Independence, using his newfound, widespread popularity to win converts and change lives in every town he entered?

The man who wielded the sword of the Word as skillfully as he'd brandished his grandfather's sword to conquer his enemy on a Tennessee battlefield?

He certainly seemed more like a dignified pastor than a fierce warrior. And at this moment, he looked downright humble.

As well he should, after what he'd said. Even if he was impossibly handsome and even charming in his embarrassment.

Clarissa touched Emma's arm, urging her up the aisle. As they approached the reverend, Graham Talbot and Grandmother, Emma drew a noisy, halting breath that had to come from her toes. Fearing more tears from her, Clarissa dropped an intentional twinkle into her eye and her smile in the hopes of lightening the mood. "Reverend Montgomery, Grandmother Euphemia and I welcome you to Natchez and to Christ Church."

He opened his mouth as if to reply, but Grandmother cut him off.

"I am capable of introducing myself." Grandmother turned her dark disapproval from Clarissa to the reverend. "You are three days early."

"Yes, he is, and that's good, because Missus Euphemia Geraldine Mathilda Duncan Adams will tolerate a three-days-early arrival. But never four." Clarissa leaned over and gave Grandmother a peck on the cheek to distract this most undemonstrative of ladies. "You've escaped her wrath, Reverend, at least as punctuality is concerned."

Grandmother's wide eyes and Emma's little giggle

made Clarissa laugh. The girl looked lovely when she smiled, until she caught her father's glance and steeled her face.

"I heard your interim pastor was to leave town tonight," the reverend said, "so I wanted to be in the pulpit tomorrow."

"But you are not scheduled until—"

"The reverend did just as Grandfather Hezekiah would have done."

The hard lines in Grandmother's face softened just a bit, as Clarissa had known they would, and she paused. "My Hezekiah would have done that, yes."

Clarissa drew a great breath of relief and caught the tiniest gleam in the reverend's eye as he gave her a nearly imperceptible nod. So he knew she was maneuvering the conversation—and her grandmother. With this man as pastor, she'd have to think things through more than ever.

Grandmother straightened her back in her maddening way that always meant she'd allowed herself to be manipulated long enough. "However—"

"I haven't properly introduced you, Miss Euphemia." Graham Talbot touched her arm. "May I present my friend, former chaplain and my aide-de-camp, the Reverend Samuel—"

"I know full well who he is. He's the image of his late grandfather. I also know you're trying to prevent me from examining this candidate as the deacon board has charged me with doing."

Clarissa resisted the urge to roll her eyes, since it would only make things worse. "But the board sanctioned the Reverend Montgomery's calling weeks ago."

"Contingent on my approval upon his arrival." Grandmother set those steady hazel eyes of hers on the two men and studied them as if trying to make them squirm like schoolboys.

It didn't work. The pastor merely inclined his head, his dark curls shining in the light of the south windows. "I'm pleased to know you made my grandfather's acquaintance."

"My husband spent a bit of time with him of necessity. One can't travel far in the hierarchy of this denomination without encountering people of—all sorts."

"In other words, the Reverend Adams did not entertain Grandfather by choice."

"Precisely."

"And yet the board of Christ Church called me here—surely not without your blessing."

Grandmother leaned heavily on her ivory-handled cane as she bent toward him. "Certainly not."

"Why did you call me then, since you clearly disliked my grandfather, as did the Reverend Adams?"

"That is a topic for another day." And that clearly settled the matter, because Grandmother had decided so. "The more important question is the whereabouts of your wife."

At the sound of a sharp intake of breath, Clarissa turned to Emma. The raw pain in her face had overtaken all traces of her earlier hardness.

"Forgive me." Reverend Montgomery nodded toward Emma. "I neglected to introduce my daughter, Miss Emma Louise Montgomery."

"And this is my granddaughter, Miss Clarissa Euphemia Adams."

"I'm delighted." The parson turned his brown-eyed gaze toward her for an instant, the smile in those eyes telling her he meant it.

"This church endured a great scandal when it called a

young, single man after my husband's passing. The bylaws now state the pastor must be married. And I won't approve your call if you are not." Grandmother tapped her cane on the carpeted floor. She did have a way of shredding any scrap of joy, especially in church. "Your wife, Reverend. Where is she?"

His face paled and he glanced upward, as if seeking divine help. "The truth is, she—"

The vestibule door swung open and banged against the wall with a force that shook the gasolier.

"Stop this meeting!" A vaguely familiar, barrel-chested man took the aisle at a clip, his long, curly salt-and-pepper hair as oversize as his stovepipe hat.

Glaring at him, Grandmother muttered, "Will all of Natchez come dashing into this church today, demanding we stop what we're doing?"

"Adams, if you cannot slow down and act civilly inside the church, you can find another attorney." Uncle Joseph Duncan followed at a pace more sedate but still lively for a man of his advancing age. He smoothed his famed white moustache, his old-fashioned top hat in his hand. "And take off that outlandish hat in the house of the Lord. Even for a stovepipe, it's ridiculous."

Grandmother's gaze hardened as she took a step toward the man who'd ignored Joseph and left his giant hat on his round head. "Absalom Adams."

Cousin Absalom. Of a sudden, a fog of confusion settled over Clarissa's mind. Absalom had died in the Battle of Lookout Mountain…

"I heard the rumor about my death," he said. "I see you did too."

"I also heard Joseph tell you to show respect in this church." Grandmother Euphemia lifted her cane and swung it at Absalom's hat, knocking the monstrosity to the floor.

"What do you think you're doing? This is a thirty-dollar hat." Absalom let out a string of curses that should have brought the roof down on his now-uncovered head.

At the sound of the man's foul mouth, Reverend Montgomery stepped toward him until he stood inches from Absalom's face. "Another such word and I'll escort you out."

The low growl of the reverend's voice must have instilled some well-deserved fear into her cousin, judging from his wide eyes. "Who are you?" he asked, backing away.

The preacher closed the gap again. "I'm the Reverend Samuel Montgomery. I won't tolerate your contempt in my church."

Absalom's face paled. "The Fighting Chaplain?"

The reverend remained silent, quirking one brow, threatening him with his dark glower.

Absalom broke away and retrieved his hat from beside the nearest box pew, muttering about the unfairness of life.

Clarissa shook off the fog and stepped toward her cousin. "What do you want? You caused enough trouble before you went to war. Why did you come back?"

"When you didn't show up for our appointment, we came to you." The hat trembled in Absalom's hand as he moved a good distance from the preacher. "We need to talk about the old man's will. About Camellia Pointe and his tenement down at the landing."

"There's nothing to talk about. He left the Yazoo ground to Father and Grandmother, and Camellia Pointe and Good Shepherd Dining and Lodging to me. And Good Shepherd isn't a tenement—it's a respectable hotel." Clarissa turned from her rogue cousin toward Joseph. Her attorney's downcast gaze shot a jolt of fear through her until she glanced at Grandmother and saw her pallor. Then the jolt grew to a thunderbolt. "Tell him it's true, Uncle Joseph."

At the tremor in her voice, her cousin smiled an oily smile. "I want the Fighting Chaplain here as a witness when you do."

Emma announced she would sit in their carriage and read, leaving the others to start down the long hallway to the pastor's study. Entering it, Grandmother poked her cane at Absalom's ribs. "Why exactly are you not dead?"

"That's harsh, Grandmother, even for you." In the cypress-paneled room, Cousin Absalom pulled a cigar from the pocket of his mulberry-red frock coat and clamped his teeth around it, looking for all the world like a riverboat gambler. Which he could be, for all they knew.

"Considering how you left your entire family for dead during the yellow fever outbreak, I'd say it's a question worth asking." Grandmother rubbed the handle of her cane. "We thought we were finished enduring your treachery."

"I was captured at Lookout Mountain and sent to the Johnson Island prison in Ohio, where they kept Confederate officers," Absalom said around the fat cigar. "I stayed until Lake Erie froze over, then I escaped by walking across the ice to Canada. The Yankees reported me as dead."

He had to be joking. "Cousin Absalom, that's the most fanciful tale I've ever heard."

"You're lying, as always." Fire shot from Grandmother's eyes and she lifted her cane again.

The pastor cleared his throat and picked up his black

Bible from the desk. "In the book of Ephesians, the apostle encourages us to speak the truth in love. I suggest we heed his exhortation and get on with our business, telling the truth and speaking it in love."

Finally—a voice of reason in this emotional chaos. Fighting Chaplain or not, flaming evangelist or not, the new pastor had just silenced both Clarissa's renegade cousin and her indomitable grandmother with one Bible verse. Could he be just what Christ Church needed?

"I agree. Let's get this over with, before I make good on my threat to retire to Saratoga." Joseph set his brown leather portmanteau atop the pastor's walnut desk. "Whatever the circumstances, Absalom is here, and we need to read the alternate will."

How could this mistake have happened, leaving them to think Absalom had gone to his eternal reward—or punishment? Admittedly, Clarissa hadn't grieved overlong for her much-older cousin. But who would, considering how he had disappointed and hurt the family as long as she could remember?

Of course, Clarissa didn't wish him dead, but neither was she elated to see him. To say so would be a lie.

And now perhaps they'd learn Grandmother and Papa no longer possessed the Yazoo Delta plantations, Clarissa didn't own Good Shepherd Dining and Lodging—and her beloved Camellia Pointe…

After this meeting, everything would change. If Absalom wasn't mentioned in Grandfather's will, Joseph would merely have informed him that he'd receive nothing but the wind blowing through Camellia Pointe, and Absalom would have gone his way.

But he hadn't. Instead he stood there like a pudgy, arrogant crown prince, waiting to become heir to his kingdom.

Suddenly eager to hear the worst so she could think through her options, Clarissa took a seat beside Grandmother on the wine-colored settee near the window. Cousin Absalom pulled the fireside wing chair into the center of the room and plopped all his plumpness into it. Between them, the reverend stood alert, eyes narrowed, as if hoping Absalom would make a wrong move so he'd have the pleasure of throwing him out.

Joseph sat at the desk and removed stacks of papers from his portmanteau. "Because we had word of Mister Adams's demise—"

"That's Major Adams." Absalom puffed out his chest, making himself look even more pompous. "I was the most highly regarded officer under General Bragg's command."

Grandmother huffed at the outright lie, but Joseph didn't bother to look up from the paper in his hand. "Mister Adams was reported as killed in action. Therefore, I divided the Reverend Adams's assets according to his wishes. However, since Mister Adams is obviously alive, we will now revisit the terms of the will."

Clarissa folded her arms over the tremor in her middle. She glanced at Grandmother, whose flinty expression hid whatever emotions ran through her at the news.

But her fingers visibly tightened on her ivory-handled cane.

Grandmother Euphemia—nervous? Nothing could have frightened Clarissa more.

Joseph stood, proud and sturdy as a live oak, his gaze fastened on the page in his hand. "This is the will I was to read in the event that both his grandchildren were alive at the time of his demise. Euphemia, Clarissa, it's quite different from the will I read when we thought Mister Adams was deceased."

For the first few moments Clarissa struggled to focus on Joseph's words, her mind drifting to Camellia Pointe and the happy days her family had enjoyed there—before the sickness. But when he spoke Grandmother's name, Clarissa fixed her attention on the elderly man.

"'To my wife, Euphemia Duncan Adams, I bequeath Waverly Hall in Yazoo County, its 2600 acres, cotton and crops.'"

A bit of tension left Clarissa's abdomen at the little chortle of victory escaping Grandmother's lips.

Joseph paused and turned a fatherly gaze on Clarissa. "This part has changed, dear. 'To my granddaughter, Clarissa Euphemia Adams, I bequeath the contents of all structures and grounds at Camellia Pointe.'"

Only the contents? That unease hit her in the middle again.

"'To my son, Barnabas Hezekiah Adams, I bequeath Sutton House Plantation in Yazoo County, its 1900 acres, cotton and crops. My other two properties, however, have deep personal meaning to me. Camellia Pointe is the home of my youth, the refuge my father built against the cares of this world. Good Shepherd Dining and Lodging is the safe haven I built to shelter and protect poor travelers landing in Natchez-under-the-Hill. One of my grandchildren will receive both these properties and continue their operation. However, the one to inherit must prove himself worthy.'"

What outlandish will was this?

All or nothing? If Grandfather wanted to mention Absalom in his will, which in itself was surprising, why would he not have simply given him some property outright?

But he hadn't, and that set her on edge. Could her

rogue cousin somehow prove himself worthy of Grandfather's home and ministry?

Absalom sat straight in his chair and pointed his stubby finger at Clarissa. "She was his favorite, so she'll be the one to inherit. It's not fair. I'm going to contest this will."

"No, you won't," Joseph said, "as you shall soon see."

As Absalom muttered under his breath, the attorney began to read again. "'To receive the inheritance, my grandchildren must meet three conditions. If one of them meets the first condition, he may progress to the second, and so forth. I have given Joseph Duncan four letters to explain the details.'"

"Grandfather always did drag things out. Get to the point, Duncan." Absalom's sonorous voice echoed off the walls of the high-ceilinged room, his expression turning annoyed.

"'Counselor Duncan will give the first letter to the pastor of Christ Church. The pastor will deliver and read the letter privately to each heir. When the first stipulation has been met, the pastor will read the second letter to both parties at once, and likewise the third. If one of my grandchildren contests the will, he forfeits his chance to inherit."

"I know how the old man worked." Absalom's face exploded with the rage Clarissa had come to expect from him. Rage he'd frequently aimed at her beloved grandfather. "He made her stipulations easier than mine. I know he did."

"I've seen the letters, and that's not true." Joseph handed two envelopes to Reverend Montgomery. "Euphemia, let's allow Clarissa and the reverend to meet here, and you, Adams and I will wait in the sanctuary."

When the door had closed behind them, Clarissa sat

across the desk from the preacher, her pulse beating out her dread. “Please read it quickly. I fear the worst, and I have no idea how bad the worst could be.”

The parson reached into his inner frock coat pocket and retrieved a pair of rectangle-lens eyeglasses. When he had slipped them on, he opened the envelope, pulled out the single sheet and scanned it. “A personal note appears as page one. ‘My dear Clarissa, my first instruction may well be your hardest to fulfill. Please try to understand and trust my reasoning. As always, I hold your best interests at heart. Grandfather Hezekiah.’

“Next, we have the legal document. ‘Both potential heirs must be married before my granddaughter’s next birthday.’”

Married—

She might as well give up right now.

Except she couldn’t, because then she would also give up Camellia Pointe and Good Shepherd—her ancestral home and her grandfather’s legacy.

Samuel whisked off his specs and regarded her for a moment. “Forgive me, Miss Adams, but have you a beau? Because if you haven’t, you need to get one—soon.”

A beau. A husband.

In less than a month.

Even though Grandfather had known that falling in love would mean that, sooner or later, she would get hurt.

Chapter Two

Sitting across the desk from Samuel, Miss Adams looked as if she wanted to turn and run at his words. The defiance in her face mirrored the expression he'd often seen in his daughter's—and his late wife, Veronica's—whenever he tried to reason with them. So much so that a part of him wished he could follow Miss Adams right out the heavy cypress vestibule doors. But clearly there was no escape for either of them. Without a wife, Samuel would lose this church—and possibly his daughter. Just as Clarissa would lose her home if she didn't find a husband. And neither of them had the luxury of time.

Then comprehension softened her eyes and they turned dewy, the golden flecks deepening to burnished copper. "Grandfather always did want to marry me off."

Samuel cleared his throat of the sudden lump forming there, the sweetness in her tone affecting him in a way he'd never known. Would she calmly accept the will's terms and fulfill her grandfather's wishes, allowing the late pastor to dictate her life from the grave? Or would she whisk aside her calm resignation and refuse?

"You are, of course, free to reject the will's stipulations. But you won't inherit." Samuel brushed away his foolish sentiment. His job was to present the letter and advise her if necessary, not to become emotionally involved in this odd situation.

But his heart was involved—a full thirty minutes into the ordeal. It wasn't like him. Why would this wisp of a young woman touch his heart so?

Miss Adams drew a deep breath and closed her eyes for an instant, as if in prayer.

And the truth hit him.

She affected him so deeply because her posture, her air of acquiescence in the midst of heartache looked just like a younger Veronica.

Samuel lowered his gaze, removing his glasses. How could he not have seen it? From the day of their betrothal, Veronica had worn the same expression of cool tolerance, of gentle acceptance amid suffering. Much of which Samuel had unintentionally caused.

And now, in order to keep his church, he may be forced into the same kind of marriage again.

The thought settled like lead in his stomach.

If only Missus Adams had told him Christ Church's pastor must be married. He stood and paced to the window. The centuries-old live oak beyond his study stood sturdy, having weathered wind, fire, drought and war. As had Veronica, until—

"Reverend, are you well?"

Miss Adams's kind voice brought him back to himself, and he composed his heart and controlled his countenance as he turned toward her. "I should ask you the same. This is a troubling revelation for you."

"It is, because I cannot reject the will's stipulations as you suggest. Camellia Pointe holds too many happy memories, and Good Shepherd is my grandfather's legacy. Absalom would destroy both." A tiny frown creased her forehead. "I can't understand why Grandfather did this."

"Have you anyone to consult, other than your grandmother and attorney?"

"They're all I have, with my mother passed on and my father living…away for the past eight years."

"Can you contact him, ask for his counsel?"

Emotions flitted across her lovely face—pain, embarrassment and then shame settled there. What could her father, the son of a great minister, have done to evoke such a reaction?

He stopped the thought cold. Samuel, of all men, knew that men of the cloth were just that: mere men, capable of sin. And so were their offspring. "Do you have other uncles besides Counselor Duncan?"

"'Uncle' is an honorary title for Joseph, as he is my grandmother's second cousin. He stepped in to be an uncle to me when I was twelve." She hesitated as if deciding how much to say. "Absalom's father was my only uncle, but he and my aunt were killed in an accident. A year later, my mother died of influenza here in Natchez, and my father returned to our plantations in the Yazoo Delta. If I wrote to him today, I wouldn't get a reply in time."

Samuel opened his mouth to dispute the fact, but as her gaze turned downward, he realized she didn't mean he could not reply in time—but that he would not. When she looked up again, the single tear glimmering on her lower lashes confirmed the truth. She rose from her seat and faltered, as if her legs were none too steady.

Samuel hastened around the desk to assist her, but she recovered in an instant. "To answer your earlier question, I have no beau, although I once did. Harold Goss.

Harold was one of the first men in Natchez to receive a commission. Last anyone heard, he was in prison camp."

Harold Goss? Surely she didn't mean the greedy snake who owned the *Daily Memphis Avalanche* and had caused him no end of embarrassment with his false journalism. The poor girl…

She ran her fingertips over the desk, as if needing to feel its solidity in order to keep her balance as she started for the door. "I need to think about this. Please excuse me."

Samuel hastened to the study door and opened it for her, bracing himself for the onslaught he knew would come from Absalom. That man and his boasting annoyed him like a Yankee. How he'd made the rank of major was beyond Samuel.

"Absalom has stepped out." Miss Euphemia stood by the door with an army of pinched-faced, wrinkled men.

Samuel groaned inwardly, sure he was facing his deacons.

The deacons who had come to fire him before he could even start his work at Christ Church, since he didn't have a wife.

"Apparently my grandson has recently married," the elderly woman said, "and he left his wife to wait in his carriage this entire time. He went outside to try to appease her. If he hasn't better sense than to treat her in such a fashion, they are both in for an unhappy marriage." She waved toward the men at her side. "These are Deacons Bradley, Morris and Holmes."

She hooked her hand through the crook of Miss Adams's elbow, and the two retreated down the hall, presumably to discuss the will.

The most sour-looking deacon of the three, a balding skeleton of a man in waistcoat and cravat, stepped forward. "As you appear unoccupied at the moment, might we have a word?"

Samuel moved aside, letting them in, bracing himself for the inevitable question.

"Miss Euphemia believes your wife did not accompany you to Natchez."

She was right. But why hadn't Samuel been told they'd expected him to be married? He drew a deep breath. "My wife passed away four years ago."

The man, who must have been the head deacon, shook his bony head, a scowl overtaking his face. "That won't do at all."

To his surprise, the deacons gave no word of comfort or consolation. Rather, they looked as if they'd like to ball up their fists at him, and Samuel wondered if he should start ducking.

The deacon with the droopy eyes took a step toward him. "We don't want to seem harsh," he said in a clear basso voice that would have enhanced Clarissa's choir. "We must do what is best for our congregation. Christ Church was a laughingstock once. We won't let it happen again. Go get yourself a wife…or leave."

"I understand." The deacons were right. The well-being of the church came first. "I'd hoped to raise my daughter here. She's had a hard time since I went to war."

"It's too bad." The third deacon crossed his arms over his immoderate belly. "We all wanted the Fighting Chaplain. You're a legend throughout the South. We thought your military honors would be good for this town."

Legend or no, he needed Natchez, and it needed him. Why else would God have called him here? But, ridiculous as it sounded, he needed a wife if he and Emma were to stay.

And Miss Adams needed a husband…

"If I had a wife, I could pastor this church?" He clasped the bony man on the shoulder, spitting out the words as fast as he could, giving himself no time to change his mind—which he would if he thought about his idea an instant longer.

"Yes, of course. You're the Fighting Chaplain—"

"Wait here." Samuel patted the man's sunken chest and dashed for the door. "Don't go away."

In his mind, he applauded his idea loudly enough to keep his heart from rejecting it. As Miss Adams surely would. He'd already made a fool of himself with her grandmother, and showing up three days early with no wife hadn't worked in his favor, either. Not to mention, his Fighting Chaplain reputation must have preceded him, since even Absalom Adams knew who he was. Why should such a refined, beautiful woman want a roughneck like him for a husband? For that matter, why would anyone? Veronica had been right—war had made him common. This idea wouldn't work.

He stopped halfway down the hall and leaned against the wall. *Father, am I taking the right path? Miss Adams will think I'm crazy. Not to mention her grandmother. So if You want me to propose marriage to her, help me reach her heart.* He paused, listening for any advice the Almighty might bestow. Samuel had made enough mistakes already. He couldn't afford another.

But instead of a Scripture verse or a lightning bolt from heaven, an image of his daughter's tear-stained face flitted across his mind.

Emma. Even if she wouldn't admit it, perhaps didn't know it, she depended on him to bring stability to her life. Staying in Natchez was the only way Samuel knew to do so.

With a quick prayer of thanks, he pushed away from

the wall and hastened toward the sound of female voices, hoping to find Miss Adams as quickly as possible. If this was God's plan, he needed to take action now, before his courage could leave him, and then everything would fall into place. He could keep Emma here, and Miss Adams could inherit her property.

But a wife? Only for Emma's good would he make such a sacrifice—which is exactly what marriage would be. He picked up his pace so his common sense couldn't catch up.

Only through a move of God could Samuel convince Miss Adams this was a good idea.

The harder job would be convincing himself.

If Clarissa interpreted the Reverend Montgomery's determined stride and dark expression correctly, he had more bad news. But how could her circumstances possibly worsen? What could be more horrible than losing Camellia Pointe?

At least his rapid approach distracted her and Grandmother from their dismal discussion of the will. For that small comfort, she gave thanks.

"The parson seems not to have a wife, and this puts him in trouble," Grandmother said in a low tone as they watched him approach the ladies' parlor. "I wish the deacons had allowed me to deliver their news."

Clarissa took in the mixed emotions on Grandmother's face, the odd tenor of her voice. She seemed almost to want him to stay while at the same time wishing to hasten his departure. "What would you have done that the deacons didn't?"

"Perhaps I would have given him a ride to the landing so he could head back to Vicksburg." She dropped her voice to a whisper. "Or maybe I'd have driven him up and down Pearl Street so he could see all the young women promenading to each other's town houses. He'd be sure to find a willing bride there."

That much was true.

As the parson stopped at the parlor entrance, the intensity in his dark brown eyes somehow changed Clarissa's perspective of him. In that instant she no longer saw him as a struggling father, an embarrassed gentleman who'd interrupted her rehearsal, or even the Fighting Chaplain. She now saw a ruggedly handsome man of action, of purpose—but what purpose did he now bring to her and Grandmother?

"You look ablaze with some dire matter or another," Grandmother said with an air of enjoying an unfolding melodrama.

"I am. I need to find a wife."

The poor man was in as much trouble as Clarissa was. She needed to leave him to pray about it and discuss it with her deaconess grandmother. "Forgive me, Reverend, if I take my leave."

"Clarissa, please stay and help sort out this misunderstanding." Grandmother waved her cane at the wing chairs in the far corner, and Clarissa and the parson sat on either side of her. "How did you escape your wedding?"

"What wedding?"

"Your wedding—to Emily St. John of Memphis."

The parson let out a bark of a laugh. "I admit Miss St. John tried her best to arrange a marriage, but to no avail."

A stricken look came over Grandmother, and she lifted her hand to her chest for a moment. "I see the information my cousin Mary Grace gave me was untrue."

Clarissa couldn't pull her gaze from her grandmother's lined face as an unexpected sheepishness settled there. "What information?"

"A *Daily Memphis Avalanche* clipping, stating the Fighting Chaplain would marry Miss St. John."

"That was her ploy to trap me into marriage."

"Cousin Mary Grace has been sending you her hometown gossip column again?" At her grandmother's raised brows, Clarissa knew it was true. "Why do you believe that rag? It's shameful that Mary Grace writes such a column, and I think she makes up most of it. I'm sorry she's a war widow but, I declare, she needs to find something to do other than nosing in other people's affairs."

"And you carried this gossip to the deacon board, Missus Adams?"

Grandmother straightened, adding an inch to her height, although she again fidgeted with the handle of her cane. "The article included a picture of the two of you together at church. If you'll recall, you told me in a letter that you were eager for Emily to see Natchez, since she would enjoy our city."

"Emma. I said my daughter, Emma, would like to live here. Not Emily." The parson's low, steady voice gave authenticity to his words. "And the picture of us they included was not a photograph but a drawing. An expression of someone's imagination. Miss St. John and I were never together in that church."

A good deal of the color left Grandmother's face, as if she realized she had caused this unfortunate situation. But, of course, being Euphemia Adams, she would never admit she'd been wrong.

But could she make it right? She couldn't change the bylaws, and she certainly couldn't change the reverend's marital status. At once, Clarissa's careless joking with Emma rang through her mind.

Do you know of a lady he might like?

Well, my grandmother is unmarried...

Suddenly that joke wasn't funny anymore.

"I've thought of a remedy to this situation," he said, interrupting Clarissa's thoughts.

She frowned at the strained look in his eyes. Whatever remedy could he possibly offer?

His brow took on a sheen, and he moistened his lips. "Miss Adams, you are in a tight spot, and so am I. It appears we each need a spouse."

She felt her face blanch. Need a spouse? Could he mean…?

"I could secure a ministry elsewhere, but Natchez seems the best place for my daughter, not to mention the fact God called me here." He stood and moved to Clarissa's side, took her hand. "And you need a husband if you are to receive your inheritance."

Husband? The parson was suggesting they get—married?

She snatched her hand away. What peculiar scheme was this? Clarissa made for the door, wanting nothing more than to leave this ridiculous conversation. "My answer is no. I swanny, Reverend, if this is how you solve your problems, you may want to leave Natchez. Here we value propriety and traditional living."

Grandmother stopped her with a firm hand on the upper arm. "You have everything to lose, including my home. I suggest you simmer down and let the man talk."

"Fine." Clarissa faced the preacher, since she could hardly defy her grandmother in front of him. But this change of events was occurring much too fast for her.

He turned those dark eyes on her, his whole soul in them. To her surprise, a boyish shyness passed across those eyes. "Have you another idea, Miss Adams? Another man you prefer to me?"

His vulnerability touched something in her heart. She had to look away. "No other man."

"I need help with Emma. She and I were once close. When I went to war, I left her and her mother in Vicksburg with her mother's parents." The shyness deepened—or was it sadness? "But their house overlooks a strategic spot on the Mississippi River, and I realized the Yankees would likely shell the major port cities, perhaps even their home. I felt they were unsafe there. Her mother passed on about then, so I sent Emma to boarding school in Herrodsburg, Kentucky. Eventually she got herself into trouble—missing classes, sneaking out in the evenings. By that time, the war was over and I was traveling as an evangelist. I had to stop and give her a home instead."

Grandmother gasped and then looked as if she wanted to skin him alive. "Hezekiah and I once went to Herrodsburg. It's but a few miles from Perryville, is it not?"

He let out a giant breath, gazing out the parlor window as if suddenly unwilling—or unable—to look at them. "The site of the bloody Battle of Perryville. Sending her there was the worst mistake I've ever made. Believe me, I berate myself for my error every day of my life."

His distress cut into Clarissa, and she chose her words carefully. "You couldn't have known a battle would take place so near. Did it affect her greatly?"

"She's not the girl she once was. She's rebellious and dissatisfied, and I can't reach her. She always seems embarrassed of me." The reverend hesitated then turned his focus to Clarissa, his dark eyes unreadable. "Her one joy is singing. When Colonel Talbot let me know your pulpit was empty, he also told me of a gifted vocal teacher here. If Emma can flourish anywhere, I think that place is Natchez."

Emma—the troubled young girl. Clarissa had sensed a sweetness inside her—sweetness masked by bitterness and disappointment. How well Clarissa knew those emotions. "I've fought her battle, and I still fight it at times."

"She's taken a shine to you. I think that, as her stepmother, you could help her. I'm sure you would grow to love her, and she you."

"Loving Emma would not be hard." Loving the reverend would be another story altogether.

Clarissa stepped away to the window and gazed down upon the chinaberry trees flanking State Street. "You said Graham Talbot told you of a voice teacher. I'm the only one in town, so he must have spoken of me."

"I suspected as much, especially since you're the choir director. Your speaking voice is so melodic, I knew you must be a talented singer."

Clarissa opened her mouth to speak, but his words so surprised her, it took her a moment to respond with her thanks. What kind of man was this, giving her the one compliment that would reach her heart more than any other? How could he have known her father had always told her the same thing? And who else knew how those words would comfort her heart?

She shook her head. It was mere coincidence. And the parson had a nerve too, suggesting marriage in such a manner.

Her grandmother caught her attention then and gave her an almost imperceptible nod, her brows high and eyes wide. Then she smiled what Clarissa was sure she meant as a sweet, grandmotherly smile.

But Grandmother Euphemia was more vinegar and

lemons than sugar and spice. Exactly who was she trying to fool? And what was she trying to do? Marry Clarissa off as Grandfather had always wanted?

Clarissa narrowed her eyes at the older lady, unwilling to take this a step further without finding out why Grandmother was acting so strangely about this even-stranger proposal. Which hadn't been a proposal at all, now that she thought about it. "Parson, would you please excuse my grandmother and me for a moment?"

When the reverend had taken his leave, she closed the door with a fierceness that fell just short of a slam, making the glass rattle enough to release a tiny bit of her frustration. She opened her mouth to speak.

Grandmother beat her to it.

"Clarissa, this is a fine opportunity. It's the only way we can keep Camellia Pointe." She rapped her cane on the pine floor as she was wont to do when emphasizing a point. But this tap carried a strange finality that spiked through Clarissa like the Fighting Chaplain's famed sword. "Do you realize we could move back to Camellia Pointe? With a man in the family, we'd be safe in the country again. And with Absalom back from the dead, so to speak, we'd have to move out of his town house anyway. I say you should move forward with the reverend's suggestion."

Move forward? Clarissa longed for a cane of her own to rap at her grandmother. "You're not being rational. If I was willing to consider this, which I am not, it would take me a good deal of time to decide."

"You don't have time." Grandmother said it as if they spoke of nothing more impacting than a horseback ride before Sunday service. "The Reverend Gifford's interim ministry is over. He's leaving on the last steamboat tonight."

"I refuse to marry a stranger without thinking it through, without praying about it."

"Then pray fast. You don't want that Reverend Abernathy from Faith Bethel to conduct the service, do you?"

Not that creepy-looking, obstinate man. "We could send to Vicksburg or Jackson for a preacher. If I decide I need him."

"You know the situation of both those churches—of every church in the South, including this one. Until our economy improves, no deacon board will approve such a trip for its pastor. When members' income is low, the tithe is low. It's simply too expensive, and I can't pay for it either."

"Nevertheless, I've always said I'd never marry for the sake of convenience."

"You've always known my own marriage was arranged, and that my father brought me here from Memphis to marry Hezekiah. But we were happy." Grandmother cast her gaze through the door glass and into the hall, where a portrait of Grandfather hung. "Marriages of convenience can develop into great love."

"Great love?" Clarissa lowered her voice, having unintentionally raised it even more, enough to bring Grandmother's brows up again. "You were happy, but Absalom's parents had an arranged marriage too, and they were miserable their whole lives long. Remember how distant they were to each other, always traveling and living apart? How was their marriage happy?"

"They were—different."

"Obviously. What parent would name their child Absalom—one of the worst sons in the whole Bible?"

Grandmother Euphemia put on her "no-nonsense" face. "They have nothing to do with us now, other than the fact that their son is trying to take what's ours. Think about Camellia Pointe instead. Think about Good Shepherd and the thousands of hours your grandfather spent there, providing a safe place for less-fortunate travelers to stay at the waterfront."

"But to marry..." Clarissa ran her thumb across the bare third finger of her left hand.

Grandmother's eyes brightened with comprehension. "This is because of Harold Goss, isn't it? Do you refuse to marry the parson because you're still in love with that fool?"

"You don't understand. You never have. Harold's betrayal killed all the tender emotions I had for him. If he hadn't up and married that hateful Belinda Grimes just because her father had bigger cotton fields than we did—"

"He would have found someone else with even more money, and he would have married her."

"While he was engaged to me?"

Grandmother waved away her objection. "It could have been worse. Missy Conrad's beau just never showed up for their wedding. Left her with a church full of guests and pink azaleas."

"Yes, and she married a few months later and was the talk of Natchez. She had to endure both the pain of betrayal and public humiliation. Not to mention pity." And the pity was the worst part. Everywhere Missy went, the Natchez elite stopped to whisper. And they'd done the same with Clarissa. "I can't endure the whole town feeling sorry for me because I was the bride in a loveless, arranged marriage."

"Then think of enduring Camellia Pointe going to ruin under your cousin's management. He may well sell it, so imagine enduring the knowledge of strangers in your bedroom, in your grandfather's study—in his little sanctuary." Grandmother surveyed her a moment and then touched Clarissa's cheek. "Can you honestly say you could give it up?"

At the rare tender caress, Clarissa looked into her grandmother's eyes, a mirror image of her own. She saw something there she'd never seen before, and it looked like fear.

The bitter bite of fear welled up in Clarissa's throat, as well—fear of loss, fear of trust. Grandmother was right about many aspects of this appalling situation, but she was wrong about Harold Goss. Clarissa wasn't still in love with him. However, he had reinforced the lesson her father had taught her years before: men could not be trusted.

Clarissa choked back her own fear in light of her grandmother's struggle, pulling a painful breath into her constricted lungs. She owed everything to the older lady. And she was the only family Clarissa had left—at least, the only family member who had not betrayed her.

She caught her breath as another thought embedded itself in her mind. What if she could bring Papa back by keeping their home?

The Spring Festival was scheduled on Clarissa's twenty-first birthday, with the Mississippi Community Choir Association Contest taking place in Natchez for the first time ever. The association Papa had founded thirty years ago, back when he and Mother lived in the Delta.

And this year, Natchez stood a good chance of winning, with a larger choir than ever and a few new, spectacular vocalists. Most important of all, the Reverend Montgomery, a noted choirmaster, had agreed to lead them.

She pressed her hand to her throat as her thoughts swirled. Missus Milburn, president of the Spring Festival committee, had offered to hold the festival at her estate. But that was before the elderly woman had taken a bad fall. Perhaps Clarissa could host instead—at Camellia Pointe.

Then Papa might come back…

She'd call on Missus Milburn today. And write to Papa tonight.

She had no choice.

Drawing a deep breath of courage, she gestured toward the door. "Would you please fetch the reverend for me?"

"I will. And we can have the wedding on the front gallery at Camellia Pointe." Grandmother hastened to the door and flung it open—a little too joyously for Clarissa's taste. Within moments her cane tapped down the hallway. "Reverend Montgomery, are you there?"

Clarissa lowered herself to the hearthside wing chair, relieving her trembling legs but not her erratic pulse. She closed her eyes and drew a deep breath, but it failed to calm her. *Heavenly Father, don't let me make a mistake.*

Could she do it—marry the parson?

She'd never trust any man enough to have a true marriage, true love. So wouldn't a marriage of convenience to the parson be worth it if it meant she could keep Camellia Pointe—and see Papa again?

The reverend's heavy footsteps sounded outside the ladies' parlor, and she opened her eyes. He stepped in, his features soft with hope. He stopped beside her chair and lifted his gaze for a moment, as if to heaven.

As she had seen her grandfather do a thousand times.

Clarissa stood. "Reverend, I accept your offer."

The late-afternoon sun cast the home into shadow, throwing a duskiness into Samuel's heart as well. He pulled into the uphill circle drive and stopped his phaeton beside the graying sign with its faded letters: Camellia Pointe. He shielded his eyes from the lowering sun and gazed upon one of the largest, most austere Southern mansions he'd ever seen. At the sight of the immoderate display of wealth, he cast aside all he'd done to brace himself for his marriage.

Even in the fading light, Camellia Pointe showed herself off, her two-story galleries embellishing her white-stucco frame, her massive columns timeless, her Greek Revival lines impeccable. She stood proud, elegant—excessive.

Hardly an appropriate setting for a minister's wedding.

Everything in him wanted to turn the buggy around and head back to town. Back to Christ Church. Back to a place of sanity and safety for his heart.

Perhaps he should have stood his ground when Clarissa had suggested holding the ceremony on the front gallery of her family home. But she'd clearly set her heart on it, and he'd hated to refuse her first request of him.

A church wedding—that's what they should have had…

He stole a glance at Emma beside him and the book she'd immersed herself in every time they'd been alone since he fetched her from Kentucky. As she'd also done when Samuel announced his marriage plan. Could nothing move his daughter? Would she remain forever engrossed in her own thoughts, her own world?

She stirred as if sensing his gaze. Then she let out a squeal and clasped his upper arm with the grip of youthful exuberance. "Is this Clarissa's home?"

Samuel paused, savoring his daughter's hand on his arm—the first touch she'd given him since he'd left her at the Kentucky school four years ago. "It's Camellia Pointe."

Emma tossed the book to the carriage seat, her brown eyes gleaming. "I've never seen such a beautiful house. Can we live here?"

"This is no place for a preacher. We'll live in the church manse as planned."

With a frown, she dropped her hand from his arm and picked up her book. But as he urged the horse up the drive, she kept the book closed, her focus on the mansion.

Samuel fixed his gaze on Camellia Pointe, as well—the one thing, other than the infernal book, that had captured his daughter's attention and brought her out of her melancholy. Even for those few moments. Despite Emma's sentiments, he would hurry this wedding ceremony along and hasten his new family to the manse.

Cresting the hill, Samuel circled around to the front entrance, taking in the broken sections of the second-floor gallery railing and the missing glass in a front window. At the sight of Colonel Talbot and Joseph Duncan in a seemingly deep discussion on the lower gallery—the very place he'd be married in a few minutes—the cool winter air suddenly turned cold as a Tennessee battlefield in January. But his daughter's lace shawl lay unused on the seat between them, and he realized his own blood, not the air, had gone frigid.

And if his impending wedding affected him like this, how must Miss Adams feel?

Samuel sucked in a deep breath, the atmosphere thick with river humidity even here, a full mile from the Mississippi. The dark-haired woman must wish she'd never seen him, never taken him up on his crazy offer. But it was too late to change her mind—or his.

He pulled up behind an impressive two-horse landau that suited this grand estate. He knew nothing of his bride. What would she be like? Warm and sweet as his mother had been, or cool and distant like Veronica? Did she take tea or coffee? Was she neat or a little messy? Did she like to sit up at night and sleep late in the mornings, or did she love the fresh, dewy new day, as he did? Roses or daisies—or camellias?

Samuel dropped the reins over the dash. All he knew of her was her name—and her position as potential heiress of this estate.

He'd known more about Veronica before their wedding…

At the thought, he slipped his finger under his stiff collar, hoping to relieve the lump in his tight throat. A mockingbird flew overhead and lit on the top branch of a nearby pine. Its spontaneous song touched a raw place in his heart.

He was entering this marriage the same way he'd begun his first. He had no guarantee this one would turn out any better.

How many people would soon discover he was a fraud, unfit to be a husband, and would mock his deceit? And would he lose his church because of it—and thereby lose Emma?

He shoved aside the thought. If he couldn't control these wanderings of mind, he wouldn't make it through the ceremony. With effort, Samuel turned his focus to his surroundings. In the shade of a massive live oak, he sensed an emptiness about the place. Quite a contrast from the bustle and busyness one would expect before a wedding. Even a ceremony as hasty as this. Did Miss Adams and the dowager live in this monstrosity alone? How could they have managed?

The moment he'd assisted Emma from his modest rented conveyance, she flashed her attention toward the magnificent landau in front of them. More specifically, toward the young man now making a show of leaping down from the expensive carriage, tossing his long mane of wavy blond hair as he hit the ground. He flicked at the sleeve of his gray wool sateen suit, which must have cost more than the wedding ring Samuel had purchased this afternoon. The smile he aimed at Emma looked nothing like the grin a well-intentioned youth would give a Christian girl.

Samuel's wedding-day jitters erased any mercy he might otherwise have shown. He widened his stance and cleared his throat. When the young man in gray caught his eye, Samuel crossed his arms over his chest and issued the same dark, silent warning he'd given Absalom earlier today.

After sneering at Samuel, the youth shifted his gaze toward Emma again and then skulked off.

He would bear watching.

Absalom caught Samuel's attention then as he exited the carriage with a woman about Samuel's age, her hair the same color as the young man's. As she stepped to the ground, her giant purple hat bobbed with her effort.

Oversize hats, overlong hair—this family's tastes certainly leaned toward the peculiar.

"Is that the Fighting Chaplain?" The woman's strident stage whisper carried to Samuel and, no doubt, beyond.

Absalom took her arm and tried to propel her toward the gallery. But she pulled away and headed toward Samuel, batting her eyelashes in a way that made him unsure if she was trying for his attention or merely had a speck of dust in her eye. "I'm Absalom's wife, Drusilla

Adams, and you saw my son, Beau, a moment ago. I've heard all about your exploits…"

As she chattered on about what she thought she knew of his war experience, she gazed at Samuel the same way the young man had looked at Emma. The thought unnerved him and he turned to Absalom for his reaction to his wife's behavior. To Samuel's disgust, the man merely pulled a fat cigar from within his coat and cut off his wife midsentence.

"We're here to make sure this marriage is legal." Absalom lit his cigar and pointed it at Samuel's rented carriage. "And to give you a word of advice from a native. You think you're being pious, driving a ten-year-old, cheap phaeton and looking like you don't care about earthly goods. But your church is full of Natchez aristocracy, and they'll expect better."

Samuel held back the harsh words that wanted to explode from his lips. "Nobody has any money in the South, Adams. Including Natchez. These people won't require me to—"

"That's where you're wrong. Take a look at my landau." Absalom waved the stinking cigar at his carriage. "Belonged to Jeff Davis. I paid a small fortune for it, but I felt sorry for his wife, Verina, since she's trying to raise bail money for Jeff. She's a Natchez girl—a friend of mine. In fact, Jeff's plantation is next door to this estate."

Samuel had to escape, now. Otherwise he was liable to give Absalom a piece of his mind, speaking of the president in such an intimate way and boasting of buying his carriage.

At the sound of Emma's giggle, wafting from the other side of the carriage, an image of long-haired Beau shot through Samuel's mind and brought a sense of foreboding.

President Davis didn't need Samuel to defend or protect him, but Emma did. A feeling of unease had wormed its way into his subconscious the moment he'd seen Beau—or, rather, the moment Beau had seen Emma. Now that unease started to fester. The only way to get rid of it was to lance it before it poisoned both Samuel and his daughter. He would look for an opportunity to warn Adams to keep his son under control. However, now was not that time.

He glanced back at the gallery, hoping Colonel Talbot would summon him, but it was empty.

He'd head over there anyway—and without further comment to Adams. If the man spent half as much energy caring for his family as he did in boasting, there might be no need for this contest between him and Miss Adams.

As Samuel approached the gallery, his misgivings about the house returned to him with violent force. Clearly, Natchez wouldn't object to his wife owning this home, since it had belonged to the late Reverend Adams. And Samuel didn't wish to offend his in-laws, especially on the day of his marriage. But he couldn't easily forget his grandfather's teaching that a minister of the Gospel shouldn't have extravagant possessions such as this home. Grandfather wouldn't approve of Samuel having a wife who owned such a palace, even though they would live in the manse. What had he gotten himself into?

He reached for the knob, but someone rattled it from inside. Then came the sound of a struggle, as if the cypress door was stuck. When it flew open, Colonel Talbot stepped onto the gallery, leaving the door ajar. "I'd hoped to have the door fixed before you got here, Chaplain."

"No need." Samuel kept his eye on his daughter as

she disappeared around the house's west corner. He lowered his voice. "Colonel, I've made a grave error. You see, this house—"

"Don't worry. The roof is sound, and the broken windows are boarded, so rain can't get in and destroy the interior. Camellia Pointe is still one of the best of the grand old Natchez homes. You'll need to make repairs at some point, but it'll stand for a long time as it is."

"You don't understand. I'm not worried about its condition but rather the brazen display of wealth—"

At the sound of footfalls, Samuel hesitated, in case one of the approaching persons was Miss Adams. They would need to talk about this house, but in private.

"We're ready," an unfamiliar female voice called from inside.

The Reverend Gifford appeared from around the corner, with Emma on his arm and Beau at his other side. Other than the gray at his temples, he looked much the same as he had when Samuel last saw him, before the war. "Glad to see you've found a new wife, and a mother for this pretty girl. And I'm happy to see you taking the pulpit at Christ Church."

"He's the perfect choice for both the church and Clarissa," Talbot cut in, pointing to the right. "The groom stands over there, or so the women tell me."

The dowager exited the house and stood at the gallery's edge, next to a square pillar, a camellia bush at her back. Behind her, Miss Adams seemed to float through the doorway, her dark hair contrasting with her high-necked white dress, its skirt narrower than current fashion dictated. The pink bridal glow in her porcelain cheeks made her even more lovely than before. Equally beautiful to Samuel was the look of adoration on his daughter's face as she gazed upon her soon-to-be stepmother. Emma's eyes shone as they had when she'd taken in the beauty of Camellia Pointe only minutes ago.

And had clutched his arm.

Father, I believe Miss Adams is the answer to my prayers for Emma. And if so, couldn't Samuel manage to tolerate his wife owning a showy home like this?

Yes, he could, especially since he would rarely see it.

The colonel clasped his shoulder and gave him a soldierly shove toward the spot Samuel was presumably to occupy. A blond woman followed Miss Adams outside, wearing a more modern pink dress, and took her place beside Talbot. Joseph Duncan stepped out next, his stern gaze settling on Absalom's family as they approached.

When the Reverend Gifford stood before them and started the ceremony, Samuel adjusted his frock coat, laid aside his misgivings and set his face like a flint. He'd failed his late wife and he'd failed Emma. For no reason could he do it again.

Samuel went through the motions, saying, "I do" and placing the ring on his bride's finger when prompted. Finally, the words "man and wife" penetrated the fog of his brain.

"You may ki—"

At the tiny shake of Miss Adams's head—or was she Missus Montgomery now?—the minister cut off his words. "You may…greet your guests."

His wife's sigh of apparent relief cut through Samuel's own discomfort and shamed him more than an open rebuke.

Samuel mindlessly accepted congratulations from the lady in pink, the attorney and the reverend, and a fierce army backslap from his former commander. He stepped over to Emma, who, he now realized, carried a bouquet of white flowers.

"Miss Clarissa picked these camellias," his daughter said, touching the petals. "They're the first ones to bloom, and she said I was her bridesmaid."

It seemed his new bride had made herself quite indispensable already.

Joseph meandered his way, a grim set to his mouth. "Reverend Montgomery, as inopportune as this seems, I must ask you to deliver the next stipulation of the will."

At his wedding? "Can it not wait?"

"I fear not. This letter is to be read immediately after both parties fulfill the first condition. I'm bound to follow Hezekiah's instructions."

Samuel's pounding headache of this morning threatened to return and finish him off, and he rubbed his skull. "I'll collect my wife and meet you inside."

"And I'll get Absalom. Both parties are to hear this letter together."

Samuel hardly knew how to approach his bride, engaged as she was in whispered conversation with the lady in pink, so he merely stood beside her and cleared his throat.

She turned to him with a smile so genuine it took his breath. Hardly the reaction he'd anticipated from her, since she'd been visibly relieved to avoid a wedding kiss. But then a black-and-white bird dog, one he hadn't seen before, jumped down from one of the carriages and headed toward them. His wife gave it the same smile she'd bestowed on him.

So much for winning her favor.

"Reverend, this is Graham Talbot's wife, Ellie," Clarissa said, "and their dog, Sugar."

"Clarissa, you'll need to begin to call your husband by his given name." Missus Talbot offered Samuel her hand. "And you, Reverend, will need to think of a pet name for her."

Pet name? He'd rather pet the dog. After releasing Missus Talbot's gloved hand, he did just that. At least Sugar and Missus Talbot didn't shrink from his touch. But neither of them apparently knew what a roughneck he was.

"We must step inside a moment," he said as the dog ambled toward Emma. "Your attorney asked us to meet him."

Miss Adams—Missus Montgomery—turned those hazel eyes on him, their gold flecks shimmering in the late-winter sunlight. "The next stipulation."

Samuel pushed the door open the rest of the way and stepped aside to allow her to pass.

Inside the center hall, he hesitated. This house was even more grandiose inside than out. However, dusty sheets covered each piece of the hall furniture.

"The mural is French Zuber wallpaper and the gasolier is Waterford." She said it without pretense or pride, as if she'd grown up playing around these priceless items. Which she apparently had.

When they entered the dining room, Joseph Duncan waited silently, his portmanteau on the sheet-covered table in front of him. Absalom sat at the head of the table as if he belonged there, first complaining and cursing their grandfather and his will, and then boasting about his "much-larger home" in Memphis.

Surely Samuel could tolerate this home easier than he could stomach the blustering braggart. And judging from the tension in those big hazel eyes, Absalom affected Clarissa even more deeply.

"It is extremely poor taste to talk business at a wedding, and I apologize," Joseph said when Samuel had unshrouded a chair and seated his wife next to the gray-veined marble fireplace. He handed Samuel an envelope. "Unfortunately we have no choice. Reverend Montgomery, please read this letter from the Reverend Hezekiah Adams."

Samuel took his specs from his pocket and slid them on. He opened and scanned the letter.

No. This couldn't be. His aching head suddenly felt as if a dozen horses' hooves pounded it. He glanced up at Joseph, who nodded his encouragement.

"'To fulfill my second stipulation, both my grandchildren must live at Camellia Pointe for one year, beginning the day the first condition is fulfilled. Since the War has wreaked havoc on this estate, my grandchildren must live as family here and work together to complete its necessary repairs and restore it to its former glory.'"

Samuel drew a deep breath of defeat. But when he saw the way his new bride bit her lower lip, as if to stop it from trembling, he wanted to throw this hateful letter into the fire.

She didn't want to live with Absalom any more than Samuel did—that much was clear. And if they'd known this stipulation before the wedding, would she have gone through with it? Would Samuel?

He shoved the thought aside. No matter what they would or would not have done, they were married now. And it was up to Samuel to make sure they kept this home, as much as he didn't want it. Something about the desperation growing in her eyes made him want nothing more than to send President Davis's carriage—and its owners—down that long, winding drive to the road, so Clarissa would never have to see them again.

And by the grace of God, he'd make sure to do just that.

Chapter Three

"I won't have it!" Cousin Absalom slammed his fist onto Grandmother's fine mahogany table, eyes blazing like the flames in the fireplace opposite him. "Clarissa will twist this whole situation to her advantage, and I wouldn't put it past you to help her, Duncan. Now that she's married the Fighting Chaplain, he will too. I'm calling in another attorney to examine this will, and I'll pay him whatever it takes to defend what should be mine."

Any shred of hope Clarissa might have held for a quick, easy end to this calamity now faded in the span of a heartbeat. Her cousin truly would fight to the death for their grandfather's property, even if that death was Grandmother's rather than his own. Which, despite her attempt to appear calm and unaffected, could happen if her current angst caused her health to deteriorate as it had after Grandfather's passing.

In a sudden flash of clarity, Clarissa recalled a moment earlier that day, when Grandmother had offered her wedding dress to Clarissa. She'd pressed her wrinkled hand to her chest as if her heart palpitations had returned. Thinking back further, Clarissa remembered seeing the same gesture even before that, when her grandmother realized she'd mistakenly caused the parson's dilemma.

Had her heart malady come back?

As this possibility sunk in, Clarissa clenched her teeth before her fear could steal her determination. Losing Camellia Pointe would be heartbreaking. But losing her grandmother would be almost as bad as…

She drew a halting breath as a tragic, long-ago night invaded her thoughts. A night before they'd left Camellia Pointe, before they lost Grandfather, before the War. A night that had formed her future. For a moment, she lived it again: the labored breaths, the little involuntary cries of pain, the goodbye kisses on soft, feverish skin—

Her vision blurry with tears of remembrance, Clarissa set her gaze on the family portrait over the mantel, painted during the last days they were happy. For the first time in two years, she focused on the dark hair, much like her own but longer, thicker, and the soft lips that would never kiss her again. It was true—losing Grandmother would be almost as hard as losing Mother.

No matter the cost, Clarissa couldn't allow it. Not if she could somehow prevent it. She hadn't been able to avert the tragedy of her mother's death or the heartache that followed. But perhaps she could somehow find a way to shelter her grandmother, keep her healthy.

The only way to do that was to hold on to Camellia Pointe.

An idea suddenly coming to her, she whisked away her tears and turned to her cousin. "Absalom, you never were sentimental about this home, and certainly not about Good Shepherd. Let's divide the Camellia Pointe land. I'll keep the house and five acres, and you can have the other twenty-five. Build on it, sell it—do what you want with it—and we'll somehow divide Good Shepherd too."

"You think I'm going to settle for a mere twenty-five acres of useless ground and half of a worthless tenement, leaving you with everything else? I'll knock every inch of stucco off this house and tear it down brick by brick—and go to jail for it—before I'll accept an agreement with you." Absalom shoved back his chair and shot to his feet, thickening the air with his tone and the weight of his words.

"It's all I can offer. This is a country villa, not a plantation. You know our acreage lies in the Delta."

"By all rights, I should get half of that too."

"By all rights," Joseph said in that threatening tone he reserved for unruly clients, "I should record your statements and conduct so they can be taken into consideration at the end of the year. And if you continue, I'll do it."

The Reverend Montgomery stood and positioned himself behind Clarissa, one hand on the back of her chair. "I'll be watching every move you make—you and your family. Keep that in mind if you take a notion to start swinging a sledgehammer."

"You'd better hope I don't swing one at you," Absalom muttered under his breath.

"Simmer down and listen. He hasn't finished reading the letter." Joseph looked at Absalom with unveiled contempt, the kind only the very aged could get away with in polite Natchez society.

Samuel continued. "'My grandson will make any needed repairs to the main house. My granddaughter will repair and restore the gardens, landscaping, bridge, sanctuary, gazebo and pergola. All work must be completed one month from today. The pastor of Christ Church of

Natchez will determine whether each party has successfully completed the task.'"

"This isn't fair." As Absalom bellowed his outrage, the heat of his breath hit Clarissa in the face. "She has an advantage, marrying the parson. He's supposed to be an unbiased party in this contest."

Joseph gathered his documents into his ancient portmanteau and stood, cloaked with the dignity of a man who'd spent sixty years advising the best and the worst of Natchez aristocracy. "Adams, you have a nerve. Waste your money on another attorney if you like, but it's not in your best interest to insult your cousin or the reverend. You know the Fighting Chaplain's reputation, and Clarissa has made herself invaluable in Natchez during the recent hard times. She's a favorite among the citizens. Better keep your bitter opinions to yourself if you hope for a fair judgment in this town."

"What's she done that's so great?"

"Besides helping to stabilize the church after it lost its founding pastor, overseeing her grandfather's waterfront mission for the poor, keeping the city orphanage running and caring for her grandmother?"

Absalom kicked his chair, sending the Duncan Phyfe antique sailing against the wall, and stormed toward the door. "None of that will make a bit of difference. I intend to have this property, Clarissa. You might as well get used to that—in fact, don't even bother moving back in."

As his thundering footsteps pounded down the center hall toward the front entrance, Clarissa fought the urge to head out the back. This was her wedding day, and she'd scarcely looked into her husband's eyes since the ceremony ended. It was also the first day of her year-long contest with her cousin, and she wished she hadn't seen the vitriol in Absalom's face, heard it in his words. At the moment, it seemed the year would never end.

Upon remembrance of Grandmother's hand pressed against her chest, she realized the year might end too soon, cutting short Clarissa's time with her.

"Don't worry about Absalom. He talks big but it's mostly blustering." Joseph turned to the reverend, an expression of sympathy flitting across his eyes.

Well, Clarissa felt sorry for Reverend Montgomery too, considering the mess she'd brought him into.

"He won't hire an attorney, but I'll let you know if he does. Stay as far from him as you can, which won't be easy while living in the same house." Joseph made for the hall then stopped in the doorway and smoothed his magnificent white moustache. "And his wife, and his stepson. I don't trust them any more than I trust Absalom."

Yes, Absalom's family was no more honest than her cousin himself. Suddenly the coming year felt more like ten.

"I'll let myself out," Joseph said. "And best wishes on your marriage. May it be long and happy."

Joseph's footfalls sounded in the center hall, then the front door opened and closed, leaving Clarissa alone with her husband. Sitting across from her, he looked anything but happy. His Adam's apple bobbed a bit as if he were swallowing back some dark emotion—anger, fear? Regret?

He turned his deep brown eyes on her then, and something there made her wish she hadn't done it, hadn't married him out of convenience. For that instant, his eyes reflected the vulnerability she'd seen in the church parfor just before he'd proposed marriage. Did he long for a woman's love? If so, she had stolen that dream from him, taken away his hope of romance. She was now his only chance for that and, of course, she couldn't bring that dream to pass. Even though he was a minister, he was still a man—and men couldn't be trusted.

The parson tugged at his lapels as if his coat had suddenly shrunk and was cutting off his breath. Then he took a long look around the room, first at the Duncan Phyfe sideboard, scarred now with what looked like sword slashes from the house's days of Yankee occupation. Next he gazed at the faded, dusty, gold draperies and smudged paneled walls, and his expression changed, took on a more disapproving air. "This home…"

His appraisal startled her more than her grandfather's strange will. What Southern estate had escaped marring from the Yankees' hands? Certainly none in Natchez. "I know it needs a good cleaning, some repairs…"

His brown eyes radiated concern as he pulled his gaze back to her. "I meant no criticism of its condition but rather its opulence. I have always lived humbly. You see, my grandfather taught me that the manse should be the pastor's home. But to fulfill the will's conditions, it appears we must live here."

We must…but Clarissa would have said *we may*. Before this morning, she'd all but given up hope of living in her beloved Camellia Pointe again. But now she would, because of Reverend Montgomery. She owed him her gratitude, and she'd make sure he got it. "If only Absalom didn't have to live here too."

"Indeed."

"I need to find my grandmother and tell her of the new development in the will."

"And I need to inform Emma. She'll be overjoyed to

learn this will be her home for a year. She loved Camellia Pointe from the moment she saw it."

Just a year? "Of course, she will be welcome to stay here until she marries."

His expression changed quicker than an eighth note. "Not without us here."

"But we'll be here. I intend to win the contest and inherit this estate."

"I'll do everything in my power to make sure you do, and we'll keep it as long as we can afford its upkeep and taxes." He crossed his arms over his chest. "But after the year is up, we must move into the manse."

What was wrong with him? Didn't he understand how much Clarissa needed to live here, in this house? Then she realized he couldn't know, because she hadn't told him. "I couldn't bear to live in it for a year and then move away. And what of my grandmother?"

"She's welcome to live in the manse with us."

Clarissa suppressed a sigh as she realized her new husband also didn't know about their current living arrangements or why they'd moved from Camellia Pointe. She could hardly expect him to make the right decisions until he did. "We need to have a long talk—"

The front door squeaked open, and then light footsteps and the tapping of a cane sounded. Within moments, Grandmother Euphemia appeared, clutching the handle of her cane as if it would otherwise run away. Samuel stood and seated her next to Clarissa. "Was it good news or bad?"

"The worst." Clarissa braced herself for Grandmother's oft-repeated lecture on how charity believeth all things.

To her surprise, it didn't come. "Whatever it is, tell me, so we can decide what to do next."

"We have to live here for a year. With Cousin Absalom."

Grandmother's hand fluttered to her chest. She hesitated. "Is there no way around it?"

"Joseph thinks not." Clarissa leaned closer to her grandmother. "Is your heart bothering you again?"

She dropped her hand to the table and scowled for a second. "Not so much that I can't hold my own with that renegade grandson of mine. He gave your grandfather and me so much heartache that, when he was reported dead, I felt a measure of relief with my grief. And now here he is, resurrected, so to speak, and no doubt ready to cause more trouble than ever."

Reverend Montgomery opened his mouth but got no chance to speak. Instead, Grandmother shifted her gaze to him, a defiant glare in her hazel eyes. "And don't you lecture me. You'd feel the same if you'd lived through his backstabbing and treachery as I have. I hardly know whether to call him Absalom, Lazarus or Judas."

"In light of that parade of biblical troublemakers—well, other than Lazarus—I won't give you a sermon on love this time. But next time, I will."

Clarissa sucked in a breath of horror. If there was one thing Grandmother hated more than tardiness—or early arrivals—it was receiving a personal sermon. Or correction of any kind. Even Grandfather Hezekiah hadn't gotten away with that.

The smirk on Grandmother's face took Clarissa back. Her grandmother was enjoying being threatened with a sermon? Clarissa glanced over at the reverend, who sat with brows lifted and a hint of a grin on his face—a friendly warning.

And Grandmother let him do it.

Before she could fully grasp this new side of her

grandmother, the older woman straightened, eyes snapping. "You're more like your late grandfather than I like to admit. However, we haven't time to discuss it. Everyone needs to get settled in."

"You're right," Clarissa said, although her grandmother's tone told her she simply didn't want to keep talking about any of this. "I assume you want to keep your old rooms, but where would you like to put Absalom and his wife? And what about his stepson?"

Grandmother was on her feet and halfway to the door before Clarissa could stop her. "Where are you going? I need you to tell me where to put these people."

"Figure it out yourself. Put them anywhere you like."

Clarissa scrambled to keep pace with her grandmother, who was now in the hall. The reverend caught up with them at the front entrance.

"I'm not staying. I barely survived the last time he lived here."

Clarissa clasped her grandmother's arm. "That's a bit of an exaggeration."

"It's not." Grandmother snatched her arm away and opened the door. "You were young, and we didn't tell you everything."

"Then tell me now."

"I don't have time. I have to make arrangements to leave town."

What was she thinking? "Where will you go?"

"Back home."

"The Delta?"

"No, I'm going to my home. To live with Cousin Mary Grace." With the tip of her cane, she pushed open the already-ajar door and stepped onto the front gallery. "As soon as I can get the money together, I'm buying a steamer ticket and moving back to Memphis."

* * *

"Grandmother, you can't—"

Missus Adams slammed the door hard enough to make the case clock chime.

Samuel glanced over at his new wife as the surprise on her face quickly gave way to fear. Then she yanked open the door and ran onto the gallery. "Grandmother, come back inside."

"I'm not leaving yet. I want to think. Alone."

"Fine." Clarissa strode inside and toward the back door. There she gestured for Samuel to join her at the six-over-six detached sidelights. "If she truly wants to think, she'll sit under the pergola. But when she wants to pray, she goes to the sanctuary."

Samuel peered out at the vine-covered, open pergola in the garden, perhaps a hundred yards from the house. "Then I'm glad I don't see her in the pergola, because she needs to pray about leaving us. But if she wanted to pray, why didn't she say so? And where's the sanctuary?"

"She thinks private prayer should be just that—a private matter, not to be spoken of. And you can't see the sanctuary from here." She grasped the double door's knob, turned and pulled, but this door was stuck too.

"Let me try." When she'd stepped back, Samuel took the knob and applied his strength to the door. When it finally flung open, he stood back so she could exit first. "I'll make sure Absalom has these doors fixed first thing, Miss—Missus..." He shook his head. Veronica had insisted he call her Missus Montgomery, and it would be wise to keep an emotional distance in his new marriage as well. However, she should be the one to decide. "What do you want me to call you?"

Her tinkling laugh—guileless, melodic—took him aback. He should have expected her to have a beautiful laugh, since she had such a sweet-sounding speaking voice. Nevertheless, he was unprepared for it. Of a sudden, he couldn't wait until the next choir rehearsal so he could hear her sing. He couldn't keep a smile from his face. "What's so funny?"

"You are, with your formality, although it will help you fit into our church and our town. You haven't been here long enough to know, but Natchez is the strictest and most conventional city on the River. Or in the entire South, for that matter, including Charleston."

No, but he'd been here long enough to believe it.

"Grandfather used to tell me stories of Grandmother Euphemia calling him 'Reverend,' even when they were alone, until long after they sent my uncle to boarding school."

"And what did he call her?"

"Ducky dearest."

He could just imagine the dowager's response. He grinned at Clarissa, hoping to draw her sweet laugh again. "Hmm…it has possibilities."

As her laugh tinkled, the warmth in Samuel's heart shot him a grim warning, reminding him that romantic love was not for him. Sure, the dark-haired beauty before him was his wife, but only because she needed to hold on to this home and he needed to keep his pastorate. So from now on, instead of enjoying the sound of her laugh, he would need to steel his heart against it. He couldn't treat her as if they had a real marriage, a real relationship. She didn't want it any more than he did.

"I think we'll leave Grandfather's terms of endearment in the past." Oblivious to the darkness of his thoughts, of his heart, she stepped outside to the weedy brick courtyard and the sprawling, equally weedy terraced gardens beyond. "Custom dictates that I call you

'Reverend' in public, and you refer to me as 'Missus Montgomery.' But at home, please call me Clarissa. As may Emma."

"And please call me Samuel."

She smiled, settling this issue, if nothing else. Although the arrangement seemed too casual, too intimate, for a wife who would never truly be his wife.

"How long have you been a widower?" she asked with a hint of compassion in her voice, unlike the deacons.

"Almost four years." As painful as it was to discuss Veronica and his marital failure, he needed to get the conversation behind him. Clarissa had a right to know. In fact, she had a right to know the whole story of Samuel's failure, although he didn't have the courage to reveal it. "My first marriage was an arranged union. My father wanted me to move up in our denomination, and Veronica's father was assistant to our national superintendent."

She stopped and turned to him, her hazel eyes bright green in the sunlight. Or had her natural empathy colored them so vividly? "Did you have a happy marriage? It's rare for marriages of convenience to lead to true love."

"We did not." Something in Clarissa's demeanor—perhaps the sad little droop of her lips—made him long to tell her all about his disastrous first marriage. But even more, he dreaded seeing pity in those most expressive eyes. However, Clarissa was his wife now, and she deserved to know as much of the truth as he could bear to tell. "Emma was born a year after we were married, and her birth was our only happy moment. Unfortunately for me, Veronica was in love with another man and had been for some time before our wedding."

Clarissa's dainty hand fluttered to her chest and then he saw it—the pity he hated. If he didn't tell her the rest of his story now, he never would, and that wasn't fair to her. "Her beau, Reuben Conwell, was a businessman and heir to the Southern Bank of Louisiana and Mississippi. Conwell had a reputation as a swindler with an uncanny ability to spot and exploit his competitors' weaknesses. The man was ruthless, heartless. Veronica's father felt he was not good enough for her."

"So her father promised you advantages within the denomination if you would prevent her from marrying Conwell."

"He promised my father, not me, but yes. But in time, I loved Veronica intensely." At least, he'd thought so at the time. He gazed out over the expanse of lawn and gardens. His late wife had never taken walks with him, had rarely had this much conversation with him. She'd seemed barely able to tolerate his presence. What a change to have a wife who wanted to be with him. "I thought I could make her love me. I did everything I could think of to make her happy, to make her like me, let alone love me."

He should probably tell her the rest, lay bare his heart and confess the event that had sealed their marriage's failure. Though he couldn't uncover the wound to share it, he relived it now—the moment he'd realized his love for Veronica. Six years ago, as they were about enter the elegant Burnett Hotel ballroom, where the district's dignitaries and guests had gathered to witness his appointment as presbyter. His tender confession of love, the kiss he'd tried to give to seal his newfound affection…

Her shocked response, her acerbic laugh. *Reverend Montgomery, do you mean you* love *me?*

His stammered response, her back as she'd fled the room.

Her shrill laugh as he'd discovered her alone with

Conwell minutes later, betraying Samuel with her mocking voice, regaling his rival with her story of Samuel's confession of love. The realization of his failure as a family man.

The withering of his heart as his love for Veronica died.

"Were you able to win her love?" Clarissa's sweet voice mercifully brought him back to the present.

He shook his head. If only he could forget those words he'd heard all those years ago. But that would never happen, and besides, it was time to change the tone of this conversation. It was his and Clarissa's wedding day, after all. She should have some measure of happiness today. "But I have Emma. Other than the Lord, she's the delight of my life."

"I'll help you with her." Clarissa laid her hand on his arm, her voice a whisper. "I'll do everything I can."

How could he respond to that? He'd placed all his hopes on Clarissa to help him rebuild his family—on her and on the Lord. If this didn't work, he didn't know what would.

They moved through the gardens, the cool evening air settling upon them as the sun lowered in the clear sky. Clarissa waved toward the west, shifting the tone as if she wanted to sweep away his disappointment in himself. "There's my grandmother—just where I thought she'd be."

Samuel looked beyond the expanse of flower beds with pink and white buds popping out here and there, past the pond with its arched white bridge and nearby gazebo. The entire estate held an air of grandeur faded to a dismal shabbiness, from the chipped paint on the bridge to the unkempt herb garden. Then he spotted a crumbling brick walk leading to a small stone chapel in the Greek temple style, its front open and supported by four white columns. Clarissa's grandmother sat on a stone bench next to a statue of a bowing angel, facing the diminutive altar.

"My grandfather built the sanctuary," Clarissa said, lowering her voice, "as a memorial to God's faithfulness in healing him and Grandmother of the illness that took my mother."

For all its compactness, the little chapel was as dignified and classic as its occupant.

They turned and started toward the pergola to give Missus Adams her privacy while keeping an eye out for Emma, who was likely curled up somewhere, reading her book. And Absalom. As much as the man annoyed Samuel, he'd rather have him where he could watch him.

"I think Grandmother is serious about going to Memphis, if she can scrape together the money for a steamer ticket."

The concern, the pain in those big hazel eyes, could have melted Samuel's heart once. Before Veronica, before his mistakes, before he'd known the power of guilt—and that he didn't deserve a second chance at love. Didn't deserve more than a marriage of convenience, a loveless union, a wedding sham.

But even though this marriage was based on necessity rather than love, he now had the responsibility of Clarissa's family. He mentally reviewed his financial state, including the modest inheritance from his parents. "I'll be glad to cover the cost of her ticket."

Clarissa's eyes turned cloudy, like a thunderstorm on the river. She hesitated, glancing toward the sanctuary and the feisty woman sitting there, holding her cane like a spear at her side.

She faced Samuel again, fear in her countenance. "Must we help her leave me? She's all I have."

He might have thought he understood, since Emma was his only living relative. But Clarissa's pained silence told him her story may have been more complex than his. Perhaps he understood less than he thought. "What happened to the rest of your family?"

Clarissa gazed into the sky, the waning sun setting fire to the gold flecks in her eyes. "When I was twelve, yellow fever hit the town just after we arrived in the spring. My father came down with it first, then Mother."

Her voice dropped, and he leaned toward her to catch every nuance. "Then she went away to heaven."

Her sigh came from someplace deep within, a slight duskiness now shadowing the tender, fair skin under her eyes. Samuel shifted a fraction closer to hear her low voice. "And then what?"

"By then, my grandparents were also sick. Cousin Absalom left us to seek his fortune somewhere or other. And my father—" She turned suddenly and gazed behind them, toward the house, as if expecting him to stride up the brick walk toward her. Her shoulders stooped for just an instant, as if she'd been disappointed he was not there. "I haven't seen him since."

Samuel had been right. Her childhood had been much worse than his.

As they passed another stunning marble statue of an angel, Clarissa reached out and brushed her fingers over the tip of one wing, as if greeting an old friend. She stopped and lowered herself to the stone bench near the statue, her eyes turning misty. "We came to Natchez thinking we'd be safe. The yellow fever hadn't hit yet, and we'd be in the country most of the time, leaving Camellia Pointe only to attend church and interview the new music teacher. He was Mister John Charles Oglethorpe, of the Savannah Oglethorpes."

"One of the most noted vocal instructors in the South."

"That's why I wanted to study under him. Mother didn't want me to move here to study because she was afraid of the fever. But I insisted, and Papa gave in to me as usual. As you know, the fever took my mother." She hesitated so long, Samuel feared she couldn't continue. Then she cleared her throat. "She was barely gone when I looked down the stairs and saw my father dashing for the door. Since he didn't have his hat, I thought he was walking around the grounds. Later Grandmother sent me to Joseph's house on the bluff to see if he knew where Papa was, since I was the only one who wasn't sick."

"And he knew?"

"I never got to ask him. The steamer whistle blew while I was standing on his front gallery, and I somehow knew my father would be on it. I looked down the bluff in time to see him walking up the gangplank, wearing the sky-blue velvet coat Mother had given him."

In Samuel's twelfth summer, he'd spent nearly every waking hour with his father, learning the work of the ministry. Translating Bible passages into Greek, Hebrew and Aramaic. Calling on the sick. Watching Father labor over sermons. Meeting with the deacon board. All the while wishing instead to be outside with his friends, fishing or frog gigging. "I'm suddenly sorry I took my father for granted."

She reached inside her sleeve, pulled out a lacy handkerchief and dabbed at the corners of her eyes. Her gaze turned soft as she surveyed the gardens, the woods beyond. "The last time we were all together—the last time we were happy—was at this place."

And she believed she could be happy here again. She didn't have to say the words. Samuel knew it instinctively. She might have been right, had she not married him.

The thought invaded his mind and embedded itself there. What was done was done, but today Clarissa had forfeited her chance of a happy union. In years to come, would she still think this place was worth the price she'd paid for it?

Would Samuel regret letting her pay it?

And what of her father? Could he not somehow have made her life easier, happier? "Why does your father stay away?"

"He and I have always been opposites. What brings me comfort brings him pain." Clarissa slipped her hanky back into her sleeve. "Although I posted a letter to him this afternoon, inviting him home for the Spring Festival and telling him of our marriage."

The scoundrel, minding his own pain and leaving behind his motherless child. What kind of man would—?

He stopped the thought cold as an image of Emma, crying and begging him not to leave her at Daughter's College in Kentucky, shot through his mind. He'd been that man, leaving her with strangers a mere two weeks after her mother's passing.

His head pounded again at the insight. At least Clarissa's father had left her with family, unlike Samuel…

"And now that my grandfather's gone," she was saying, "and Papa never comes to Natchez, Grandmother Euphemia is all I have for family. Besides Absalom."

"Having him for a relative is worse than having no family at all, I'm sure." He pressed the pad of his thumb against the scar at the base of his skull, the spot that always throbbed at the most inopportune times since the battle that had changed his life. He gave it a rough massage.

"Precisely." Missus Adams's voice rang out beside Samuel, no more than twenty feet away.

He hastened to rise. How had he become so careless? Engrossed in his wife's story, he hadn't noticed the elderly woman tapping her cane on the brick walk beside him as she approached. His wartime alertness must have gotten rusty.

Clarissa stood, too, and hastened toward her grandmother as if she feared she'd never see her again. Which might not be too far from the truth, given the older woman's dislike for her own grandson.

With a spryness that surprised Samuel, Missus Adams made for the house. "Please take me to town, Reverend."

Clarissa lifted her narrow skirts and sailed along after her. "Where do you intend to go?"

"Back to Callaway House."

"You can't. Absalom won't let you."

"He has nothing to say about it. He can try to throw me out if he wants."

"Grandmother, please…"

Still rooted to the spot where he'd stood from the bench, Samuel breathed a quick prayer for wisdom. Did he have the right to step in and make suggestions, offer help, give guidance? *Lord, what would You have me do?*

Probably act like the head of the Montgomery household, which now included Clarissa and Missus Adams. And probably take responsibility for their safety and well-being. They might not like it, but for some strange reason, God seemed to have chosen him for such a time as this.

He hastened to catch up and wedge himself between

Clarissa and Missus Adams in her huge black hoopskirt. He offered his arm to each. The grandmother immediately hooked her bony hand into the crook of his elbow, but Clarissa held back. With what he hoped was a mock-severe expression, he waved his elbow at her, coaxing her. She smiled and took it, if only to keep it from jabbing her in the ribs. "Now, please tell me what Callaway House is and what it has to do with us."

"It's our place of exile—"

"Grandmother, it's nothing of the sort." Clarissa's laugh tinkled again as they took the slight rise to the big house. Samuel steeled himself against its allure. "It's Cousin Absalom's town house. Before the surrender, a dozen Yankee officers occupied Camellia Pointe. Callaway House was empty, since Absalom had already gone to war, so we moved in."

"I inherited it when we thought Absalom died," her grandmother said, "and believed I owned it until today."

"You still live there?" That would explain the run-down condition of Camellia Pointe, the sheets covering every piece of furniture he'd seen so far.

"We did until Joseph got a man to move our things here this afternoon. Before you came, we felt safer in town. Of course, Natchez is still occupied and overrun by Yankees." Missus Adams's tone said all Samuel needed to know about her opinion of those Yankees. "But at least in town we have our friends nearby if we need them."

Samuel couldn't hold back a grin. "More likely, you were the one to rescue them from the Yankees, Missus Adams."

A glimmer of friendship twinkled in her eyes. "I might have done just that on occasion."

And Samuel believed it. "But surely you don't intend to stay there alone while we all live at Camellia Pointe."

"I told you I intend to stay at Callaway House until I can get to Memphis, and I meant it."

Samuel glanced around the grounds. "I'll take you to town as soon as I find Emma. I don't want her here alone with Absalom and his family."

"I'll look inside," Clarissa said, starting for the house.

Fifteen minutes later Samuel met Clarissa in the courtyard as she burst out of the massive two-story brick dependency behind the house. "She's not in here. I've searched the house from attic to basement too."

Missus Adams rounded the corner from the front. "Absalom's carriage is gone. Could she have left with them?"

Surely not. But they'd looked everywhere except the dense woods behind the gardens, and she wouldn't have gone there. He headed toward the house, the women keeping pace with him. "Where would they have gone?"

They rounded the corner to the front. Only Samuel's carriage stood under the oaks.

"To Callaway House, no doubt." Missus Adams picked up her pace, heading toward Samuel's rented phaeton. "Let's go."

Clarissa looked down at her dress. "In your wedding gown?"

"It survived sixty years in the cedar chest. A trip to town won't hurt it. Get in the carriage." She turned and glared at them both in the waning winter light. "Now!"

Ten minutes later, they turned north onto Pearl Street, the three of them crowded into the phaeton's single seat. "You'll have to drop me off at Callaway House before you look for Emma," Missus Adams said. "This meager buggy of yours won't hold all of us."

As they pulled up to the single-story town home, a tousle-haired young man in grimy work clothes bounded down the front steps, a toolbox in his hand.

"What are you doing here?" Samuel called from the carriage.

"You don't need to get out. Major Adams paid me before he left."

"Major? Do you mean Absalom?"

"He told me to call him Major Adams."

Missus Adams craned her thin neck and peered at the man. "Justin Bellows, what were you doing?"

"Changing the locks, ma'am." He dashed through the gateway and down the street.

"Changing them?" She pointed with her cane. "But we won't be able to get in. Reverend, stop him."

"He's already half a block away."

"Try the doors anyway. All four of them." Her voice followed him up the walk and onto the gallery.

After hastening to check the doors, Samuel returned to the carriage. "All locked. You'll have to ride along—"

The thundering of horses' hooves racing up Pearl Street cut off Samuel's words. He turned that way as a runabout sped toward them, pulled by a chestnut French trotter and careening up the wrong side of the street. Who would take this sort of risk with such a beautiful horse? Or had the horse run away? With only the thin light of dusk to illumine the road, the animal could easily step in a hole and cause an accident.

As the carriage flew nearer, it rocked back and forth with the horse's speed and then whipped around the next corner, balancing on two wheels. Samuel caught a glimpse of a bareheaded man and a woman in a cream-colored bonnet—a woman in danger.

Hearing the carriage race around the block, Samuel

hastened into the middle of the street, prepared to leap at the horse and grab the reins if he could. As soon as the conveyance came back into his sight, he waved furiously. “Stop! Whoa!”

Samuel braced himself to make his move.

The driver snapped his whip near the horse’s head.

He was racing at this speed—on purpose?

A mighty wind blew Samuel’s hat from his head as the carriage flew by, much too fast for him to catch the reins. In the driver’s seat sat Absalom’s stepson, Beau.

Looking back at Samuel, holding on to her hat with one hand and the carriage brace with the other, was Emma.

Chapter Four

Whisked away to her beloved estate in a fine brougham pulled by two black horses, a devoted husband by her side…

Such had been Clarissa's girlhood dreams of her wedding evening.

But instead, Samuel swung his wooden-seated phaeton into Camellia Pointe's lane after a bumpy, silent drive in the waxing moon's cold, white light. The conveyance seemed barely able to hold together as Samuel raced along, seemingly hitting every rut and hole.

She couldn't blame him for his intensity. Seeing Emma alone with a young man in the twilight was bad enough. But their wild ride—Clarissa would not soon forget the shock. Or Samuel's futile attempt to catch up to the wayward couple, making their ride almost as bad as Beau's.

Nor could she fault him for being a less-than-enthusiastic bridegroom. Their arrangement was just that—an arrangement.

"Reverend, your daughter needs guidance," Grandmother said as if she was the only one who'd recognized the fact.

"Agreed. But first I'm going to have a long talk with Absalom and Beau."

If the timbre of Samuel's low, measured voice was any indication, the talk may not turn out well for her cousin.

"If you like, Samuel, I can settle Emma in her room," Clarissa said.

As he murmured his agreement, she formed her plan for accommodations. Emma could have the second-floor bedroom next to Clarissa's in the original part of the home, and Grandmother could stay in her ground-floor rooms in the rear wing. Absalom and his wife could have one of the second-story rooms above Grandmother's, and Beau the other—and what of Samuel?

Where did one house a man who was one's husband in name only?

They pulled under the canopy of live oaks, their Spanish moss swaying lightly in the damp winter breeze and the light of the brightening moon, and stopped behind Beau's runabout. Before Samuel could alight and assist the women from the carriage, the front door banged open. Absalom strode out, holding a burning ten-light candelabra.

"What do you mean, locking your grandmother out of the house?" Samuel swung out of the phaeton and faced Absalom head-on, his stance wide, his tone ominous.

Clarissa stepped onto the granite carriage block and caught Samuel's blazing eyes, his set jaw, a menacing contrast of shadow and light. Was this what the Yankees had seen in him the day he'd defied them to save his platoon? If so, it was a wonder any of them had stayed around for the fight. The handsome parson could look downright intimidating when the need arose.

"Come this way," Grandmother Euphemia whispered as she stepped down, a spark of interest in her eyes. She tightened her grip on Clarissa's hand and pulled her into the shadow of the nearest low-hanging oak branch. "If Absalom forgets we're here, he'll speak more freely."

"What? Hide in the trees and eavesdrop like children?"

Grandmother shushed her, her finger to her lips.

Apparently so. Clarissa turned her attention to the men.

"Callaway House is mine and has been for ten years." Cousin Absalom's voice boomed in the darkness, echoed back from the trees. "She's a squatter and so is Clarissa. I had to protect my home."

"From an elderly lady and a young woman?" Samuel took another step toward Absalom. "Callaway House was in no danger from them."

Absalom backed up, holding the flames out before him. "You don't know that. Houses burn to the ground all the time."

"If I wanted to burn down your house, I'd have done it after you left us during the fever epidemic." Grandmother Euphemia stalked up to the gallery, apparently done with her spying, her cheeks crimson in the candlelight. The silence of the night turned deafening until an owl hooted from the direction of the kitchen wing and a clattering sound came from the upstairs gallery. "And you know why."

The smirk on her cousin's face revealed that he did, indeed, know why.

But Clarissa didn't. Her grandmother's words of this afternoon rang through her mind.

Considering how you left your entire family for dead during the yellow fever outbreak...

What had she meant by that? And why had she never spoken of it to Clarissa?

"Regardless, you can't stay at Callaway House. And I hear you won't live with me, either, so perhaps you should go back to the Delta." Absalom smiled that heinous smile that had always made Clarissa run from him when she was a child. "Or somewhere even farther."

"That's enough." Samuel strode to the door and held it open. "We'll continue the conversation inside. Alone."

Grandmother swept past them, her skirts swishing. Absalom's grip visibly tightened on the candelabra, and he raised it slightly as she sailed into the hall. For a fleeting moment, Clarissa feared he might strike Grandmother with her own coin silver. She rushed to step between them.

Samuel beat her to it. "Give it to me, Adams."

"I'm the head of my own family. Why should I take orders from a preacher?"

An image came to Clarissa's mind, one she had fabricated the first time she'd heard of the Fighting Chaplain's exploits in battle. A man with fire in his eyes and a saber in his hand, defending his vulnerable men from the enemy's merciless onslaught. She leaned forward and whispered, "Because he brought his sword with him to Natchez."

Absalom's mouth slackened for a moment then he reached out, holding the candelabra an inch closer to Samuel.

Apparently her cousin was still a coward.

Samuel took the candlestick. "We have much to discuss, including your stepson's conduct with my fourteen-year-old daughter this evening. Please collect him and meet me in the dining room."

Grandmother had been right about one thing—they'd be safe at Camellia Pointe as long as the Fighting Chaplain was there.

Clarissa glanced around the hall and into the parlor. “Where do you think Emma is?”

“You’ll find her where you find Absalom’s stepson,” Grandmother said, heading down the hall toward the sitting room. “Mark my words, that boy’s going to cause us more trouble than Absalom will.”

If so, this contest would be harder than any of them had thought. “Maybe he won’t. He might simply be a bored young man of privilege and won’t do any real damage—just make a lot of noise…”

She hesitated, remembering the sound on the upper gallery. Too loud to be a squirrel or other rodent, it had to be Emma and Beau.

“I know where they are.” Clarissa took another candelabra and matches from the piano that sat in the curve of the staircase. She lit the candles and started up the stairs.

She took the steps as fast and silently as she could. However, a part of her would rather have slowed down and put off the confrontation that might take place when she found Emma.

She wouldn’t put it past Beau to lure the girl away to take advantage of her. *Lord, help me to “be ye angry, and sin not.”*

If she was right about Beau and took out her anger on him, she could turn Emma against her. Clarissa was a mother now, and this may be the first test of her love for her new daughter.

And she did love Emma, although they had met only today. But how could Clarissa manage to discipline her, teach her, when they were too close in age to be mother and daughter?

Perhaps she should act less like a mother and more like a young aunt.

She had to admit the role of aunt would come more

naturally. Love the girl, guide her, be her friend—that, Clarissa could do.

She crossed the second-floor center hall, the floorboards making their familiar popping sound under her weight as she passed her room to the right. A muffled soprano giggle sounded from outside.

She grabbed the knob, flung open the door and stepped out to find Emma and Beau sitting mere inches apart on the floor. On Great-grandmother Anne's quilt from Clarissa's room.

Eating apples and cheese by candlelight.

In her relief, Clarissa couldn't help letting out a peal of laughter. "Wherever did you find food in this house? No one has lived here since Lee's surrender."

"None of your business." Beau scrambled up, dropping a pocketknife on the pine floor, sounding just like the noise Clarissa had heard in this spot before they'd come inside. Apparently she'd been right—they didn't have squirrels living on the gallery.

The knife slid across the boards and stopped at Clarissa's feet.

She bent and retrieved it. "I don't blame you for finding yourself a snack. With all the excitement, we hadn't been thinking of food. But it's a nice evening for a picnic on the gallery."

Beau snatched the knife from her hand and stomped inside, his childish temper evident with every loud footfall.

Emma stood, also, and took a shaky step back. "We didn't do anything wrong..."

Other than racing through town at dusk and risking their lives and Emma's reputation... "Let's take the rest of the cheese and apples downstairs. Now that I've seen them, I'm getting hungry, and I'm sure everyone else is too."

"You aren't mad?"

"No, but Grandmother will be furious if she sees her mother's quilt outside. She had it and the silver stashed in a secret compartment under Absalom's stairs since the Battle of Antietam. Until this afternoon."

Emma lifted a corner of the quilt and gave it a half-hearted shake. "Your friend—the blond-haired lady from the wedding—left some food in the kitchen."

Clarissa checked the back side of the quilt. A few live oak leaves stuck to it, and she plucked them off and tossed them into the breeze. "Don't tell Grandmother you had it out here. It'll be our secret."

"A secret..." Her gaze turned dreamy, the way Grandmother said Clarissa always looked whenever she took a bite of her favorite bread pudding. "I won't tell."

So the girl had a fascination with secrets. Clarissa would have to keep that in mind. "What else did Missus Talbot bring?"

"Ham, fried chicken and fresh bread. And bread pudding."

Clarissa's grin brought a quizzical look to Emma's face.

Emma grabbed the food and candleholder from the floor then stepped inside. "Missus Talbot didn't bring the apples and cheese."

"Then who did?"

"The old gentleman. The lawyer. He brought them in right before the ceremony, along with potatoes, flour, baking powder and salt. And he put milk and butter in cold storage. He told your grandmother it was everything we need for breakfast—"

Light footsteps and the sound of a cane thumping on the stairs stopped Emma.

Grandmother.

Clarissa thrust the quilt into Emma's arms and gave her a little push toward the bedroom. "Put it away before she sees it."

Another set of footsteps, too heavy for Beau and too fast for Absalom, sounded on the stairs as Emma came back into the hall and Grandmother reached the second floor.

Grandmother paid them no mind, holding out a key on a tattered red-velvet ribbon. "It's no big surprise, but Absalom is acting the fool."

Clarissa reached for the unfamiliar key. Ornate and oversize, it wouldn't fit any door in the house that she knew of.

"That's the key to the suite. Make sure you use it, because I put your grandfather's silver communion set in the study. I don't trust Absalom's wife any more than I trust him. She's the kind who will sneak in and steal the stays right out of your corsets."

"Why do I need a key to the suite?"

"There you are," Samuel interrupted, entering the hall from the stairway. "Emma, I don't know which was greater, my fear for your life during that wild flight in the runabout, or my anger at Beau."

Emma faced her father and glared at him, her jaw tight. "I've been in worse danger."

Samuel's shame smoldered in his eyes until he averted his gaze. "I suppose you have. Nonetheless, in the future, please exercise both caution and wisdom where Beau is concerned."

"At least this time you weren't a thousand miles

away." Emma's bottom lip plumped and stuck out in the hint of a pout.

He gave an almost inaudible groan. "I was never a thousand miles from you."

"You may as well have been. You wanted to be."

"Emma Louise, that is not true."

The girl stamped her foot. "All you've ever wanted was to get away from me—from my mother."

The shame in Samuel's countenance deepened into a level of guilt that drove a spike into Clarissa's heart. He turned away as if he couldn't bear the sound of his daughter's rebuke, the sight of mistrust shimmering in her eyes.

The same mistrust Clarissa held for her own father.

An early moonbeam slanted across the floor and stopped at Emma's feet, seeming to shed light on her pain. Clarissa could feel the girl's longing for her father's attention, his approval, his love.

And her complete inability to make him see it.

Clarissa certainly understood this kind of heartache, since she felt it every day, each time she thought of the men who'd failed her. Now her stepdaughter's guarded expression made Clarissa reexamine her own shielded heart.

How could she help Emma when she couldn't change her own feelings toward her father?

Lord, I'm either the most qualified person to help Emma—or the least. I'm not sure which.

Samuel turned his now-pounding head from the sympathetic gazes of Clarissa and Missus Adams. Would he ever convince Emma of his desperate love for her? Her dainty finger had touched a shard of truth, and that hurt as much as her rejection. He had wished to be a thousand miles from Emma's mother—in exactly those words—after her betrayal of him at the presbytery reception. Apparently he'd failed even in keeping that fact from his daughter.

The thought made him want to run, to head back to the army, to hide himself in some distant place where no one had ever heard of him or his failure.

Or the Fighting Chaplain nonsense.

But he'd done that once, had run off to "serve the Lord and the Confederacy," although even the War couldn't take him a thousand miles away. In the agony of his late wife's ultimate treachery, he'd compromised his convictions, and he'd regretted it every day since.

He'd not make that mistake, commit that sin, again.

"Emma, dear, it's been a long day, and you're overtired." Clarissa's soothing voice broke through his musing and somehow comforted him. Although it was surely a false comfort. She'd overlooked Emma's harsh words to ease the tension, to console his daughter, not because she thought he was innocent of the sin Emma had uncovered.

And yet he couldn't quite stop the echo of her sweet voice that still rang softly in his mind…

He looked up to see his new wife brushing her fingertips over Emma's windblown hair, drawing her close and murmuring in her ear. The sight brought a mistiness to his eyes and he blinked it away. When had Emma had a motherly caress such as this? He'd certainly never seen Veronica showing love to her as Clarissa did now.

"Regardless of all that," Missus Adams said in her no-nonsense tone, "we all must eat and sleep tonight. I'm not sure what calamity my grandson has caused now, but I saw him storm out of the dining room and the back door."

"Absalom is angry because I told him to control his

stepson and his wife—what's her name again?" Samuel asked, glad for the diversion.

"She insisted I call her *Miss* Drusilla. You can imagine the turn of that conversation."

Samuel surely could. "Drusilla has already chosen rooms for them and is unpacking as we speak."

"Which rooms?" Clarissa cast her lovely hazel eyes, a deep green now in the dim light, about the hall and its four bedroom doors.

"She and Absalom are taking a ground-level suite in the west wing, and Beau the room above them."

Clarissa dashed to the back gallery door. "Grandmother, she's in your rooms—"

"Let her have them. I'll stay in this part of the house. If I must sleep under the same roof as Absalom, I'll at least be in a separate wing. Perhaps then he won't murder me in my bed."

Under different circumstances, Samuel might have laughed at Missus Adams's acid tongue. It reminded him much of his grandfather's.

The downstairs case clock chimed the hour before he could formulate a reply. Clarissa consulted the timepiece pinned to the front of her dress. "Nine o'clock. May I suggest we all help ourselves to a cold supper in the kitchen and then retire?"

The thought of food turned Samuel's stomach. If only he could skip the meal and withdraw now, to a place of calm and quiet…

"I doubt any of us has much of an appetite. I'm going straight to my room." Clarissa's grandmother laid her hand on her flat stomach as if calming it. "Your parents' room."

"I was thinking of putting Emma there. If you take that one, where should she sleep?"

"In your room."

"But—"

"She's taken a liking to you. She'll feel more comfortable staying in the room where you slept as a child."

"But where will I—?"

"I want the reverend to have use of your grandfather's study, so you and he will take the second-story suite." Missus Adams lowered her voice and spoke in gentle tones that held none of her usual harshness and reminded Samuel of Clarissa. "Where my Hezekiah and I started out."

A suite. Two rooms, bedroom and study. He nodded his thanks to Missus Adams.

The two women bustled about, gathering linens and who-knew-what to make Emma comfortable in her new home. Samuel headed for the rooms Clarissa directed him toward.

Alone. As he should be. As he always would be.

As he deserved.

Chapter Five

The next morning, Samuel stirred the embers in the study fireplace at the church, the coals mirroring the sunrise outside the window but not the dreariness in his heart. A cheery fire on a damp winter day usually spawned in him a prayer of gratitude. But today it made him feel lonelier than ever. What good was a comforting fire when he had no one to share it with?

And what had caused his uncharacteristic bout of melancholy? He'd spent his adult life without the love of a woman, so why should today be worse than any other day? He had much to thank the Lord for. Yesterday he'd been alone with a daughter who'd seemed unable to tolerate his presence. Today he had a beautiful wife who had formed an immediate bond with his daughter and seemed both capable and willing to be a mother to Emma. Perhaps more of a mother than Veronica ever had been.

So why could he not curb his foul mood?

It must have been the hard daybed in his study at Camellia Pointe. Or the fact he'd gone to sleep hungry and thirsty—and still was this morning. Or perhaps the river air didn't agree with him.

Whatever the cause, Samuel would take the matter to prayer. If continual musing over his situation could change it, that would have happened an hour ago when he'd first arrived at church.

He looked about the study for a spot to designate as his prayer closet, his secret place of prayer. Upon finding a tiny room with a few shelves of hymnals, Bibles and commentaries, he entered and shut the door.

Dropping to his knees, he began his custom of praying aloud, the sound of his own voice keeping him focused and free from woolgathering. As soon as he'd mentioned his new wife's name to the Lord, her voice called to him from the study.

"Samuel, are you here?"

He hastened to his feet and stepped out of the closet. "I'm surprised to see you so early. I was going to bring my phaeton for you, your grandmother and Emma later."

"I drove in alone. Grandmother's cousin-in-law Ophelia Adams loaned me her little one-seat runabout while she visited at Camellia Pointe this morning." The corners of her mouth turned up the tiniest bit, as if she was holding back a smile as she doffed her pale green shawl. "You were—in the closet with the door shut?"

Samuel's face flushed hot in the chilly room. "I understand how I might look silly. Jesus said when we pray, we should go into the closet and shut the door." The trace of a smile lingered on her lips, and it brought a grin of his own. "I took Him literally."

Clarissa's eyes twinkled as her smile spread across her face. She was even more beautiful this morning, standing before the window in the tentative early morning light, the dim rays bringing a hint of a shine to her dark hair. The sprinkling of green leaves in the fabric of her white dress turned her hazel eyes to a near-emerald shade, and her gentle smile tugged at Samuel's heart. Her gold-colored pendant, decorated with a purple stone, caught his attention as it rested against her porcelain skin.

At last, he noticed a covered pail and basket in her hands. She set them on the desk and removed her dark gloves, then pulled out plates, a cup and a leather-bound book marked with a dark green ribbon. "I brought breakfast for us. I've heard soldiers like their coffee strong, so I added extra grounds to the pot for you."

The robust aroma of coffee wafted toward him and lifted a bit of the gloom from the room. How long had it been since a woman had prepared food or drink just for him? For Clarissa to serve him this way—the thought stole his breath for a moment.

Then Samuel realized he was alone with his new wife. If he'd lost his breath a moment ago, he now sensed his pulse betraying him, racing like sniper fire. How was he to act with her? He'd never figured that out with Veronica, had never been able to please her in all their years of marriage.

And now duty dictated he try again.

Could he do it? He and Veronica had had separate interests, separate lives, and eventually, separate rooms. Perhaps he and Clarissa should maintain that kind of marriage too.

Except that he remembered how unfulfilling that had been…

Clarissa lifted the lid from the pail, took a dipper from the basket and filled his cup. Then she set the pail on the cast-iron trivet on the brick hearth, where it would stay warm. She moved closer, handing him a napkin and the cup, and another, sweeter scent mixed with the coffee's bite. A flower fragrance, light and delicate, drifting from her hair.

He drew another whiff then stopped himself. What was he thinking, enjoying her perfume that way? He stepped back, sloshing his drink onto the floor and his boots.

Before he realized what she was doing, Clarissa stooped down with her napkin, cleaning the spill from the leather of his boots and then from the cypress boards. The distracting fragrance hit him again.

"I'm a clumsy oaf. Let me clean it up." Samuel bent on one knee and attempted to take the cloth from her, but before he could manage the exchange, she finished her wiping and stood again.

"No need. It was only a few drops."

He scrambled up and reached for the napkin, but she was already tucking it into a corner of the basket.

When Clarissa had made them each a ham and cheese sandwich with the provisions she'd brought, she cut the sandwiches in two, then took a seat in the straight-backed chair across the desk. Far enough away that he missed her flowery scent. Then was glad he could no longer smell it.

After his word of prayer, which calmed his racing heart somewhat, she opened her book to the page where the strip of green lay. She ran her finger along a list. "Early this morning, I jotted down a few things I thought might help you in your first days at Christ Church."

Help him? The thought gave enough comfort that food appealed to him again, and his stomach rumbled. He glanced down at the plates Clarissa had prepared. The bread was nicely browned and his sandwich fat with generous amounts of ham and cheese. Exactly as he liked it.

Samuel forced his gaze from his plate and waited for

his wife to take the first bite. If she didn't do it soon, he'd be sorely tempted to start anyway, despite Clarissa's strict Natchez manners. He took a long swig of his coffee instead.

Its overwhelming strength and bitterness made his eyes bulge. When he'd managed to get it down, he couldn't stop the cough that exploded from his assaulted throat. Army camp coffee was milk compared to this concoction. It was a wonder it hadn't eaten holes in her tin pail.

Was this how they drank coffee in Natchez? If so, he'd be in trouble at pastoral calls and church socials. But wait, she'd said she made it strong for him, obviously thinking he'd like it that way. He cleared his throat. "Are you having coffee this morning?"

She kept her focus on her book. "I prefer mine quite weak, so I took a cup at home. I made this pail especially for you."

For him? The whole pail?

He couldn't possibly drink a whole quart of that kerosene coffee. He opened his mouth to say so but, of a sudden, something nudged his heart—quiet, gentle—the way the Lord often warned Samuel he was about to make a fool of himself. Apparently, He understood something about this situation that Samuel did not.

He closed his mouth. *Then what do I do, Lord?*

When no clear answer came, he assumed he was to drink it. Breathing a prayer for his health, he held his breath and emptied the cup. As he set it down, his stomach roiled. If he didn't get some food in it fast, that coffee would do more damage than a minié ball to the gut.

He laid his hand over his abdomen. Gut shot—by his own sweet wife's coffee.

At the sound of the cup hitting the desk, Clarissa

looked up from her list. Seeing the empty vessel, she flashed him a warm smile that made her eyes gleam.

And Samuel understood why he'd had to drink that coffee. She was trying to be a good wife on the first morning of their marriage. He took in the pretty curve of her cheek, her delicate brows and lashes, the innocent set of her lips. Refusing her attempt at pleasing him this morning would have crushed her. It was far too soon for him to make a mistake like that. He'd have to drink her coffee every time she made it for him. And as for his stomach—well, if God was leading Samuel to drink the stuff, it would be up to Him to keep it from killing him.

However, he knew better than to hope this could mean they'd be happy in the future. Even Veronica had tried—a little—in the beginning.

Clarissa pushed the book to his side of the desk. "I've written down the church's regular meeting schedules, community activities, names and addresses of the deaconate—details like that."

She finally took a bite of her sandwich.

At last, he bit into his, its good salt-rising bread and salty ham, the smooth cheese…

Footsteps sounded in the hallway and drew nearer. "Did I hear someone mention the deacons?"

The severe tone of the man's voice brought Samuel's gaze up. The skeletal deacon he'd met yesterday—was it Bradford? Bradley?—stuck his balding head inside the door, the other two deacons behind him.

As Samuel hastened to finish his bite of sandwich, Clarissa smiled her encouragement to him. The three men, clothed with every bit of their dignity, filed into the study and all but circled the desk.

"I don't understand why you're still here," the bony one said.

Finally able to speak, Samuel stood and faced his tormentors. "I've had a change of circumstances, Deacon..."

"Bradley."

"Deacon Bradley. I'm happy to report I'm now married." And it was true—he was happy to report their nuptials because it meant he could stay at Christ Church. Being happily married was a different story altogether.

"You're married? To whom?" The ample-bellied deacon's astonishment showed in both his tone and his wide eyes.

"To me, Deacon Morris." Clarissa waved her left hand, displaying her wedding ring. "The Reverend Gifford married us at Camellia Pointe before he left town last night."

Deacon Bradley snatched her hand and held it close to his face, peering at the ring as if wishing to bite it to make sure it was real gold. Then he dropped her hand and turned to Samuel. "I trust Miss Euphemia will give us the same story when we ask her."

"She was at the wedding. So was Joseph Duncan." And Absalom Adams, but he saw no point in bringing up that unpleasantness.

"I suppose you now meet our criteria, so you may stay," the third deacon said, the one with the smooth voice. "However, we have already retained Deacon Bradley to preach today."

"I will preach, and you may take your stipend from my salary, Deacon." Their plan had worked. Nothing could keep him from pastoring in Natchez now. His new life would certainly hold its challenges, but Emma would settle in here and forget her notion to move back to Vicksburg to live with her mother's parents. *All is well. Thank You, God.*

Deacon Bradley pointed his skinny finger at Samuel, interrupting his silent prayer. "A hasty marriage is better than no marriage at all, I guess, although it's quite shocking. You may stay at Christ Church, so long as you manage to avoid any more scandal—"

The sound of running feet, heading in their direction, cut him off. The deaconate turned toward the hall. A tousle-headed boy of about nine, his rough clothing in tatters and a drum sling around his neck, burst into the study. Running toward Samuel, the redheaded boy slid the sling over his head and dropped the drum to the floor.

"Papa Samuel! I finally found you!"

Papa?

Yesterday's life-changing events must have somehow destroyed Clarissa's sense of understanding, of reason. Because, for the life of her, she couldn't figure out why this disheveled-looking boy had called her husband "Papa."

Samuel bounded to his feet and bolted across the room toward the child. "Willie! How did you get here?"

Clarissa caught both the mistiness in her husband's eyes and his wide grin as the boy flung himself into Samuel's arms.

Could Samuel have a son—another child—but had neglected to tell Clarissa? That would have been bad enough, but he must also have left the boy behind somewhere—alone. Clearly, Willie had been fending for himself for some time, judging from his dirty, shabby clothing and filthy hair and hands. The only presentable thing about him was his drum, its head worn but clean, its brass shell decorated with bright stars and polished to a shine. Even its ropes looked new.

Watching Samuel ruffle Willie's russet-colored hair, she could hardly believe he'd deserted the boy. She moved a few steps closer as Samuel took the child's right hand.

"Remember how to shake like a man?"

Willie lifted his head. "Strong grip, look him in the eye."

Samuel's laugh rang out, the first laugh she'd heard from him. He couldn't have abandoned Willie. Her husband's pleasure at seeing him was not the behavior of a man who had betrayed his son.

Then again, no one would have thought Clarissa's father would abandon her either.

"Reverend, who is this boy? Your son?" Deacon Bradley shouted, pointing at Samuel and the child, teetering a bit as if this new development might knock him off his feet. "How much more disgrace do you plan to bring us?"

"What disgrace?" Deacon Morris bellowed in a voice that could have been heard on Wall Street. "We don't even know who he is yet. Give the reverend a chance to explain."

"Why's everybody so angry?" Willie looked down, blinking as if holding back tears. "Guess I shouldn't have come here."

"No, you did the right thing, and I'm glad you did." Samuel looked over Willie's head and glared at the deacons for a moment. Then he held out his hand to Clarissa. "Willie, I want to know how you got here and why, but first, I have a surprise for you. I have a wife now."

She hesitated at the vulnerability in his tone as he called her his wife. Did he fear she would fail to live up to the title? That she would resist the touch of his hand?

Or was it something unrelated to her, some long-ago rejection he'd not yet shaken?

Whatever the cause of his uncertainty, her job was to dispel it. As she was not doing by making him wait for her to come to him. She hastened to her husband's side and took his hand.

He held it, steady and safe, as if trying to convince both her and himself that all would be well. Samuel's tenderness with her and the child, coming so quickly after his firmness with the deaconate, made her catch her breath.

"Missus Montgomery," he said, his voice low, "this is Willie Bigelow."

Bigelow, not Montgomery. Apparently, the boy was not her husband's son. Still clasping Samuel's hand, she held out her other to Willie.

To her surprise, he did as Samuel had said—held her hand in a grip just tight enough and with a steady gaze, a sense of wonder in his big blue eyes. "Pleased to meet you, ma'am."

What good manners. His eagerness to please Samuel touched Clarissa's heart. And his distinct East Tennessee twang might mean he came from the area where Samuel had fought the Yankees.

"I want to meet him too, Reverend," Deacon Bradley said, stalking over to them. "Who is he, and why did he call you Father?"

Samuel opened his mouth as if to explain, but Willie spoke first. "I called him Papa Samuel, not Father."

The head deacon gave Samuel a menacing look, as menacing as a six-foot, one-hundred-twenty-pound man could give. "I warned you. No scandals."

Samuel dropped Clarissa's hand and faced him, that Fighting Chaplain light in his eye. "I fear your mind leans toward the unsavory, Deacon. But the apostle taught us that charity believeth all things, and by that he meant all good things. There's nothing scandalous about an orphan drummer boy giving an affectionate nickname to his army chaplain."

Bradley took a step back, swaying like a leaf in a summer breeze, his taut skin reddening. His gaze shifted to the drum on the floor. "Drummer boy?"

"Do you object to a man of the cloth caring for an orphan?"

An orphan who called her husband Papa Samuel. It seemed Clarissa had married a more noble man than she'd realized.

"Of course not." He hesitated, then glanced at his deacon-cohorts. "But he's not dressed as a drummer boy. I thought that drum was just a toy."

"It's more likely that you simply paid no attention to him. The drum is standard size, not small like a toy. It has eleven stars for the eleven states of the Confederacy. You'd have noticed that if you'd had any interest in him."

Deacon Morris crossed his arms over his girth. "You're right. Deacon Bradley, you owe an apology to both the reverend and the boy. But I'm not going to waste my time waiting around for it."

Morris headed for the door, and Clarissa silently applauded him for his newfound courage. It seemed Samuel's influence had already begun to make a real man of at least one deacon.

However, judging from the scowl on Deacon Bradley's face, he hadn't yet surrendered to the Fighting Chaplain. He fidgeted with the pocket watch chain on his baggy forest-green waistcoat, his sparse jaw tremoring. "I'll be watching you, Reverend."

He stalked out, Deacon Holmes trailing along behind him like a puppy, as usual.

Clarissa followed in their wake to close the door to further interruptions.

"Now, Willie, tell me how you found me here." He seated Clarissa at the desk again, Willie in the chair next to her, before he took his place across from them. "And why you didn't go to live with Major Dandridge as I arranged before I left to attend the surrender."

"The major took sick while we was going home. Corporal Wilder and me buried him north of Batesville." He spoke fast, matter-of-factly. "The corporal had taken to drinking again. He didn't ask me to go home with him, but I didn't want to anyway. So I left before daybreak the next morning while he slept it off."

Twice an orphan. And now Clarissa could see glimpses of his ordeal in the way he looked at Samuel, the way he cared for his drum while neglecting himself. But even more, she recognized his nonchalant manner when speaking of his major's death and his corporal's failure to take care of him. Being left behind was devastating, but enduring people's sympathy made it even worse. As well she knew.

Contemplating the boy, she caught him stealing glances at the sandwiches. She touched his arm, opened her mouth to offer him her breakfast, and he turned big blue eyes on her—trusting eyes. Trust she hadn't earned but had been given because of her association with Samuel. The weight of that trust pressed upon her mind and heart—not only regarding Willie, but Emma as well.

And Samuel.

She froze at the thought. Her husband had no reason to trust her, but he clearly did. Not only to be a proper wife and helpmeet, at home and at church, but also with his most precious possession: Emma. Clarissa turned to him and his brown-eyed gaze and saw for the first time how much he counted on her.

The fact shook her to the marrow.

Could she do it? She had understood she needed to be a mother to Emma. But was that all? Had Clarissa given enough consideration to the depth of her new responsibility? She feared not. Her hand trembled as she reached for her plate and set it before Willie.

She would need to spend much time in prayer about this. But for now, she had an orphan to care for.

"Have you had time for breakfast?" Instinctively she knew she mustn't shame the child, mustn't let him know she could see how poorly he'd been able to care for himself. He probably thought he was a man, or at least should be, and she didn't want to shatter the little confidence he likely had. "Had I known you were coming, I'd have brought something for you too. But I find I'm not hungry, and this ham is so good, it's a shame to waste it. Won't you finish it for me?"

The boy's eyes steady with determination, he shook his head. "No, thank you, ma'am. I eat only what I've paid for or earned."

Well. She hadn't expected that.

"But if you have any jobs you need done, I'll work it off."

She stole a sideways glance at Samuel, who reached up to cover his smile, his eyes twinkling. Apparently, during the war, he had taken the opportunity to begin to teach Willie how to be a man. And for some reason, the fact made her handsome husband all the more attractive.

Not wanting to pursue that thought at the moment, she turned her attention back to Willie. "I need some work done at my home, and the reverend has his hands full here at church. You may consider the sandwich part of your pay."

"Much obliged, ma'am. I'll eat half, but not unless you eat the rest." At her nod, he picked up one half of the sandwich, then hesitated. "After you."

She bit off one corner of her half before moving Samuel's plate closer to him so he could eat too. He merely shook his head as Willie took an impossibly large bite.

"Would you care for coffee, Willie?" Clarissa asked, moving toward the fireplace. She took it from the trivet and brought it to the desk. "It's nice and strong, just like you had in the army camp."

She thought she saw Samuel rub his stomach for a moment, but she couldn't be sure.

Willie drew a deep breath, smelling the coffee, and then pushed it aside. "No, thank you, ma'am."

What fine manners and table etiquette. If he were cleaned up and dressed properly, even the oldest Natchez families would receive him.

"How did you find me, Willie?" Samuel leaned back in his chair and studied the boy, elbow on the armrest, chin in his hand.

"I've been following you ever since the major died," he said between bites. "I was afraid I wouldn't never see you again."

"When did he die?"

"Three days after the surrender."

Nine months on the road, no one to care for him. How hungry had he been, how lonely? Clarissa's thoughts drifted to her twice-weekly visits at the city orphanage. Children like Willie came to them every week, all hungry, all alone.

All wanting a real home.

"How did you know I was here?"

"When I got to Vicksburg, the preacher told me."

"How'd you know I was in Vicksburg?"

"The preacher in Jackson."

Samuel laughed as if the boy had been on an adventure. Which, in a way, he had. "Let me guess. Before that, you went to Memphis, Birmingham, Atlanta and Savannah."

"Yep. Saw a lot of the South."

This couldn't be true. No child could travel so far on his own with no money. Did Samuel question his story as she did? Considering the amused grin on his face, probably not. And she had the feeling she should keep those doubts to herself, at least for now.

Samuel let Willie finish the last bite of his sandwich, then he pushed his own plate toward him. "Eat your fill."

"No, sir. While I was traveling, I was hungry sometimes, and I thought of you and how many meals you skipped." Willie shoved the plate right back at him, then turned to Clarissa. "He never ate until all the soldiers had been fed. I was just a boy then, and I didn't understand why he did that. But I'm not a boy anymore, and I'm not taking his food. Please eat, Papa Samuel."

"Very well." An undertone of pride resonated through Samuel's casual tone, and he took a bite.

Perhaps Clarissa had been wrong and Willie told the truth about his travel exploits. Certainly he had more character than Deacon Bradley. "How did you manage to go all the way to the coast? You couldn't have walked that far."

"Same way I got here from Vicksburg. Worked my way. The preacher in Vicksburg had an old shed that needed torn down at his house. I did the job, and he gave me my meals, a bed and a steamer ticket to Natchez."

"And what did you have to do to get all the way back from Savannah?" she asked.

"That was harder."

"The work?"

"The ride. It's easy to get on a steamer and let it carry you down the river. But coming back from Georgia, I had to hitch rides, since Grant tore up all the railroads. I couldn't always find somebody going my way who would take work instead of money for pay, so I had to walk some."

"Why did you look so hard for me?" Samuel asked, having eaten a hearty portion of his sandwich while Willie told his story. He gazed at the pail of coffee for a good long time and then reached for it and dipped himself another cup.

Clarissa had a hard time keeping a smile from her face, hardly able to believe she'd been able to make coffee to his liking the first time she'd tried. She'd be sure to have a pot ready when he got home every night. In fact, she'd make the next pot a little stronger, since he enjoyed it that way.

Samuel took a long sip, set down the cup and gazed heavenward for a moment. Giving thanks to God, no doubt.

"I heard you was traveling and preaching. I thought you needed someone to look after you, and I missed you and didn't have nowhere else to go." Willie set the empty plate to the side. "The preacher in Jackson tried to put me in an orphanage. I broke outta there, right quick. Now I've come here to help you."

To help him? Did he mean he wished to work for Samuel—to live with them?

The sympathy she saw in Samuel's dark eyes told her he, too, thought Willie was leading up to that.

When Samuel turned to her, the sun broke through the morning mist, brighter now and shining on his thick, dark curls. With it came a flash of understanding. Samuel wanted to invite Willie to live with them, to invite him to be their son.

Grandmother would be scandalized.

She had already said she wouldn't live at Camellia Pointe with Absalom, but Clarissa had held on to hope that she would change her mind. Grandmother loved her disciplined, orderly life. Would a rambunctious boy with a drum make her the more determined to leave?

The thought nearly smothered Clarissa, took her back to a place and time she'd often wished would vanish from her memory forever. Mother's eyes, closed forever in a humid, hot room that was quiet as the tomb. Alone, afraid…

Then an image of Willie's face flitted across her mind. Dirty, hungry. Alone.

Willie was the abandoned child Clarissa had been. Surely Grandmother wouldn't refuse him—would she?

Samuel wanted him, anyone could see that. And were it not for Samuel, Absalom and his family would own Camellia Pointe. Clarissa couldn't imagine her cousin letting her and Grandmother continue to live in Callaway House either. Instead, they would be without a roof over their heads today.

If they didn't take some time to think, to pray, she was sure they'd make the wrong decision…

Or would Samuel decide himself, without consulting her?

She pushed away her empty plate and bounded from her chair. Willie hopped up as well, beating Samuel to his feet.

"Reverend Montgomery, Willie, would you excuse me a moment?" she said as she sailed toward the hall.

Hearing Samuel calling to her to wait, his footsteps trailing behind her, she hurried all the faster. He caught up to her in the sanctuary, near the pulpit. The cooler air in the high-ceilinged room helped her catch her breath.

"Sit and talk with me awhile." Samuel took her arm, his touch as warm and gentle as his voice.

When they reached the first box pew, he waited for Clarissa to enter first. He closed the pew door behind him, clicking it shut as if sealing them in until they made the right decision. Until they embraced God's will for themselves, for Grandmother and for the boy who insisted he wasn't a boy.

"Willie was always the bright spot in my days," Samuel said as he sat near her, his abruptness and lack of preamble telling her as much as his words. He wanted to take Willie home with them, there was no question. "His father was killed in the Battle of Chattanooga, and his mother died in childbirth, along with her baby girl. We passed by his farm just as he had begun digging their grave."

Tears stung her eyes as she tried to imagine the depth of darkness she'd have felt had she dug her mother's grave.

"Colonel Talbot allowed us to stop, and we dug it for him. I preached her funeral, and as soon as it was over, Willie packed a few clothes and marched out with us. I kept him near me, and for the next year, the colonel and I tried to finish raising him the best we could."

His tone had turned gentle and he rested his hand on hers. In the dimmer light of the sanctuary, Samuel's large, sinewy hand brought a measure of comfort and warmth that hardly made sense, that passed her understanding. The gentle pressure brought up her gaze. She looked into those brown eyes, even darker in the dimness, and saw an emotion she couldn't describe, a nameless nuance that vowed to change her world forever.

Again.

Chapter Six

The sheer anguish in Clarissa's beautiful, dewy eyes pierced Samuel like a dragoon saber, throwing him off-kilter for a moment. He breathed a silent prayer for wisdom. By no means could he afford to make a mistake now.

"Clarissa, dearest—"

Samuel cut the word short. Where had it come from? Certainly not his heart.

He tugged at his collar, hoping to relieve the sudden heat in his face and neck. Perhaps she hadn't heard. Perhaps he'd just imagined he'd said it. Perhaps—

With wide eyes, she looked up at him, lips parted and trembling. Then she closed them, as if she had no words for the gravity of his blunder.

No doubt about it. He'd said it. She'd heard. And every single word of explanation he could think of would only make things worse.

Finally he removed his hand from hers and edged farther from her until his side touched the door. "Forgive me. I didn't intend to be forward..."

That sounded pathetic. But how could he explain when he had no idea why he'd done it, why he'd called her "dearest"? He had no dearest, not in a romantic sense. His first wife had been dear to him but hadn't been truly his. Her heart had belonged to another…

"No need to apologize." Clarissa laid her hand on his forearm, somehow bringing a measure of comfort. The soft pressure lured his gaze to her again, and from some deep reserve, she drew a smile. "And you don't need to crowd yourself into the corner. It was just a mistake."

A mistake. The worst thing she could have said.

Nevertheless, if she could make a valiant effort to dispel his embarrassment, he could return the favor. Of course, she was uncomfortable too. He forced a smile of his own, which wasn't as hard as it might have been had she not done so first. Could he make her smile again? "It could have been worse. I could have said 'ducky dearest.'"

As he'd hoped, she smiled, this time with twinkling eyes. He moved an inch closer.

"I know you were married before and loved your late wife," she said. "It's perfectly natural for you to fall into habits from that marriage, including terms of endearment. Please think no more of it."

She was wrong about the words of affection—after Veronica's betrayal, he'd stopped using them. But Clarissa's maturity astounded him, especially considering how frightened she'd looked when he got to the sanctuary. Perhaps her influence would truly be the best thing for Emma, as he'd thought.

"That's kind of you," he said. "But we should discuss the matter at hand. I feel I have direction from the Lord concerning Willie, and I'd like to take care of it as soon as possible. Then we can turn our attention toward settling in as a family and making repairs at Camellia

Pointe. We can't let ourselves get distracted from fulfilling the conditions of your grandfather's will."

"Agreed. But how can you know God's will so quickly?"

He shifted in his seat as if this was the first time he'd been questioned on the topic. "I know it may seem rash. But I'm a man of action, not contemplation. Always have been. The Lord seems able to work within my temperament and give me instant insight in some cases. This is one of them."

"Did that happen yesterday too?" Her voice carried a note of hope, of yearning to believe they'd done God's will. "Did you immediately know He meant us to marry?"

"I did."

"I shouldn't be surprised. Grandfather often said the Lord worked with him the same way. It bothered him at times, made him question himself."

The great Reverend Adams struggled with this, as well? Samuel couldn't help but chuckle. "Wish I'd known that when I entered the ministry. Talking to him might have saved me many long hours of doubt."

Although a part of him wished to continue this satisfying conversation, he needed to finish their discussion about Willie before he lost his nerve. "I'm entirely confident of God's plan for us to take Willie home. He has no one but me. No relatives that he knows of." He looked beyond her, toward the north window and his Vicksburg home. "We might be able to find someone else to take him, but I believe God is directing us to be his parents."

"I understand his need, and were it not for one concern, I wouldn't hesitate to take him."

The same distress settled in her eyes again, even more

intense than before. What could worry her so much? "Tell me."

"It's Grandmother. She's the most orderly, disciplined woman in Natchez, and she won't quickly welcome a boy in her home. She doesn't have your heart for orphans."

What—the widow of Hezekiah Adams not interested in orphans? If that was true, Clarissa's reaction to Willie's appearance made more sense. "But your grandfather was known across the state for his work with the local orphanage."

"He comes from a long line of preachers on his mother's side. Absalom's father was the first in their line to go into business since they came over on the *Mayflower.* But Grandmother is from an old planter family, and their interests lay in finances rather than charity. Grandmother changed through the years, but she has difficulty welcoming strangers into her home."

He took a moment to absorb this news. "That would give her all the more reason to move to Memphis."

Clarissa drew a hankie from her sleeve and pressed it to her eyes. "She's all I have, and she needs me too..."

A part of him wanted to tell her she had him now, and he would always protect and care for her. His rational side protested. He wasn't a true husband and didn't know how to be. No matter how much he wished for—had always wished for—a true marriage.

Still, Clarissa and her grandmother were his responsibility now...

He took her hand again, to calm her, comfort her, impart his strength and support. Of course she wouldn't want her grandmother—her only relative, other than Absalom—to leave.

But what if...

"I think we can keep both Willie and your grandmother. He's an excellent boy, and he'd be a big help to us," he said. "We have to begin to fulfill the second condition of the will, and my time will be limited. I'll get a tutor for him and Emma, and after their studies are over, he can help with the repairs at Camellia Pointe."

"How will that keep Grandmother from leaving?"

"Willie himself will do that. When we were in the army, we had some hotheaded men in our platoon. But they all loved Willie so much that they wouldn't fight and argue when he was around, because they wanted to protect him and make him happy." As he spoke, he began to convince himself. "Now he'll be the buffer between your family—our family—and Absalom's."

Clarissa twisted her hankie as if wringing her cousin's stout neck. "I'm not so sure Grandmother will give in to his charm. You know how jaded she is."

"I think she will. Willie is respectful and responsible, but he's still a nine-year-old boy and needs a woman's influence. When your grandmother gets to know him, she'll want to help. I'm certain of it. Trust me."

Clarissa looked away, a tremble to her lip.

He took her hand again. "I won't force you. The final decision will be yours."

She jerked away from his grasp, a spark flashing in her eyes. "You move too fast for me. This crazy plan of yours will either keep my family together or destroy it, and I have to decide what to do. How am I to make such a huge decision without taking time to think it through?"

"You can, because Willie is here now and doesn't have a place to sleep tonight. Not to mention, he's going to be hungry again in a couple of hours. He needs us."

The fire in her eyes died down, and he sensed her struggle.

"I promise, if your grandmother wants to leave because of Willie, you'll be the one to decide whether we let her go or find a different home for him." He stood and opened the pew door. "You're the granddaughter of the Reverend Hezekiah Adams. You'll do the right thing."

"Are we now to be nursemaids to a ragamuffin?"

Grandmother Euphemia and her cousin-in-law, Ophelia Adams, had apparently not moved from the parlor sofa where Clarissa left them early this morning. Which suited her fine, since Miss Ophelia would likely turn out to be a diplomat, if not an ally, in the war that was breaking out in the parlor.

"He's not a ragamuffin, Euphemia," Miss Ophelia said, her gentle eyes taking in Willie and his drum. "He's from fine stock, with those clear eyes and strong jaw. All he needs is a good bath and some fresh clothes."

"And just where am I to find clothing for him? We've been remaking our clothes for three years now, without a single affordable bolt of new fabric in the whole town."

Willie met Grandmother's gaze and held it, a feat many grown men couldn't do for more than a few moments. "All I want is to work for you and the chaplain, ma'am. I'll earn the money for my own clothes."

"You'll need to speak to the reverend about earning money. Mine is all but gone."

The rustle of skirts drew Clarissa's attention to the center hall as Emma glided in, wearing a modestly cut blue taffeta gown suitable for a girl her age. She spun in the spacious hall, making the skirts dance. "Miss Ophelia says I can wear this to your wedding reception."

"It's lovely on you." Clarissa guided her to the parlor. "I want you to meet your father's friend, Willie Bigelow. He's moving in with us."

Rather than the jealousy Clarissa would have expected, Emma gave him the condescending smile of an older girl who perhaps saw an opportunity to be a younger boy's boss. "I'm Miss Emma," she said, lifting her chin.

"You're not yet old enough for that title, young lady," Grandmother said as Miss Ophelia hid her smile behind her handkerchief.

Emma paused a fraction, then swirled back out the parlor door to the hall. "Nevertheless, I'm older than you, Willie, and I was here before you. So don't take any foolish notions, and don't put on airs."

In Emma's wake, Miss Ophelia dropped her handkerchief to her lap. "I declare, Euphemia, she reminds me of you."

"What? Me? I was never that bossy." At the sound of a carriage approaching, Grandmother craned her neck toward the window. "Who's coming up the lane?"

Never bossy? Clarissa held back a grin and glanced outside to see Samuel in his rented phaeton, taking the drive at a more sedate pace than he had last night. "It's Samuel, come to fetch us for church."

Miss Ophelia hastened to the window as the open carriage approached the house. "Just as you said, Euphemia, he's his grandfather made over. I can see it, even from this distance. That will stir up memories among our friends."

"Some memories are best left alone." Grandmother's tone turned even grumpier.

"Left alone? Then why did you call him here?" And why had she gotten downright bristly both times the elder Reverend Montgomery had come up in conversation since Samuel arrived?

Grandmother straightened her back, if it was possible for her to sit any more upright than she already was, and turned her focus to Willie. "Run outside, child, and help the reverend with his horse. Then come back and we'll decide what to do with you."

After settling his drum in the farthest corner of the parlor, Willie headed for the door.

What would Grandmother do when she discovered she didn't have a say in this matter?

"Samuel already invited him to stay with us."

"Without consulting me?" Grandmother looked as shocked as she had yesterday when Absalom appeared in church. Could Samuel have been wrong to insist Clarissa break the news to her grandmother without him? By saying the wrong thing, could Clarissa drive her away?

"Why not continue this discussion after the reverend gets in, and after I've gone?" Miss Ophelia said, always the peacemaker. She turned to Clarissa and gave her a too-bright smile. "Let's change the subject. I certainly hope Handsome Boy didn't give you any trouble on your drive to town this morning. And I'm referring to my horse, not your stunning-looking husband."

Stunning-looking—yes, Clarissa had to admit Miss Ophelia's assessment was true. She dismissed the thought before it could grow roots in her heart.

Footsteps hit the slate gallery floor, mercifully giving her no time to answer, and the front door opened and shut. Then Samuel burst into the parlor, full of confidence and purpose, as always, and drawing attention and admiring glances from all in the room, Grandmother included. No wonder everyone still called him the Fighting Chaplain a full two years after the battle. He seemed incapable of entering a room like an ordinary man. Which she was beginning to learn he was not.

"Good morning, Missus Adams, Madam," he said,

whisking off his silk high hat and giving a proper, understated bow to Grandmother and Miss Ophelia.

Judging from the looks on the older women's faces, Samuel's courtly manners had certainly won Miss Ophelia's favor, if not Grandmother's.

Willie, having taken in Samuel's actions and the women's charmed smiles, snatched his own battered brown cap from his head. He swept the cap before him in exaggerated imitation of Samuel's bow, brushing the brim across the carpet.

Clarissa hastened to introduce Miss Ophelia and Samuel as she laid her hands on the boy's shoulders, urging him to an upright position.

"I'd say your work is cut out for you, Reverend." Miss Ophelia's eyes shone with amusement.

"And I'd say he's bringing it on himself," Grandmother said. "But I can clearly see that somebody has to teach this urchin to become a gentleman."

"You'll have the perfect opportunity to begin that instruction Friday evening, when I host a reception in your honor, Reverend," Miss Ophelia said. "My nephew, Colonel Graham Talbot, insisted we hold it in his home, where I also live."

"I look forward to it." But the almost-imperceptible tightness in his tone suggested otherwise. "Is this a church event or private?"

"By invitation. The guest list includes the deacons, their wives and the choir. The singers are eager to get to know you, especially since you're the new director of the community choir. And the deaconate seems to need reassurance that you're happy in your new marriage."

"As they naturally would, considering the former pastor's indiscretions," Samuel said, looking around the room. "Where's Emma?"

Miss Ophelia waved away his concern. "My nephew's wife, Ellie, sent along a few gowns she feels are too girlish for her now. Emma is upstairs trying them on."

Loud, heavy footsteps sounded on the back gallery, then the door opened and slammed shut.

Absalom stalked into the parlor. His head was bare, his almost waist-long curls billowing behind him until he plopped his oversize frame into the gold upholstered shield-back chair next to Grandmother. "Ophelia. We meet again."

Grandmother whacked his knee with the tip of her cane, none too gently. "Call her Miss Ophelia. And take it easy on that chair. It's—"

"One of the Hepplewhites that Great-grandfather Peter brought back from London a thousand years ago. Trust me, I remember." He rubbed the offended limb. "And quit using your cane on me. I have a war injury, you know."

"I didn't know." Grandmother let the cane hover over his knee. "Did a Yankee give it to you, or did one of our own do the Confederacy a favor by taking you out of battle?"

"Taking me out?" Absalom's roar filled the parlor and bounced off the high ceiling. "If the Confederacy hadn't been so short-lived, I would have been decorated for bravery in that battle. You and your roughneck preacher could both take a lesson from my heroism. I fought like a gentleman, not a saber-slashing madman—"

A loud thumping sound pierced the air, startling even Absalom into silence.

Clarissa spun toward the corner, where the noise had originated, just as Willie lifted Miss Ophelia's reticule and slammed the drum head with it again.

"Nobody talks about my chaplain that way." Eyes

flaming, Willie grasped the drawstrings of the pink, frilly purse and held it aloft as if he were about to launch it at Absalom like a tomahawk. Which he might just do if the long-haired ruffian insulted Samuel again. "Nor Miss Phemie neither."

Miss Phemie? *No, no, no.* Not Grandmother's most hated nickname…

"Willie, stop." Samuel crossed the room in an instant. "Why'd you bang that bag on your drum?"

"I had to make him listen to me." Willie raised his chin and studied Absalom's openmouthed, once-handsome face, his forehead and cheeks now lined and his eyes droopy as if he'd lived a harder life than he probably had. "He ain't the kind of man to obey a drum call. I had to use force."

Samuel guided the boy, hand on his shoulder, toward Miss Ophelia, whose eyes danced in the bright morning sun streaming through the window.

"I won't argue with you on any point except the lady's purse," Samuel said. "Gentlemen don't touch those. Ever."

When Samuel raised his brows and cocked his head toward the reticule, Willie slowly held it out to Miss Ophelia, his narrow gaze fastening again on Absalom.

"Willie," Clarissa said, laying her hand on his shoulder and praying for wisdom in her words and tact in her tone, "I think my grandmother would rather you call her Missus Adams. Not Miss Phemie."

"Oh, let it go." With a little wave, Grandmother dismissed Clarissa's concern, dispensing with a hundred years' tradition with four words. "I've always hated nicknames, and that one in particular, but it sounds rather charming when Willie says it. Reverend, you may as well call me Miss Phemie, too, when we are home, and

I will call you Samuel. All this 'Missus' and 'Reverend' stuff has become tiring."

Clarissa opened her mouth to speak but had no idea how to respond. What odd change of heart, of habit, was this? No one in Natchez would believe this transformation. Clarissa closed her mouth and glanced out the window, half expecting the sun to fall from the sky with this new order of things.

"Who is this little hooligan? What's he doing in my house?" Absalom rose to his feet, no sign of a knee injury now, and pointed to the door. "Get back to the dirt farm you came from, boy."

"You can't boss me around. I'm the assistant to the chaplain, who is also the aide-de-camp." Willie puffed out his chest as if he had gold Confederate stars on his collar. "I outrank you."

As Absalom took a menacing step toward the boy, Samuel moved between them. "Don't get too close, Adams. Willie's pretty good with a sword."

Absalom circled around them and made for the hall, his steps quick for a man with a bum knee.

"And it's not your house," Grandmother screeched to Absalom's retreating back.

Grandmother—shouting? Until today, Clarissa had never in her life heard anyone, let alone her proper Natchez grandmother, yell inside this home. What renegade influence was Absalom having on them all? And as long as he was here, how could Clarissa ever hope to bring back the peace and order they'd once cherished at Camellia Pointe?

"I love to get in the last word with him." Grandmother lowered her voice and grinned like a schoolgirl as soon as they heard the squeaking of the dining room threshold board. She turned to Samuel. "What did Willie mean about outranking Absalom?"

"The men made him an honorary lieutenant. They pretty much did what he said."

Grandmother Euphemia cocked her head and glanced sideways at the boy, the corners of her mouth twitching. "Absalom says he was a major. So he outranks you, child."

"He never acted like no officer, so I thought he was a private." Willie turned those bright blue eyes on Grandmother, drawing a smile from her. "Even if I'd known he was a major, I wouldn't have let him insult you, Miss Phemie."

For the space of a moment, Grandmother's expression softened. Then she drew her brows together in a frown and rapped her cane on the parlor floor. "Samuel, you ought to make sure my grandson doesn't gobble up the entire breakfast Ophelia brought us. And don't let him tear up anything. If he doesn't respect the Duncan Phyfe pieces in there any more than he does my Hepplewhite, we'll soon have nothing left to sit on."

"I'm on my way." However, Samuel hesitated and set his gaze on Willie, as if silently imploring him to curtail any further outlandish behavior.

With Samuel out of the room, Willie moved in closer to Grandmother and finally sat next to her on the parlor sofa. Bless the child. He'd help to counteract the damage before Grandmother could get a chance to buy a steamer ticket and flee this house that was becoming more disorderly by the minute.

Clarissa fidgeted with the amethyst in her pendant, its facets cool against her fingers.

"Come over here and sit down, Clarissa," Grandmother said in her "take charge" voice. "That man has you as jittery as a June bug."

Clarissa hastened to the sofa and perched on the hassock, her skirts flowing at her grandmother's feet.

"Ophelia, you may think I'm an old fool, and you're probably right. But I've decided to stay at Camellia Pointe for a while, so I can tell Absalom 'I told you so' when this is over."

She wasn't going to leave? Clarissa bounded up from the hassock and hugged her, breathing in the familiar scent of her lavender soap. "I'm so glad. I need you here—"

Grandmother reached up and took a firm hold of Clarissa's arms, unwrapping them from around her neck. "You weren't listening. I said I would stay for a while. If Absalom makes things unbearable, I'm heading straight to Memphis. Don't forget that."

Clarissa settled back onto the stool. Of course Grandmother wouldn't commit to staying at Camellia Pointe the entire year. Was it possible that she valued her freedom from Absalom even more than she valued her home?

A sound erupted from the other side of the house, a sound like a fist hitting an antique mahogany dining table. Then Absalom's boisterous voice rang out with a string of foul words Clarissa wished Willie hadn't heard.

Yes, freedom from Absalom could be more desirable than a country villa.

"Ophelia, go in there and try to reason with that man," Grandmother said. "Tell him there are ladies and a child in this house who don't want to hear his riverboat-gambler language. You always were the only one who could talk any sense into him."

"That didn't happen often, but I'll try." Miss Ophelia

gave Willie's arm a squeeze as she passed him on her way to the dining room.

When she had gone, Grandmother fixed her hazel gaze of steel on Willie and pointed her gnarled finger at him. "Within the last twenty-four hours, Camellia Pointe has undergone the invasion of my insufferable grandson, his wife and stepson, and a new husband and stepdaughter for Clarissa. I had no control over any of it. But this is my home. And from this moment on, I will decide who does and doesn't live here.

"Now, as for you, young man..."

Willie gazed at her, wide-eyed, with the innocence of a cherub. "I want to live with you, Miss Phemie, so I can protect you and Miss Clarissa."

Clarissa leaned closer to her grandmother and breathed a silent prayer, recalling the older woman's immunity to Clarissa's own childhood pleadings. No amount of charm had ever swayed Grandmother from what she'd thought was right.

But if she had softened earlier, she all but melted at the boy's feet now. For about two seconds. Then she pressed her lips together for a moment, narrowing her eyes at him. "You're as courageous as Clarissa's father was at your age—and as cheeky. But yes, I'll feel safe with you in the house."

As a grin emerged on Willie's face, Grandmother patted his knee. "You may stay at Camellia Pointe."

Her new protector let out a whoop and dashed into the hall. "I'll help Papa Samuel keep an eye on ol' Absalom."

When his clomping footsteps died away, the parlor felt as empty and cheerless as cold ashes on a winter night. "Willie has a way of brightening the room, doesn't he, Grandmother? Surely you can see it."

Grandmother rose from the sofa and made for the

hall, her cane-tapping a little softer than usual. "I see only that he's the enemy of my enemy, and that makes Willie my friend."

How had Camellia Pointe come to house so many enemies—first Yankee soldiers and now Absalom?

The Yankees had left of their own accord, but Absalom? Never. He'd proved that by refusing her offer of a compromise.

No, the only way to get free of her cousin was to fight. But who would suffer? She got up and paced to the doorway in time to catch sight of Grandmother leading Willie up the stairs, presumably to make him presentable for church. Did Clarissa have what it would take to hold together her family—both natural and newfound—at Camellia Pointe for a year? Could she defeat Absalom, outwit him? Outwork him?

Grandmother must have heard her in the hall, because she turned and peered down at her from the top step. "Willie can't go to church in these rags. Come help me get him some clothing that looks respectable, even if his tongue isn't."

Clarissa hastened up the stairs, spotting the apprehension in her grandmother's eyes and the trust in Willie's. If she couldn't beat her cousin in this contest, how much more would she lose than just a home?

At ten minutes of eleven, Samuel set the matter of Willie and Miss Phemie—he wasn't sure he'd ever get used to calling her that—from his mind.

What would happen at his first service at Christ Church of Natchez? If attendance dropped with his arrival, the deaconate might boot him out.

And if people came just to see the Fighting Chaplain,

as many had during Samuel's evangelism circuit days, might the deacons take offense to that, as well?

Either way, he'd certainly need the hand of the Lord on the service today.

He'd never appreciated the custom of the pastor making a grand entrance into the sanctuary as if he were some celebrated singer or play actor. So, in keeping with his habit, he left his study early, climbed the seven steps to the pulpit and surveyed his new congregation.

Every single one of them was there, so it seemed.

Scanning the rows, Samuel couldn't see a box pew without at least one person in it, and they hadn't yet stopped coming in. But in Miss Phemie's first letter to him months ago, she'd said the war had caused the attendance to dwindle to around two hundred and membership to three hundred.

Well, Grandfather Jonah always said it was easier to preach to a full house than a half-full one, and Samuel learned long ago how true that was. And perhaps the drastic increase in attendance would give him a little favor with Deacon Bradley—

Interrupting his thoughts, Miss Phemie, with Emma at her side, strolled down the aisle on the arm of a slicked-down, dressed-up boy.

It couldn't be Willie.

Samuel held in a laugh. Somehow, the women of his new household had apparently trimmed the boy's unruly hair and cleaned him up, dressed him in trousers, shirt and morning coat.

How had they accomplished such a feat in two hours?

Willie tipped his battered but cleaned cap to each lady he passed in the aisle, drawing twitters from the women and a tap of reprimand on the shoulder from Miss Phemie. Then she sat him and Emma in the front pew and headed toward the stairs to the second-story gallery and the choir. Samuel turned his back for a moment until he could control his smile. At least they'd arrived early so the fuss would die down before the service.

A quick clatter of light footsteps drew Samuel's attention to the gallery. Clarissa hastened toward the assembled choir near the front, her white, lacy dress and fern-green hat brightening the morning.

Following her, a blond woman perhaps ten years older handed a baby to an elderly woman near the choir and then took her place next to Clarissa in the soprano section.

As he'd instructed in his last letter to Miss Phemie, Clarissa started the choir anthem at eleven o'clock sharp. Ah, the new hymn "Jesus Paid It All." Excellent choice. Samuel stepped back from the pulpit and stood just in front of the trompe l'oeil "niche" there, soaking in the harmonies and lyrics. Slower and sweeter than he'd heard it before, the song sounded nearly perfect.

At the beginning of the fourth verse, Clarissa took the solo. Authentic, rich—smooth; her voice seemed timeless and left him breathless. The kind of voice that came around once in a lifetime. As she sang, her face glowed with the truth of her lyrics. Lyrics she meant; lyrics she lived.

This was his wife? *Dear God, what treasure have You given me?*

When she sang of Jesus's power melting the heart of stone, the mood shifted as if a soothing wind had begun to blow through the sanctuary. The sound of a deep sigh or the catch of a breath wafted up to him from a front pew. Surveying the crowd, Samuel discovered the source of the sound in Deacon Bradley's box. The skeletal man held a snowy handkerchief under his nose, tears raining down his sunken cheeks.

Was Samuel seeing right?

Looking around, he saw similar responses throughout the sanctuary, felt an inner warmth himself. The tenderness of Clarissa's heart seemed to flow from her sweet voice, assuring them all of God's love and desire to soften their hardened hearts.

When the song was over, Samuel feared to move, to break the moment. When he sensed the time was right, he began his sermon with greater freedom than ever before.

To his surprise, the congregation's response far surpassed any he'd seen on the circuit. If he'd thought he'd traded an exciting traveling ministry for a sedate pastorate, he'd been wrong.

When he concluded the service, Deacon Bradley rushed to the front, nearly climbing the pulpit steps in his enthusiasm. "I've never seen anything like the combination of Missus Montgomery's song and your preaching. The Reverend Adams used to talk about the music paving the way for the Word, but this is the first time I've seen it happen."

Music paving the way? Samuel had never heard anyone except Grandfather Jonas say that. Had the Lord planned this for him all along?

Or would the novelty of the Fighting Chaplain wear off in a few weeks and leave them with a smaller congregation than before he'd come?

He'd often thought ministry would be easier without the fame, without the expectations. Now he was sure of it.

Chapter Seven

Late that afternoon as Samuel roused himself from his Sunday afternoon nap in the now-chilly upper gallery rocker, his first waking thought centered on Clarissa and her stunning choir anthem. He'd done nothing to deserve the blessing she was to him already. But why had God chosen him for this woman who'd begun to graft herself into his heart?

He shook away the thought. He'd promised to meet Clarissa, and the shadows had already started to fall in the gardens. But first he needed to retrieve his Bible and his ministry ledger so he could record the details of the morning service. Now if he could only remember where he'd left them and his eyeglasses.

Samuel trotted down the outdoor stairs to the ground-floor gallery then let himself inside to search the lower level. Having no success, he climbed the stairs and unlocked the second-floor suite he shared with Clarissa. Or rather, his room within the suite. Inside, he pocketed the key. When Miss Phemie had given it to him and insisted he use it, he'd thought a lock on the suite was foolish. After getting to know Absalom Adams, though, he saw her wisdom.

"4 for 4" MINI-SURVEY

We are prepared to **REWARD** you with 2 FREE books and 2 FREE gifts for completing our MINI SURVEY!

You'll get...

TWO FREE BOOKS & TWO FREE GIFTS

just for participating in our Mini Survey!

Dear Reader,

IT'S A FACT: if you answer 4 quick questions, we'll send you 4 FREE REWARDS!

I'm not kidding you. As a leading publisher of women's fiction, we value your opinions… and your time. That's why we are prepared to **reward** you handsomely for completing our mini-survey. In fact, we have 4 Free Rewards for you, including 2 free books and 2 free gifts.

As you may have guessed, that's why our mini-survey is called **"4 for 4".** Answer 4 questions and get 4 Free Rewards. It's that simple!

Thank you for participating in our survey,

Pam Powers

He cast his gaze about the room and spied a small, clear vase of white camellias on the bedside table. He picked up the little vase and sniffed the sweet scent. Clarissa had thought of him this morning and left the flowers for him to find. The idea of a woman giving him this kind of attention—he hardly knew what to make of it.

Returning the vase to its place and his thoughts to the need at hand, he made a quick search, to no avail. He sat for a moment on the edge of the narrow daybed. It seemed almost as if someone had purposely furnished it for a bachelor—or a husband who was no husband at all.

His gaze fell upon the large trunk, the one he always kept locked, and his mood plummeted. Why had he even brought it here? He reached into his pocket, pulled out the key to that offensive box and tucked the unpolished key onto the highest shelf of the wardrobe. He'd not need anything that trunk held as long as he lived in this house. In fact, if not for sentiment, he'd throw it and all it contained into the depths of the Mississippi River. He'd be happier if he never saw the contents again.

Light footsteps in the hall broke into his melancholy and reminded Samuel of his responsibilities here. As well as his blessings. Emma was with him, he had a new pastorate, and his wife would be a help in the ministry. If she didn't kill him with her coffee first. He'd not fail to remember the good gifts God had given him.

The footfalls drew nearer and stopped at his door, then came a soft knock.

"Samuel?"

Clarissa's tentative, halting voice made him bound to the door. He flung it open to find her still in her pretty white Sunday dress and holding his black Bible, ledger and eyeglasses.

"I found these on the front gallery and thought you might want them."

Of course. He'd set them on a wicker chair when he'd arrived from church, meaning to come back for them. He held up the Bible. "I'll need this if I'm to continue to fight with your cousin. The sword of the Word, you know."

Clarissa had the grace to smile at his lame joke. "Have you noticed how nervous Absalom gets when anyone mentions swords?"

He hadn't, but now that he thought of it, it did seem true. "Perhaps it has something to do with his war experience."

"I have no idea, but if you hang your Fighting Chaplain sword over the doorway, do you think he'd move out?"

Her wicked grin made him laugh, his gloom somehow lifting. How had that happened so quickly? "Unfortunately not."

"Then let's take a walk through the gardens and grounds and discuss our options for repairs. I want to fulfill the second term of the will before Absalom does."

Samuel laid his Bible on the trunk and glanced around, memorizing the locations of his belongings, just in case. Then he locked and double-checked the door. "Thank you for the flowers."

"They're off the bush I cut my bridal camellias from. I wanted your room to feel cheery."

Funny how the little blooms had done just that, at least until he'd started to feel sorry for himself.

"Let's take Willie and Emma along, if we can find them. Willie is probably outside somewhere. And my daughter is enamored with Camellia Pointe and would enjoy a guided tour."

Clarissa's smile budded again at the mention of Emma's name, and it warmed his heart. "I haven't seen her since dinner."

"She told me she planned to find a secluded, quiet spot and read her book."

Clarissa started down the narrow stairs, her skirts touching the wall on one side and the railing on the other. "What book?"

What difference did it make? "The one she's hardly had out of her hand since we left Kentucky. It's *Our Mutual Friend* by Dickens."

"That book's full of people with secrets. Perhaps that speaks to her in some way." On the bottom step, she stopped and gazed up at him, the thin winter light now drawing the gold from her eyes.

Samuel paused, considering both her idea and her eyes. What other golden insight might she have, what gilded vision? And how did her interest in Emma make her even prettier to him?

He reined in the thought as he would a runaway stallion. Outward beauty accounts for little, as Grandfather used to say. And well Samuel knew the old preacher was right. Veronica had proved it.

Clarissa took the last step and as he navigated around her hoopskirts to open the back door for her, he caught a whiff of her sweet flower fragrance.

Samuel braced himself against the scent. He considered holding his breath until she passed by. Instead, he hastened through the door after her and kept a respectable distance. "You did wonders with Willie this morning. He looked like a native Natchez boy."

Her tinkling laugh made him smile. "It was certainly a challenge. Grandmother cut his hair while my neighbor

Tessa Collins, the woman sitting next to me in the choir, and I made over Grandfather's oldest suit."

"So quickly?"

She gave him a smile that could have warmed even General Grant's heart. "We didn't have time to do more than cut and tack it. All through the service, I prayed it wouldn't come apart."

He laughed with her, and it felt good. Surprisingly good.

"I'm sure I know where Emma is—the same spot where I read *Wuthering Heights* four times the summer I was fourteen," she said, looking about the grounds. "But what would catch a boy's attention at Camellia Pointe?"

As they strolled across the brick-paved courtyard, Samuel took in the expanse of lawn, the gardens, the many structures and pond beyond. "The water, especially the bridge and the far bank with the cypress knees."

"And I see Emma in the gazebo."

By the time they reached it, only a blue hair ribbon lay on the seat.

"How did she disappear so quickly?" Clarissa's skirts swished as she whirled around, looking behind her. "I know I saw her. There's no mistaking her beautiful auburn hair."

Samuel picked up the ribbon. "Is it hers or yours?"

Clarissa's tinkling laugh made him think of glittering snowflakes he'd seen drifting through a north Tennessee meadow. "I'm a little old for hair ribbons."

Of course. What a foolish question. But the laugh it brought dispelled what had remained of his earlier glum mood. Today he could ask for nothing more.

"Should we search the grounds?" she said, her hand shielding her eyes as she scanned the area.

"Her teachers in Kentucky told me she'd developed the unsavory habit of eavesdropping, and had gotten quite proficient at it. I suspect she's hiding somewhere nearby, listening." He raised his voice. "Right, Emma?"

He got no response from his daughter and hadn't expected to. However, Willie must have heard, since he bounded up to them, a can of worms, a small hook and a length of line in his hands. He set them on the gazebo railing and snapped off a salute. "I just got back from scouting the area, sir."

Samuel returned the gesture. "Where have you been, and what have you to report, Lieutenant?"

"Just here in the yard. The enemy is hiding behind that bush, listening. Spyin'."

"Spying?"

"And writing everything in her dumb ol' book."

Of course. Samuel strode to the bush Willie indicated, a thick, tall one with white flowers. His daughter crouched there on all fours, dress and hair in disarray, and peered back at him.

"Come for a walk with us, Emma. Clarissa is going to show us around." Samuel clasped Willie's shoulder and pulled him a little closer. "I want you to make Willie feel welcome."

Her stony eyes made him pause. He moved a step closer. "I'm getting a tutor for you both, and I'd like your input on your studies. Do any particular subjects interest you?"

"A tutor for us? Him and me—together?"

The raw look on his daughter's face sent him a twinge of confusion. He reached for her hand to help her up, needing but unable to understand what pained her so. "How else would you both get your education?"

"I won't do it." She jerked her hand from his and shot

to her feet. He tried to stop her, but she ran off across the croquet lawn and toward the stables, her precious book and what looked like a little diary in her hands. "Leave me alone!"

"Emma, wait…" He may as well have shouted to the air.

Clarissa called to her too, but she raced on like a foot soldier with a platoon of Yankees on her tail.

With a whoop, Willie took off after Emma, dangling a worm before him. At Samuel's gentle rebuke, the boy wandered back over to them.

"She isn't usually this rude." Samuel spat out the first words to come to his mind. Then he hesitated. According to the Kentucky school headmaster, she was, indeed, this rude. But now, since both Samuel and his new wife had witnessed her behavior, he could no longer deny it. "I should have accepted her conduct problem long ago. And I should have told you about it before you agreed to be her mother."

And if such behavior continued—or worsened—would Clarissa regret the arrangement?

"I knew it would be hard, especially at first." If she wanted out of their agreement, neither her words nor her tone betrayed it. "Give her time."

"I have no idea why she's so upset." Samuel let out a groan. "I'd say your grandmother was right. Between Emma and Willie, we have our work cut out for us."

"True, but Grandmother thinks it's a worthy cause."

Willie explored a short distance from Clarissa and Samuel as they walked through the gardens, past the angel and the vine-covered pergola. The boy returned to them every few minutes as if needing reassurance that his chaplain was still there.

"This means your grandmother is staying?"

"For now." Her tone carried less relief than he might have expected. "Let's go straight to the stables in case Emma stopped there. We need to mend this rift between you."

She wanted to see his failure up close—even closer than she just had? That made no sense. "Let her cool off instead. She won't talk about it. She never does."

"I'm afraid your method doesn't work well with young girls. They need to be lovingly convinced to talk about their troubles."

Clarissa's calm but insistent tone stopped him cold. "I'm merely giving her time to overcome her wayward emotions, not applying some method."

"But you are, if it's what you do every time she misbehaves."

Samuel clenched his jaw. How could Clarissa know more than he did about raising a child? He glanced at her impossibly huge hazel eyes, green in the bright sunlight, and saw deep serenity, even peace. Which further proved she understood neither Emma's problem nor his response.

Entering the stable, Samuel heard a quiet sob from the area of the stalls. When he called to his daughter, the sound stopped. He hastened toward her and found her petting the nose of his rented bay roan, her back to Samuel. Clarissa moved to the horse's other side, running her fingers through the mane the color of her own hair. "Her name is Strawberry," he said, vaguely recalling Emma's affinity for horses.

"I know," she said in a whisper.

"What's the matter, Emma?" Didn't she know she was ripping his heart out? He took a tentative step closer.

Her cold stare stopped him from taking another.

"Remember, fathers don't always understand their

daughters." He barely heard Clarissa's sweet, low voice. "But not because they don't try or don't want to. It's because they're men and don't understand women."

That much Samuel could attest to.

"For example, your father doesn't realize how embarrassing this is for you."

Samuel hesitated, struggling to make sense of her words. "What's so embarrassing about having a tutor?"

"I'm a grown woman." Emma stamped her foot on the straw-covered ground. "Willie is just a child."

"Grown woman?" Samuel chose not to point out that he'd often seen Willie acting more mature than Emma had this morning—had just now, stomping like that.

His expression must have given away his thoughts, because his daughter's petulant look quickly turned to anger, her eyes a roaring fire that burned into his heart. "Yes, and if you were ever around, you'd know it."

"I was at war." Samuel lowered his voice to hide the pain she shot into his heart like a cannonball.

"It's all right. I didn't really miss you." Emma's tone hardened all the more, making him wince. "I had my mother."

Clarissa held up a hand to each of them as if trying to separate two sworn enemies. Which, in his daughter's eyes, they were. Then she cast a pleading glance in his direction, and he couldn't help but nod, ready to listen to whatever she had to say. Clearly, Samuel wouldn't be the one to solve this issue.

"Let's stop and think about this," Clarissa said. "Is there a way to alleviate Emma's embarrassment and still provide an education for her and Willie?"

Samuel began with the obvious. "I'm sure there's a school in Natchez."

"A private school?" Emma's face brightened a fraction.

"Our private schools closed during the war." Clarissa smoothed Emma's auburn hair as her countenance fell. "All we have are the Freedman's Bureau schools, and Emma has already passed their highest grade. But I could instruct her in French, the classics, religion—"

"And music," Emma said, a hopeful lilt in her voice.

"I think not," Samuel said. "I'd like you to guide her and oversee her education, and of course give her voice lessons, but you'll have extra church responsibilities as my wife. And you must give attention to the conditions of the will." For that remark, he earned a glare from his daughter.

Clarissa's face lit then as if she'd hit upon the solution. Or at least thought she had. "Yesterday, Absalom said he'd retained a tutor for Beau. He starts tomorrow, and he could teach Beau and Emma together. Willie could study separately, since he's younger."

What? Emma under the influence of that renegade youth for hours every day? It would never work. "Surely we can think of—"

"I'll do it." Of a sudden, the atmosphere seemed charged with Emma's new enthusiasm.

Apparently it was less embarrassing to take lessons with an older boy than with a younger one. But that didn't make this idea acceptable. "Since Beau nearly got you killed last night, I'm not sure this is the wisest solution."

Emma's disappointment cut through him as her earlier outburst had. If only he could agree to this arrangement, he might win a bit of her favor. But Beau was undependable at best…

Clarissa caught his gaze and tilted her head toward the door, nearly imperceptibly. She wanted Samuel to leave? Fine. He nodded slightly and made for the outside, the wind feeling like the cold hand of death on his cheeks.

Why was this transition so hard? He'd left his traveling ministry to make a home for Emma, but nothing had gone as planned. A beautiful stranger for a wife, a mansion unbefitting a pastor's home and a money-grubbing braggart for a cousin-in-law. Perhaps Samuel had been unrealistic, thinking a change of address and a new music teacher could make him and his daughter into a real family. But he'd thought he'd heard from God.

Then he heard Grandfather Jonas's voice in his memory. *God shows us His glory in the hard times.*

Samuel didn't like those words any better now than he had as a boy. But if they'd been true back in Grandfather's time, they were likely still true today. If so, one thing was sure: they'd all better get ready to see a whole lot of glory.

Oh, Emma...

The girl had a way of making Clarissa feel twice her own age while simultaneously hauling out every youthful yearning she'd thought she'd put to rest. Of all people, Clarissa understood the difficulties of a daughter whose father didn't understand her.

And yet Samuel certainly tried harder than Father had.

The unrelenting thought pounded through Clarissa's mind as Emma melted into her embrace. The rawness of the girl's pain, her hesitant desperation, somehow brought Clarissa's own shallowly buried desolation to the surface. Refined it. Even redefined it.

And it was the last thing she wanted now. Why must revelation always come at inopportune times? And at such a cost?

She forced herself to push aside her traitorous thoughts of her father. Emma's needs came first. But before long, Clarissa would need to take out that thought again and wrestle with it until she could make peace with it.

If peace were to be found…

As the girlish frame trembled in Clarissa's arms, she whispered a prayer for her, for Samuel. Emma's emotions clearly ran deeper than mere embarrassment over being seen as a child. Something more foundational was at stake, some crack in the deepest part of her.

Then she remembered the tears staining Emma's face the first time she'd seen her, when she'd wondered if Samuel had somehow hurt her. Could Emma be unsure of her father's love?

Did she doubt her late mother's love as well?

At the thought, a chill shook Clarissa's bones—a chill as deep and unsettled as the Mississippi. If she was right, Emma's pain ran even deeper than Clarissa's. At least she'd always known Mother loved her, even if she hadn't been able to show it in ways that would have reached the more hidden crevices of Clarissa's heart.

Crevices that remained empty today.

The thought gripped her harder than the arms encircling her waist. She forced herself to relax, not wanting Emma to notice her sudden rigidity and think she'd caused it. The girl didn't need to feel more rejection.

As she held Emma, calming herself, Emma's arms loosened until she pulled back and met Clarissa's gaze. "Sometimes I almost hate him. It's a sin, but I can't help it."

The poor girl. Clarissa smoothed the auburn hair, dark in the dim stable. "You don't hate him. You simply haven't learned to control your emotions, but you will as you get older."

"I can't study with Willie. He's just a child."

Clarissa held out her hand as a notion came to her. Dare she act on it now, rather than take time to think it through? It seemed she must. "The sun is shining now, so let's get out of this cold stable and walk around the grounds. I have an idea…"

Emma snatched her book and notebook from the upturned pail they rested on, and they started outside and down the walk past the woods' edge.

"Your father is disappointed because you went riding with Beau last night without permission. You're a good girl and didn't mean to do wrong, so I'll try to help you prove yourself to your father and get back in his good graces." As further inspiration hit, she smiled into Emma's brown eyes, drawing a tiny grin. "If you'll help me with something, as well."

Emma nodded, her cinnamon curls bouncing as they started across the lawn.

"I'll ask your father to let you take French with Beau—"

"Perfect!"

Now the hard part. "And the rest of your classes with Willie."

Emma's enthusiasm died like the wind at sunset, the glow leaving her face and a cloudiness overtaking her eyes.

"I'd also like you to teach basic music theory to Willie. You'll be the adult and assign his lessons. If you do a good job, your father will notice and, in time, he might let you take more classes with Beau. Of course, you'll need to use good judgment when you're with him, so your father will trust you."

From the distance, Clarissa heard the slamming of a door on the rear gallery. Turning toward the sound, she caught sight of Beau stepping out of his second-story room and lowering himself to the wicker chair beside his door. He gave a flirty wave in their direction. Clarissa ignored it and hoped Emma hadn't noticed.

Judging from her quick smile and wave, she had, indeed, noticed.

"Remember, we need your father to trust you if this is to work."

Emma didn't look at Beau again but rather cast her gaze downward, a tiny smile on her lips.

Perhaps this arrangement would bring more grief than relief.

They rounded the bend in the path and spotted Samuel at the sanctuary, his head in his hands, looking as if he were in either prayer or agony. Or perhaps his headache of yesterday had returned and he merely needed another cup of her good coffee.

As they approached the little chapel, he raised his head and then stood. A tiny spark of hope lit his eyes when he saw the two of them together and Emma smiling.

"Emma, I'm not sure what to do about this disagreement..."

When his daughter made no response, acting as if he hadn't spoken or wasn't even there, Clarissa nudged her arm, her touch gentle. Emma looked up at her and Clarissa mouthed the word *trust.*

After a moment's hesitation, Emma lifted her gaze. "Clarissa has a solution."

They sat together, and when Clarissa had explained her idea, he turned to Emma. "Is this what you wish to do?"

"No, I wish to take all my classes with Beau, but Clarissa says I first must earn back your trust. That's what I want."

He hesitated, the air suddenly thick as if he fought a rise of emotions, some tide of expectation he dared not dream he'd fulfill.

This tender, vulnerable side of him drew Clarissa against her will, and she couldn't pull her gaze from him, from the heart she could see in those deep brown eyes. Sensing his struggle, she entered into it herself, fighting alongside him with silent words of prayer. Why not expect God to hear, to answer? Why not dare to believe she could help Samuel regain his daughter's heart, to make her a home and give her a real family?

A real family...

For the span of a moment, the thought of a happy home and warm marriage flitted through Clarissa's mind, teasing her with its sweetness. She stole a glance at Samuel, his strong profile, his dark hair shining in the late-morning sun...

Then he turned those brown eyes on her with an intensity that suggested he'd been thinking similar thoughts. Thoughts neither of them should entertain.

Samuel's eyes lost their hint of yearning at the same moment she stopped her own dangerous line of thinking, before its appeal could take root. They couldn't have a real family, because they didn't have a real marriage. And never would. She rose and turned her back to him, setting her gaze on the sanctuary's stone walls. No matter how kind and protective he was, how gentle and handsome, she could never give her heart to him. He was a man, and men weren't to be trusted...

"That's what I want too, Emma. Trust."

Now how did he know what she was thinking? She

faced him again, but he focused on Emma as she fidgeted beside him. A bit squirmy herself, Clarissa turned toward the sanctuary. "With this issue settled, we should probably discuss the repairs we need to make. Emma, would you please make a list in your notebook?"

Emma opened her book, found a fresh page and poised her pencil over the paper as Clarissa told them her plans for hosting the Spring Festival. Samuel ticked off projects for the grounds. Replace broken and missing bricks in the walks, repair the garden terrace steps, weed the lawns. Paint the bridge, gazebo and outbuildings.

"We need to clear the brush around the sanctuary." Clarissa wandered to the rear of the little chapel and stopped under her grandfather's favorite live oak, its branches sprawling and all but touching the west wall. "The woods took over back here."

Samuel approached the tree. "Emma, add 'prune sanctuary tree branches' to the list."

"No, let's leave them," Clarissa said, gazing upward. "Grandfather always let this tree grow wild. He loved the way it shaded his special place of prayer."

"As you wish." Samuel ran his hand up the wall. "There's an inscription on this stone near the top. 'LA III XXII.'"

Clarissa hastened to see it and reached up to touch the crude etching. "Grandfather etched this himself. It refers to his favorite Bible verse. Lamentations, chapter three."

"'It is of the Lord's mercies that we are not consumed, because his compassions fail not.' A comforting verse." Samuel consulted his pocket watch and then glanced up at the noonday sun. "I'll start trimming the trees as soon as I can. But for now, let's have dinner before I go back to church for the afternoon."

As they turned toward the kitchen, Emma peered over her shoulder. "What's Drusilla doing?"

Clarissa looked that way. Absalom's wife stood beside the duck pond, a thick, leather-bound book in one hand. She kept glancing from the book to the sanctuary and back, her pencil gliding over the pages as if she was sketching the building.

An unsettled feeling hovered around Clarissa's heart. She shook it off. "I wish she'd help with the cooking instead."

She turned around, putting Drusilla from her mind.

With Emma beside her, Clarissa felt every step Samuel took behind her. His nearness and helpfulness with the estate went a long way toward easing her mind about Camellia Pointe's future. He seemed as eager as she was to win this contest. Then again, perhaps he was merely impatient to get it over with and move them all out.

Inside the kitchen, they found Grandmother Euphemia rattling the skillets and saucepans. "Clarissa and I survived on our meager kitchen skills these past years, but we aren't good enough cooks to feed this household. And Drusilla's no help. I've asked Ophelia to cook our dinners for us, starting tomorrow."

Emma straggled in behind them and flopped onto the corner rocker, opening her book.

"You may help prepare the meal," Samuel said, gently taking her by the elbow and guiding her to her feet.

"Me? Cook?" Emma's eyes grew as large as the lid Grandmother set on the pan of potatoes.

"Yes, you. This is a good opportunity to learn a practical skill."

"But I don't like kitchen work." She sat in the chair again and dropped her gaze to the pages.

"You can either help cheerfully, or Miss Ophelia can

give you cooking lessons in place of your French class." Samuel slid the book from her hand and stuck it into his morning coat pocket.

"My book—"

"I'll give it back after you serve dinner."

Emma turned from him, eyes closed and face red.

Grandmother set the ham before her and gave her a bone-handled knife. "Take out your frustration on the ham, sugar."

Sugar? When had Clarissa ever heard her grandmother use a pet name?

Silently, Samuel crossed the room to the east window and laid Emma's book on the sill. The poor man, having to discipline Emma in front of them all, and now he must be starved and in need of a hot drink. Well, since Grandmother had Emma well in hand, Clarissa might as well focus on her husband.

As she hastened to the coffeepot and spooned in the grounds, she heard a little baritone moan. Well, if she was going to uphold her side of the bargain and be a good wife, she'd do it with all her heart, mind and strength.

She opened the coffee can again and added an extra spoonful to the pot.

Chapter Eight

Finally, a place of tranquility, of sanity.

In Christ Church's sanctuary early the next morning, Clarissa introduced Samuel as the community choir's new choirmaster as well as her new husband. Then she settled into her usual spot beside Grandmother in the first soprano section. On her other side, where Clarissa's friend Tessa usually stood, Emma stopped flipping the pages of her sheet music and pressed it to her chest.

"'Misty Morning.' I know this song," she whispered.

Good. If she did well at rehearsal, Clarissa would ask Samuel to give the girl a duet part.

With the music distributed, Samuel tapped his baton on his rosewood music stand. "We have less than a month until the spring festival, so please work on your parts between now and Saturday's rehearsal. Remember, practice is personal, and we should learn our parts at home. Rehearsal is when we put those parts together and learn to sing as one voice to the Lord."

Apparently there was a lot Clarissa didn't know about her new husband, including his aptitude as choirmaster.

"Let's run through 'Misty Morning.' I've made phrasing and articulation notes in your individual scores. Just sight-read the best you can for now." He glanced up at Missus Porter, seated at the piano in the gallery. Then he counted out three beats, setting the tempo, and led them into the verse.

To Clarissa's surprise, Emma sang out with certainty, her pitch sure and her tone clear. Her sweet voice was mature for her age, something Clarissa didn't often hear from a new student. Yes, she should definitely ask Samuel to let Emma sing a duet part.

After the grand ending, Samuel gave them a few instructions on dynamics and timing. They'd just begun the verse again when the vestibule door swung open, and a woman in a hooded gray cape crept in, her head down, carrying a baby wrapped in a blanket.

A few yards down the aisle, she pushed back the hood. Tessa Collins. As she came nearer, the tears on her cheeks glistened in the early morning lamplight. And she had little Lilliana with her, so she wasn't here to sing.

Something was terribly wrong.

Clarissa handed Emma her music score and hastened toward her friend.

Tessa had taken a few more steps, now stopped, swaying as if she could barely stay on her feet. By the time Clarissa reached her, she'd clutched the back of the nearest pew, her face pale beneath its veil of tears.

Clarissa swung open the pew door and helped Tessa in.

"I can hardly bear it." Tessa's voice wavered, tinny. "The others were hard, but I don't know if I can do it..."

"What don't you know? What happened? Is it Hugo?" Tessa's brawny husband had suffered enough during the War and afterward. Surely he hadn't taken a turn for the worse.

"It's Hugo, it's me, it's the children..." She pulled in

a shuddering breath. "He tried his best, but a man needs two legs if he's to grow cotton. If only he hadn't been too proud to sharecrop out his family ground. Even though he worked the fields as hard as he could, we couldn't scrape together enough money for our mortgage. The bank has called our note."

Not another Natchez family farm lost. Not the Collins family. "What are you going to do?"

"Texas is less war-torn than the rest of the Confederacy, and Hugo can't bear to leave the South. He hopes he can eventually get a Texas land grant." She anchored her faded blue gaze on her sleeping child. "Carl is going with us because he's fifteen and old enough to get a job. And our neighbors took in the other boys, to let them work on their farms. But I don't want them to raise Lilliana. We heard you've taken in an orphan…"

"Oh, Tessa…"

"We can't provide for her." Tessa's staccato words shot out as if she feared she'd lose her nerve if she didn't say them fast. "And your home is so large, and you love Lilliana. It's just until Hugo can find work in Texas and we can save a little money."

"But I've never taken care of a baby…"

"You'll know what to do, and Miss Euphemia will help." Tessa swiped at the tears coursing down her cheeks. "Believe me, I'll be knocking on your door the moment we can take care of Lilliana again."

"Surely there's work somewhere in Natchez."

"If there was, Hugo would have found it."

"There has to be another way." But for the life of her, Clarissa couldn't think of one.

"He's outside in the wagon, waiting for me. He couldn't bear to come in and see me leave Lilliana. This is breaking his heart even more than mine." The choir's song faded to an end as Tessa pulled the baby's blanket more snugly around her and then laid her in Clarissa's arms. "You're the only person I trust with her," she whispered.

Tessa's quick hug was over almost before it began. With an agony that seeped into Clarissa's heart as well, she kissed the still-sleeping baby's pink cheek and tore herself away from her child. Pulling her gray hood over her head again, she stumbled from the box pew and up the aisle.

The vestibule door slammed behind her, a cold draft in her wake.

In her sleep, the baby snuggled against Clarissa's body, warm and content and oblivious to the fact that her mother was gone. For how long? Perhaps forever?

Would Lilliana see her mother again?

Samuel hastened to Clarissa and the baby, his face awash with questions. "Isn't she your neighbor?"

"She—used to be."

Quick comprehension flashed across his face. "What happened?"

Indeed, what? Hugo's small cotton fields had provided for his family for three generations. Now they'd had to farm out three of their four children—break up their family—

And the same thing could well happen to Clarissa.

Her heart skipped a beat and she pressed her hand to her chest as Grandmother had been doing more frequently these last days. Just as poverty had taken Lilliana's mother from her, Absalom could separate Clarissa from her grandmother if he beat her in the contest for their home.

Absalom had only to repair a few doors and windows, restore some minor damage the occupying Yankees had caused. He had the money to hire laborers, and the cost would be minimal. Clarissa, on the other hand, had acres of grounds to restore…

And who knew what the third stipulation would require?

Could she do it? Could she save this home while caring for a baby, a new husband, a new stepdaughter and an orphaned drummer boy?

She drifted her gaze over the church and thought of home. The gazebo, the sanctuary, the gardens. The statues she'd pretended were her childhood friends. Could she give them up?

Yes, if Grandmother would live elsewhere in Natchez, with Clarissa and Samuel. But she clearly would not.

As it was, Camellia Pointe—that most elegant of Natchez manor houses—was the place her family had always been happy, had laughed, had loved. The place her mother had drawn her last, precious breath. The place Clarissa and Grandmother wanted to live—together.

Had they not decided to try to fulfill Grandfather's will, they could find a different home together, perhaps in Memphis, and be happy there. But they had. And so Clarissa was married, had a stepdaughter and now a baby, and had to stay in Natchez.

It all came back to Camellia Pointe. The place where she still hoped her father would return to her. Because if he ever did heal of his grief over her mother's death enough to reunite with Clarissa, Camellia Pointe was the only place that could happen. She knew it as if he'd told her so.

She looked at the child sleeping in her arms, glanced at Samuel by her side, Emma and Grandmother in the choir. They all depended on her now, and she couldn't let them down. And if she lost their home, she would never reunite with her father. She had to save Camellia Pointe, so her father would hear and would come back to her. At this year's Spring Festival.

Then she caught Grandmother's gaze. She knew exactly what was going on, both with Lilliana and with Clarissa's heart. Clarissa could see it in the set of Grandmother's head, in the little glint of fear in her eyes.

Her grandmother depended on her too, to save her home, preserve her heart. Even if everyone else turned against Clarissa, Grandmother rooted her on, cheered for her. Believed in her.

And Clarissa would not let her down.

The baby shifted in her arms. Clarissa looked down in time to see tiny eyelashes flutter and tiny lips smile at her. She would care for this child and love her, as she'd love Emma and Willie.

She would also save Camellia Pointe.

No matter what.

Late the next afternoon, Samuel pulled up at Camellia Pointe to refresh himself before their wedding reception, although he would rather face a line of armed Yankees than the deaconate at a social function.

A high-pitched whine burst forth from beside him, and Samuel picked up the black-and-white puppy Colonel Talbot had given him this afternoon. He got out and held the squirming pup in the crook of his arm as he fastened Strawberry's reins to the hitching ring.

But wait—the weeds were gone from the camellia beds on either side of the porch. And from the drive in front of the house. Someone had replaced the dining-room window glass as well. What was going on here?

Hearing voices from the east side of the house, he ventured that way. Moments later he found a tawny-haired young gentleman in the east flower beds with Willie and Beau, all on their knees, pulling weeds. The new tutor? With his broad shoulders and muscled arms, he looked as if he'd be as proficient in a game of tug-of-war, or archery, or even swordplay as he would in a classroom.

"Reverend Montgomery?" When he looked up, his bright blue eyes and quick smile, not to mention the fact he'd gotten the boys into the flower beds, made Samuel like him instantly.

"Mister Forbes, I presume. I'm relieved to have you here. None of us will get into a disciplined schedule until we get our three hooligans into school."

"Oh, these two already are. This is part of horticulture class."

Which Absalom would put an end to as soon as he saw Beau helping with the gardens. Samuel set the pup on the ground, and she immediately wobbled over to Willie.

"A dog!" Willie scooped her up, the weeds clearly forgotten, and let her lick his face.

"An English setter," Mister Forbes said, striding over. He rubbed the dog's floppy ears. "What's her name?"

"I thought I'd let Willie name her. Her mother is Colonel Talbot's dog, Sugar."

"Then I'll call her Honey." Willie set her on the ground and ran with Honey around the nearest magnolia tree, the pup nipping his heels.

With the dog in good hands, Samuel stepped to the front gallery, where piano music greeted him. He must have stumbled upon Emma's voice lessons. He braced his shoulder against the door, turned the knob and shoved as usual. This time, the door didn't stick. He all but fell into the center hall, as if Absalom had planned it.

As Samuel caught himself on the door frame, he recognized the sweet strains of "Meet Me by Moonlight." His mother's favorite song—the one she used to sing to him on summer nights when he couldn't sleep in his hot, second-story bedroom…

Eager to hear more, he hastened farther into the hall, in case the song could bring him some healing balm as it had in his youth.

There, Clarissa's dulcet soprano voice flowed, pitch-perfect and clear-toned, from some deep well of liquid love within her heart. He paused just inside the door, savoring the honeyed sounds. The old-fashioned love song touched something within him, something he'd neglected for more time than he wanted to admit. Unwilling to break the moment, he crept closer to where Clarissa held court from her piano stool. She'd captivated her audience of Miss Phemie, baby Lilliana and Emma, who stood next to Clarissa at the polished Steinway as she sang of shewing the night flowers their queen.

And "queen" Clarissa was. Were he to meet her here at moonlight, what those beams might do to her raven hair, her porcelain skin. She would surely rival the night flowers in beauty and sweetness.

Emma stood as close to her teacher-stepmother as she could get. She mimicked Clarissa's every move, her lips moving along with the lyrics.

No one seemed to notice him, which was no great surprise, considering Clarissa's extraordinary talent and stage presence. He headed toward the stairs and started up, determined to extricate himself from her captivation. He dared not let his mind, his heart, take him down a dangerous path.

As he passed her at the bend in the staircase, she smiled into his eyes.

"'Meet me by moonlight alone…'"

It brought him to a halt on the third step.

Her intimate smile, her rapt attention—he felt as if she'd meant the lyrics just for him, as if the two of them were the only ones in the room. Her words sounded like an invitation, one he would be hard-pressed to decline—

Wait—what was he doing, standing there like a schoolboy with his first crush? He broke the moment quickly, tearing his gaze from her and bounding up the stairs.

What was wrong with him, making a fool of himself in front of his entire family? Clarissa had merely been performing the song—playacting, so to speak. Yet he'd all but agreed to meet her by moonlight.

Samuel unlocked their door and stormed into his study. His bedroom. His hiding place. He had to keep his heart from becoming entangled. And he may accomplish nothing more in Natchez. His plan for Emma wasn't exactly working out as he'd hoped. Not only had she ignored him just now, but she hadn't spoken a word to him since he took away her book Sunday evening. They were no closer to being a family than the day he'd picked her up in Kentucky.

Clarissa had said it would take time, and she was right. But his daughter seemed barely able to tolerate his presence, and each time he tried to change that, she merely ripped out another piece of his heart.

Of course, Clarissa wasn't to blame. Their problems started long before he'd met her. In fact, he'd felt as if he'd been bleeding inside since the day he learned he'd sent Emma to live next door to a battlefield.

He'd come to Natchez to stop that flow. Married Clarissa as a last-chance effort to repair his relationship with Emma. But now, after his foolish response to Clarissa's innocent singing, he had to admit he was developing feelings for his wife. Feelings that, if not checked, would result in the same kind of heartbreak he'd endured with Veronica.

Instead of healing his wounds by marrying Clarissa, he'd sliced an artery.

Would things ever get better? Could he have a happy home like his grandparents'?

In a flash of nostalgia, Samuel retrieved his trunk key from the wardrobe and knelt before the old chest. Dare he open it, bring back to light those reminders of another day, a happier day? Or should he throw trunk and all into the river?

Thoughts of the past held him captive for minutes that felt like hours, and then he jammed the key into the lock. How could things get worse? If he took one more look, endured one more reminder of the happiness of youth and the hope he'd once held for his future, perhaps he could finally set those dreams to rest.

Because some dreams weren't meant to come true.

Or were they? Rusty from neglect, the lock fought him, refusing to relinquish its simple treasures. With a final, wrenching twist, Samuel broke the box free. He lifted the lid.

First he took out his sword—Grandfather Jonas's sword. Its weight still felt right in his hand, and he stood and swished it about the room. Next, his battered uniform and hat, and his father's portrait. He set the frame facedown on the carpet, as he'd packed it.

Then he reached for the only item in the trunk that he'd longed to see. An old-fashioned velvet box, light green and heavy. Samuel touched the hasp and the waning afternoon rays lit the emeralds in Grandmother Esther's lavaliere. The one that carried a blessing.

The one she'd instructed him to give to the woman who would fall in love with him.

Would he ever give it away?

Would he ever be worthy to give it away?

His thoughts drifted back to the moment Clarissa sang to him. To the day he'd called her dear, to her sweet response. To her obvious love for Emma and even baby Lilliana, her care for him at church, even her attempt to please him with her terrible coffee.

Could she care for him? Perhaps not with the kind of love she sang about. He was too much of a roughneck. But might she grow to admire him, just a little, in time?

If so, could Emma also come to care for him again? Probably not. The hardness he saw in her mirrored her mother's contempt for him. From that fateful evening of his presbytery appointment until the last time he'd seen Veronica over three years ago, her scorn had grown almost daily. She wouldn't speak to him, wouldn't even glance his way, despite his year-long absence at war.

To deny that Emma had taken up her mother's offense would be to deny reality.

He snatched his grandfather's sword and slashed the air again.

During his evangelistic tour of the South, he'd preached the same message in every city he entered: be a real man, a man of God. A man who made sacrifices, took care of his family, loved his family.

A man like Grandfather Jonas. Not like his own father. Not like Samuel.

Would he ever be half the man Grandfather was?

At the sound of footsteps pounding up the stairs, he set down the sword and tucked the jewelry box into a corner of the trunk. Perhaps he would retrieve it someday. Then again, perhaps not.

"Papa Samuel, you in there?" Willie yelled as he banged on the door. "Miss Clarissa says she's ready to go."

"Come in before Miss Phemie comes up here with her cane. She doesn't like noise in the house."

The door inched open and Willie peered inside at Samuel and the contents of the trunk strewn on the carpet. He shifted Honey to his other arm. "You lose something?"

"No..." Samuel picked up the sword. "How would you like to start your sword-fighting lessons again?"

Willie's eyes shone like the sword in sunshine. "When? Right now?"

The boy's enthusiasm gave Samuel back a little joy. "Tomorrow at sunrise. Tonight, Miss Clarissa and I have a party to attend, and then we're going to Good Shepherd."

"What's that?"

"A little boardinghouse Miss Clarissa owns."

"Why you going there? We got plenty of room here."

Samuel's laugh sounded sarcastic, even to his ears. "We're not moving in. Miss Clarissa wants me to meet the boardinghouse manager and take a look at the operation."

"All right, but let's practice a little now." Before Samuel could react, Willie set down the pup, snatched the sword and affected a left stance.

Samuel held out his hand. "Before you start hacking the drapes, remember—we practice outside. There's too much to tear up in this house."

Willie surrendered the sword. "I'll meet you on the battlefield at sunrise."

Battlefield? "The croquet lawn?"

"'Croquet lawn' sounds like we're just playing games. Let's call it the battlefield."

Well, in reality, the swordfight lessons were a game… "Battlefield it is."

The boy cast a longing gaze at the sword for a moment and then brightened. "Guess what? Miss Drusilla got on the steamboat for Memphis today. And I got to drive her to the landing in ol' Absalom's carriage. He said he didn't have time to mess with her. I say good riddance to bad rubbish."

Samuel started to correct the boy, but he felt the same way and so held his peace.

Willie made as if he would leave, but then he spotted the framed oil portrait that still lay face down on the floor. He grabbed it as quickly as he had the sword and turned it over. "Why you got a picture of yourself?"

"What? No. That's my father."

"Sure looks like you."

"No, I resemble my grandfather." But he took the portrait anyway, and held it up. Sure enough, Father had his own mother's smaller eyes and thinner lips, lighter hair. Samuel looked nothing like his side of the family.

"Well, maybe not the hair and everything," Willie said, "but you look like this when you look at Emma."

"I don't see it."

"You pull your eyebrows together like his and make your mouth kinda tight. And—scowl."

Samuel took a hard look at his father's image then at the mirror. Was it true? Had he become his inattentive, scowling father?

Nothing could be worse.

And nothing could hurt Emma more.

His hand shook a bit as he set the portrait in the trunk.

"Willie, please tell Miss Clarissa I'll be downstairs in a few minutes."

The boy scampered from the room, Honey at his heels. Samuel hastened to close the door and lock it from the inside. He looked at himself in the mirror, then he returned to the trunk, took out Father's portrait and studied it again.

It was there—the resemblance Willie noticed.

No wonder Samuel was getting nowhere with his daughter. Come to think of it, she was acting exactly as Samuel had at Emma's age. The difference was that Father had always responded with a switch.

He laid the portrait back in the box, then thought better of it and propped it on the mantel. He would need the reminder. Emma's heart depended on it.

Samuel sat at the corner desk, his gaze landing on Grandfather Jonas's sword. *God, how do I learn to be the man my grandfather was? The man I preach about from the pulpit? Whose daughter feels loved and loves him back...*

The soft rap on his door surprised him. "Samuel? Willie brought the carriage around, and I've given the children their supper. Are you ready?"

His wife's sweet voice drifted into his room, his mind, his heart. She never raised it to Emma or Willie in anger or irritation. Her mouth never scowled, nor did her brows pull together. She knew how to show them love, to be a mother to them. He lifted his head, realizing God was answering his prayer.

Clarissa would show him how.

Chapter Nine

Her first social event as a married woman, the most anticipated party of a Natchez girl's life. But Clarissa would rather have hidden in the kitchen, washing the dishes. Everyone here knew she wasn't a chosen bride, a beloved wife. And that was enough to tempt her to get right back into Samuel's carriage and race home to Camellia Pointe. At least she wore her favorite bottle-green dress, well-fitting and remade well, its frayed lace replaced with tatting she'd found in the attic.

Samuel must have sensed her fretfulness, sliding a protective arm around her waist as they entered the Talbots' crowded center hall and passed Nettie Bates playing the violin. Or perhaps he was merely trying to keep up appearances, as was Clarissa. At any rate, his careful attention to her, his strong arm keeping her close, gave her a sense of comfort.

But if anyone said one word about an arranged marriage, she'd drive herself home—or walk.

They crossed the hall and stopped just inside the parlor, where Graham's stepmother served them her new no-alcohol Roosevelt juleps, the current rage in Natchez, made with fresh garden mint and sugary syrup.

"Applesauce cookies. My favorite." Samuel selected a large one from the tray beside the juleps.

Emma sat in the corner, cradling Lilliana and rocking her gently to sleep.

"I didn't think you could look more beautiful than you did at your wedding, but you do." Graham's wife, Ellie Talbot, slipped up behind her, her honey-blond hair pulled up in a chignon instead of her usual curled style.

Clarissa set her cup on the drink table. "Your new hairstyle becomes you."

Ellie turned a pretty shade of pink. "I decided I need to look more mature."

More mature? Then her meaning hit Clarissa and she clasped her friend's arm.

"God has blessed us with a child." Ellie lowered her voice. "The Spring Festival will be my last party before my confinement."

Graham strolled over then, winking at his wife and wearing a rather silly grin, clearly understanding their secret was out.

Clarissa blinked back tears as she gave her friend a hug. With her arranged, loveless marriage, she would never have the same joy. And until this moment, she hadn't realized how much she wished that wasn't true.

Samuel rescued her by drawing her attention to the cross-shaped cake Miss Ophelia fussed over. He excused them and guided her to the cake table, his hand warm on the small of her back.

When Miss Ophelia caught sight of them, she hastened around the table, her long red curls bouncing. Grandmother Euphemia approached from the other side of the room, at a more sedate pace.

"Now, Clarissa, don't be upset with me." Miss Ophelia clutched Clarissa's hands, hers trembling a bit. "I had no idea the reception would turn out this way. I didn't invite—"

"And don't make a scene. Just ignore it," Grandmother said, a grim line to her mouth.

Whatever they were referring to must have been important, judging from the vehemence of Grandmother's cane taps to the floor. "What am I to ignore? You're not making sense."

The room grew silent then, other than Nettie playing "Old Folks at Home," when a blond-haired woman approached, wearing a bluish-green ball gown of the latest fashion.

Of a sudden, Clarissa understood the older women's anxiety.

"Belinda Grimes." How had she—the woman who had stolen Clarissa's beau all those years ago—wrangled an invitation to this party?

"It's Belinda Goss, and well you know it." She sidled in closer, and Clarissa saw her ploy. Belinda's aqua dress made Clarissa's bottle-green look positively sickly. It probably did the same for her complexion.

Clarissa took a step back. Must all of Natchez see her looking poorly beside this woman who was now married to Clarissa's former beau—her first and only love? She moved even farther away, to the spot where Samuel stood, watching, waiting.

"This is my husband, the Reverend Samuel Montgomery—"

"And I'm Clarissa's dear friend, lately of Memphis." Belinda's gaze slid from his rich dark curls and chestnut eyes to his strong shoulders as if she'd enjoy stealing another man from Clarissa. She glided toward him and held her slender hand close to Samuel's face, clearly expecting him to bestow a kiss.

He held it briefly, then released her.

Clarissa felt like giving him the hug of his life.

For an instant Belinda narrowed her eyes at him and scowled, then she flounced her yellow curls as she had the day of her wedding. To Clarissa's beau. "I've heard all about you and your hasty marriage. I never knew anybody who got married the day they met. You move fast for a preacher."

Samuel eased his arm around Clarissa's waist—bless the man—and pulled her close. Very close, and gazed into her eyes like a man in love. Or, at least, the way she imagined a man in love would gaze. "What man wouldn't hurry to marry Clarissa? She's the best thing that could have happened to me."

Clarissa's face flushed hot, from his words, from the way he spoke them with his slow, deep drawl, or from his nearness, she couldn't tell.

Clearly, Belinda wasn't buying it, judging from her raised brow. "It looks like an arranged marriage to me. I thought preachers weren't supposed to lie."

Then a man stood next to Clarissa, wearing a handsomely tailored frock coat, the diamond in his cravat pin the size of one of Grandmother's pearls. Every blond hair in place, perfect teeth and perfect smile, eyes the color of spring irises—the face she'd once thought the finest in the world. "Clarissa, you're ravishing as always. Still wearing the old family garnets, I see."

"Harold Goss." Harold—out of prison camp and here in Natchez.

At her wedding reception, celebrating her marriage that wasn't a marriage at all.

Clarissa opened her mouth to say something, anything to shatter the heartbreaking silence, but no words could ease this embarrassment, this humiliation. Harold knew her better than anybody, except Grandmother. He would see right through her wedding sham and would instantly know—probably already knew—she was an unloved bride, a wife of convenience.

She turned and saw that Samuel had left her. Where had he gone when she needed him, and where was Grandmother? Miss Ophelia? Her jaw tremoring, she cast her gaze about the room and caught sight of Samuel whispering to Miss Ophelia on the other side of the cake table.

He hastened back to her side as Miss Ophelia tapped her spoon against her punch glass. "Gather around, everyone."

How could they gather around any more than they already had? All of Natchez seemed to be right there in Clarissa's face, witnessing her shame—

"We're here to celebrate the marriage of our own dear Clarissa Adams to the Reverend Samuel Montgomery," Miss Ophelia said, her voice even more animated than usual. "And it's a good thing he wanted to marry her right away, or that handsome man would have had pecks of trouble fending off the women in town."

Samuel laughed with the rest of the guests, then raised his voice. "I don't know about that, but I certainly did want a hasty marriage. I couldn't take the risk of another man carrying off my beautiful girl while I wasn't looking."

Beautiful? Her? Clarissa tried to speak through the lump in her throat, but words wouldn't come. No one had called her beautiful since Mother passed away…

"And since the wedding was private, we didn't get to see the bridal kiss," Miss Ophelia said. "Reverend, would you rectify this for us now?"

Samuel held Clarissa's gaze, moving nearer. "With pleasure."

Did he truly mean to kiss her? Here, in front of everyone she knew?

If she assumed he'd kiss her quickly and then release her, she was wrong.

Drawing her to him and holding her closer, much closer, than Natchez manners allowed, he brushed a wisp of hair from her cheek. The room seemed to hold its breath as he held her, making her wait, not hesitating but purposeful.

After agonizing long moments, he kissed her. He tasted minty and sweet, and his tenderness made her slide her arms around his waist as she soaked in the pure bliss of his nearness, as she savored the warm scent of his woodsy soap. For an instant, the span of a breath, she let herself believe he meant this kiss, that he loved and cherished her as he made her feel in this moment.

Strong, wise, pure-hearted Samuel, kissing her as if he'd chosen her, as if she was the woman of his dreams…

What would it be like to be that woman, feeling his love and care?

Samuel finally released her and she felt a sigh fall from her lips, too fast for her to catch it. Clarissa turned from his gaze in the hope he hadn't noticed. His roguish grin told her he had.

"Well, Natchez has certainly changed since I left." Belinda Grimes, or rather, Belinda Goss's tone clearly said she disapproved.

"Looks to me like it changed for the better," Harold said, and Clarissa had the distinct impression he'd have liked to be the one kissing her.

And that was just too bad for him. She followed her

husband's lead and took Samuel's arm in a possessive, almost flirtatious way, drawing a deeper smile from him.

Then a cold realization hit her—she had kissed her husband. Kissed him and liked it.

And must never do it again.

Immediately a sense of loss bore down on her, as if she'd carelessly forfeited something precious, never to find it—or feel it—again.

She shook off the sensation. Even if she wanted a real marriage with Samuel, which she didn't, he didn't want her.

But what if someday—?

"Cut the cake, Clarissa." Miss Ophelia held out a long knife and cake server, her gaze intense upon them.

Had she guessed their pretense? Did she somehow know she had just witnessed their first—and only—kiss?

The thought was ridiculous. Of course, she couldn't know. But gazing into the wise old eyes, Clarissa wondered anew.

Could Miss Ophelia know more about them than they did?

Two agonizing hours later, Samuel bid farewell to the last guests, wanting nothing more than to get home to his study. Harold Goss and his conniving wife should have been one of the first couples to leave, not the last. As it was, Samuel had stuck by Clarissa like the most doting husband, giving Goss less opportunity to make things uncomfortable for her.

Which seared the memory of their kiss all the deeper.

He'd been right to give Miss Ophelia the idea of a bridal kiss. And he didn't regret it, since it had shut up Clarissa's old beau and stopped Belinda Goss and her talk of an arranged marriage. Clarissa was a good wife, an excellent stepmother to Emma, and nobody needed to know the details of the marriage that worked just fine for them both.

At least it had, until he'd tasted her kiss…

He'd had no expectations. He'd merely thought he'd give her the sort his late wife always demanded—quick, neat, polite. That was what nice people did, she'd said. But when he'd taken Clarissa in his arms, all thoughts of a quick encounter had left his mind.

And then she'd kissed him back, and every person in the room had seemed to vanish. Just as their family had faded away this afternoon, as she'd sung to him to meet her by moonlight.

Samuel squeezed his eyes shut for an instant to block the memory. But it didn't work. When he opened them, Clarissa still stood beside him, still sweet, still kind, still beautiful.

Still filling his thoughts.

"Please come and visit us, Reverend. And bring your *wife*, if you wish." Belinda started to raise her hand, then let it drop, as if she'd suddenly remembered he didn't play her game of hand-kissing.

"By all means. We live in the old Harborough place now," her husband said, slapping Samuel on the shoulder, hard.

Samuel stood like a rock, refusing to allow this beefy dandy the satisfaction of making him stagger under his blow. What was Goss's game? As always, the Fighting Chaplain story had come up tonight, and afterward, Goss had done his best to pick a fight. Testing him, perhaps? Most men respected Samuel's military history; some even feared him a bit, although he never encouraged it or brought up his past. This man, however, was different. Arrogant. Overconfident. With an agenda.

He would bear watching.

"The Harborough estate? It recently went to auction," Clarissa said, her voice tight.

"I've always loved that house." Belinda's eyes shone in the gaslight of the center hall.

Goss's face took on a smugness that turned his pretty-boy looks a little ugly. "Anything my wife wants, she gets."

Yes, Samuel could believe it.

"But the family came up with nearly all the back tax money." Clarissa's compassion tightened her voice and darkened her eyes. "The Freedman's Bureau officer gave them an extra week—"

"The Bureau doesn't control everything in Natchez." Goss's condescending tone grated on Samuel's nerves. Clarissa's too, if her little frown meant anything.

"Do come by and see what we're doing with the place. If I'd known you needed a host for the Spring Festival, I would have offered our home. We call it Goss House," Belinda said in her simpering voice. "We've gotten rid of those misshapen old trees in the front lawn, so we can see all the way to Main Street from our hill."

Clarissa's eyes flew open wide. "You cut down those beautiful four-hundred-year-old live oaks?"

"I wanted a clear view of Main Street. What's more beautiful than my darling husband's new stores, making us tons and tons of money?"

Clarissa's brow smoothed then, her emotions swept from her pretty face. She drew a great breath and released it, as if in an attempt to control her feelings. She extended her hand to Belinda. "I wish you both all the best in your business ventures. I'm sure your stores will help the city recover from the losses of war."

She quickly released the other woman's hand and

stepped back as if giving them room to pass through the door.

Samuel hid the smile tugging at his mouth as the Gosses stepped into the cold night. What a gracious way to throw an obnoxious couple out of the house.

After giving their hostess a warm farewell, he escorted Clarissa to the carriage and headed east, toward Camellia Pointe and his bedtime apple-mint tea.

But she clasped his arm and pointed behind them. “Good Shepherd is on the river.”

The boardinghouse. How could he have forgotten? Looked like he’d have to wait a while for his tea. He tugged the line and pulled the carriage around, following the directions she gave.

Her nearness in the carriage threatening to distract him, he kept his focus on the street. She sat closer to the door than she had on the way to the party. Avoiding his closeness, avoiding his touch. No doubt avoiding a repeat performance of their kiss. Although she needn’t have worried.

“It was kind of you to—avail yourself for me tonight,” she said.

Avail himself? Was that how she viewed his kiss? He shook his head, trying to clear his thoughts. Obviously it hadn’t affected her as it had him.

But what had he expected, hoped for? He was common, rough, a husband of convenience. Had he thought she would now fall at his feet, beg for more of his kisses? No, and he was a fool for not anticipating her response. “It was nothing.”

Not entirely true, considering the way it had made his heart pound like horses’s hooves.

“Harold is my former beau, the one I told you about.”

“I remembered him from my time at the Memphis

church." And didn't like him any more this night than he had then.

"Hence your act of gallantry to protect me."

Since when did kissing a beautiful woman make a man gallant? Perhaps she was thinking she'd been gallant to bear up under it. "Think no more of it."

And he meant it. Now, if only he could do the same.

As they drove down steep Silver Street from the bluff to the landing, he set his mind to the business at hand. No sense dwelling on things he couldn't change.

They pulled up at a sprawling, white frame building. "My grandfather had a heart for poor people traveling the river." Clarissa's voice turned soft. "Before he built Good Shepherd, Natchez-Under-the-Hill had no accommodations fit for families and women traveling alone. Now they have a safe place to spend the night."

The inn's quiet proved her right, compared to the tinny piano music and off-key singing that blared from the drinking establishments surrounding it. He helped Clarissa from the carriage and offered his arm. She took it in the lamplight. "You don't come here alone, do you?" he asked.

"Grandmother and I come together. Her position in the church and community protects us both."

"That protects your reputations but doesn't keep you from harm. From now on, I'll escort you. Anything could happen in a place like this."

"I'd be grateful. I'll not bother you more than necessary."

Bother—no. Distraction—most certainly.

Inside, he glanced around the small lobby with its pine floors and furnishings, its braided rugs and white, ruffled curtains. He drew a deep breath. Something made this place feel peaceful, safe.

"I gave rooms to two traveling families at no cost this week, ma'am," a white-haired man called from the hotel desk. "The mother of one of those families died this morning."

"My manager, Frank Reeves," Clarissa introduced him, sympathy in her big eyes. "What can we do for them?"

"Ask Missus Woods. She's with them in room eighteen."

Clarissa and Samuel headed toward the stairs to the second floor. At room eighteen, Samuel knocked on the door. A towheaded boy, smaller than Willie and with a straight-up cowlick, answered.

The son of the deceased? His hollow look twisted a raw place in Samuel's heart.

A woman in a black dress and white apron bustled to the door, her gray hair nearly hidden under a white cap. "Miss Adams, your timing is perfect. I was about to send you a message about these poor children."

"This is my new husband, the Reverend Samuel Montgomery…" When she hesitated, he looked in the direction of her gaze. A pretty little girl, about the size of the boy and with the same nearly white hair, sat on the bed and stared out the window.

Another broken heart.

"If I try to get her away from the window, she cries her little heart out."

"Why?" Samuel whispered. "Where is her father?"

"He didn't come home from war. The children's uncle brought them to town to see if anyone had heard from him." The housekeeper pulled a sodden hanky from her sleeve and dabbed her eyes. "And this morning, little Peter came out into the hall and told me he couldn't wake his mother."

"Is she—have they buried her yet?" Clarissa said, glancing at the two empty beds in the room.

"Mister Greenly and his boy come and got her and buried her right away, because we don't know what kind of sickness she had." She leaned in close. "If I'd been here, I'd not have let the girl see them take her mother away. She sat at this window and watched them carry her up the street to his place."

Waiting for her mother to come back.

"That's the saddest story I've ever heard." Clarissa withdrew her lace-edged handkerchief and held it to the corner of one eye for a moment. "What of their uncle?"

"One of the maids saw him board the late steamer for Vicksburg. Left these two as orphans, and didn't pay for the room either." She lifted her hand to her lips as if sipping from a bottle. "Drinker, you know. Probably a drifter who can't forget the war."

No, none of them ever would.

"We'd heard of your marriage, so we took care of things ourselves, not wanting to bother you right after your wedding."

Yes, a true bride and groom wouldn't have wanted the interruption. Samuel, however, might have welcomed it. "What shall we do with them? The city orphanage?"

"It's a fine home," Clarissa told the twins, "run by a nice lady who is my friend. She'll take care of you until your father gets home."

"What if he don't come home?"

Samuel had no answer. A child of Peter's age shouldn't be familiar with so much suffering.

Clarissa sat on the bed with the girl, whispering to her, but the child turned away and held her hands over her ears.

Samuel should try to help, as his wife was making no

progress, but a ruffian like him could never comfort a small girl. After a while, when it became clear the girl would have no part of Clarissa, he approached her anyway. Clarissa stood to make room for him, and he sat next to the child. "My name is Samuel. What's yours?"

"Prudy," she whispered.

The amazed look on his wife's face mirrored his own astonishment. "Peter wants to go with me to the lady's friend's house," he said in his gentlest voice.

She turned from the window and wrapped tiny arms around his neck.

Just as Emma used to do. Back when she was little, before he'd become the enemy. He blinked away the mist forming in his eyes, turning his face a little so his wife wouldn't see. Then he stood, lifting Prudy with him, and carried her to the carriage.

Ten minutes later, he and Clarissa stepped into the office of the rundown mansion that housed the Natchez Children's Home. The headmistress, Miss Caldwell, settled her bony frame into a hard chair behind a desk piled high with stacks of paperwork. The bare walls lent no cheer to the room, and the paltry fire on the marble hearth did little to dispel the chill, darkness or gloom.

After seating Clarissa on a worn and faded gold-upholstered settee, Samuel took the remaining seat in the room: a thin-spindled, pine kitchen chair unhindered by paint or decoration. The two children stood near the sorry little fire, gripping each other's hands as if afraid the woman behind the desk would rip them apart. Which she may well do, for all Samuel knew.

The thought didn't settle well.

"Miss Caldwell, these children are war orphans. Their mother passed early this morning, and their father has not returned from war," Clarissa said. "I know you take only Natchez children, but would you make an exception, since their father was a soldier in the glorious Confederate army?"

"I sympathize with them, Missus Montgomery. But tonight I received word of a fire at the Melville orphanage, and I sent a telegraph promising to take all their children temporarily. Thirty-six of them."

Clarissa sucked in a breath. "Wherever will you put them?"

"The smallest ones will double up in the beds. Older ones will sleep on the floor, under tables, wherever we can make a pallet." Miss Caldwell's kind face turned vexed, the heft of her responsibilities clearly weighing on her. "I know what you're thinking. With that many children, we wouldn't notice two more. But only thirty-six children survived the Melville fire. The other fourteen were lost due to overcrowding."

The knowledge hit Samuel hard and an image of Willie passed through his mind. "What can we do to help here?"

"Take these two children home with you."

"To Camellia Pointe?"

"I hear the surprise in your voice, Missus Montgomery, and I realize you are newly married. But you have plenty of room." She looked rather pointedly at the two children trying to warm themselves by the meager fire. "'I was a stranger, and ye took me in.' It's what Jesus taught us to do."

"I'm embarrassed that I didn't think of it." Clarissa stood and clasped her hands together, her lip trembling a bit. "I'm ashamed of myself. The granddaughter of a minister of the Gospel should do better."

Who was this amazing woman he'd married? For once, Samuel, a man who talked for a living, could think of nothing to say.

Chapter Ten

After Clarissa had put Lilliana and the twins to bed, baked applesauce cookies and retired for the evening, Grandmother Euphemia called her to her room, an ominous tone to her voice.

"This corner room is too drafty for me," she said, buttoning her white lacy bed jacket up to her neck and patting the bed. "As soon as we get rid of Absalom and his entourage, I'm moving back to my own room. After I have it fumigated and sanitized."

Dressed in her gown and wrapper, Clarissa crawled in next to her on the poster bed and pulled up the quilt, thinking of the chill in the drafty orphanage. "I can't imagine that's the reason you called me here."

"It certainly is not."

"I know—you're unhappy with me because I brought the orphans home. You have every right to be upset, but I had no choice—"

"No, I want to talk about Absalom." She paused, probably to wait for Clarissa to close her wide-open mouth. "He's up to something. This evening, just before dusk, I saw him and that Harold Goss skulking around the sanctuary. And don't tell me it was a late-night prayer meeting."

"What were they doing?"

"It looked like they were going over plans. Maybe a contract—or a land grant of some kind. Absalom had a packet of papers tied with string, like Joseph uses for his contracts—"

"Wait, you saw string?"

Grandmother gave Clarissa a look that said she'd like to shake some sense into her. "Would I know it was tied with string if I didn't see string?"

"Where were you when you saw it?"

"In the gazebo."

"You could see string from there?"

"Well, no, not with my eyes."

"Grandmother…"

The old dear let out a puff of air. "All right, I used Emma's binoculars."

Despite all she had on her mind, Clarissa had to laugh at the image of her dignified grandmother spying on her own grandson.

"That Goss fellow's looks have improved with age."

True, but what had Clarissa ever seen in him? Hadn't she recognized his greed, his arrogance? And why had she thought him handsome? Sure, he was, in a worldly sort of way. But she now knew what handsome was, that a good-looking man looks even better when his character aligns with his outward appearance. Why, even if Samuel worked all day in a cotton field, he'd still come home looking better than—

Oh, no. She wasn't about to finish the thought. Especially with her grandmother propped up in her bed, not six inches away.

"Grandmother," she asked on a whim, "what do you think of Samuel?"

"He's the image of his late grandfather."

"I already know that. What do you think of him as a man?"

"Compared to Harold Goss?"

"Just as a man."

Her sharp eyes probed Clarissa's, looking for something there… "He's just about right for you."

Just about right...

Clarissa bounded from Grandmother's bed, her bare feet hitting the cold floor.

"Where are you going?"

She stopped and kissed the older woman's cheek. "I have things to do."

It was true. She needed to go to her own sanctuary, her refuge, her secret place of prayer. And discover what God had in mind for her, for Samuel, for their entire family.

Driven by an urgency she could neither understand nor deny, she hastened to her room for slippers and a warm shawl. Then she silently slipped out the second-story gallery door and down the steps to the courtyard and beyond.

She raced along the path toward the little arched bridge over the duck pond, its paint worn and its boards weathered. Here she'd met with God since she was twelve, the way Grandfather met with Him in the sanctuary he'd built. Clarissa picked up a handful of smooth stones from the ground near the water's edge.

On the bridge, she tossed them into the water. The ripples were hidden to her on this moonless night, but she could hear the stones hit the pond's surface. She turned her heart to prayer, listened for God's still, small voice, waited for the peace that came with His presence. Sometimes, at this spot, she seemed to remember her every encounter with the Almighty. But today, only one thing assaulted her mind: her growing feelings for Samuel. Well, two things, if she counted their kiss.

He'd told her to forget it. It had meant nothing to him. To her, it had meant more than she wanted to admit, even to herself. How had she gotten into this mess?

And Harold. Why had he chosen this day, of all days, to come back into her life? What had he been doing at the little sanctuary with Absalom? Come to think of it, she hadn't seen much of her reprobate cousin yesterday. Where had he and his family been, and what had they been doing?

She turned and gazed back at the big house, its rooms now nearly full. It felt good, felt right, to use the house this way. Even Grandmother seemed to agree.

However, in the morning, she would need to find out what new plot her cousin was cooking up in an attempt to take Clarissa's property.

When she did, her newfound sense of purpose could vanish like the pebbles in the pond.

As soon as the sun had burned off the fog the next morning, Samuel crept outside, Grandfather's sword sheathed at his side and another in his hand. If he was quiet enough, perhaps he wouldn't awaken Clarissa or Miss Phemie.

He hadn't heard Willie come down the attic steps from his room this morning, hadn't heard puppy toenails on the wood floors, but the boy was canny enough to have sneaked out silently. Not that he practiced stealth in his daily activities, however. With all the noise he made in the house, it was a wonder Miss Phemie didn't make him sleep in the stable.

Samuel glanced around the grounds. If Willie wasn't already at the croquet lawn—battlefield—they wouldn't have time for a lesson before Samuel had to get to church.

As he stepped onto the battlefield, he heard the pup growl, then Willie sprang out at him from behind a towering bush and aimed a pointed stick at his chest like a saber. *"En garde!"*

"Use this instead." With Honey nipping at his heels, Samuel handed Willie the sword he'd bought from a former soldier yesterday.

"My own sword?"

Samuel drew his weapon and assumed his fighting stance, right leg forward and left hand on his hip. "Attack in the one line!"

Willie tossed his stick to the ground and aimed the sword at Samuel's head, slow and deliberate, as he'd been taught. Samuel deflected the thrust with his sword's edge. "Attack in the seven line!"

He cut to hack Samuel's sword at his flank.

"Eight!"

After some impressive footwork for a boy his age, he lunged at Samuel's hip.

A quick parry. "Well done. You've been practicing."

"Every day, like you told me."

"We need to fashion a practice target for you." Samuel glanced about the area until his gaze landed on a pink-flowered bush, about as tall as the boy, growing near the pergola. He laid his sword on the wall and beckoned Willie to follow him. "For now, let's use that bush. Imagine where the head, chest and flank would be if it were a man."

"I'll imagine where they would be if it was Absalom."

Choosing to let the comment pass, Samuel called the parry numbers to him again, and Willie responded by thrusting, cutting and lunging at the poor bush.

A full-throated soprano laugh behind Samuel caught his attention. Clarissa. However, he dared not turn to look or Willie might cut down the whole bush. Instead, Samuel waved his sword. "Attack from the rear. Prepare to surrender!"

Willie stopped, sword in midair, and looked beyond Samuel. "I ain't surrendering to no girls." Left hand still on his hip, he spun around again and assaulted the bush with fresh vigor, tossing aside all rules of swordplay in favor of a barbaric attack. Branches and flowers fell to the lawn as he pruned the lower half of the bush.

"If you cut down all the camellia bushes, we'll have to change the name of our home." Clarissa, Emma and little Prudy drew near, Clarissa pushing a battered wheelbarrow.

"What you got in there? Where you going with it?" Willie's attention diverted, he used both hands to set the sword on the terrace wall and headed toward the wheelbarrow.

"Bricks. We plan to replace all the broken ones in this section of sidewalk before breakfast. Absalom has a lot of his repair work done already, and I want to beat him."

Willie peered inside the wheelbarrow. "You going to let them, Papa Samuel? This is men's work."

Samuel took in Clarissa's determined stance, her faded brown work dress. How was he supposed to answer? For all Clarissa's femininity, she could probably succeed in anything she tried, even bricklaying. But should he allow her to do such hard work? He should have addressed this sooner, somehow made arrangements to do the repairs himself. His first days in his new pastorate were crucial to the health of the church, but his new family's needs were important as well…

"Generally speaking, you're right." Clarissa mercifully answered for him. "But Samuel has his church responsibilities, and you have school. That leaves the work for me."

The torturous expression on Willie's face made Samuel grin. "You can work until breakfast. Go get Peter so he can help too."

"Pete? He's just a little kid. He'll mess it up."

"He's a private in boot camp. You're the ranking officer. It's your job to make a good soldier of him."

Willie gave him a halfhearted salute. "Yes, sir."

"Keep an eye on Honey too."

As Willie trudged off toward the house, Emma eyed Samuel's sword, still on the wall where he'd left it. "Great-grandfather Jonah's sword… Mama said he used it in the War of 1812."

"He did." Samuel peered at the sun, estimating the time he'd been outside. "I'll help you get some bricks replaced, since we have a half hour or so before breakfast."

He maneuvered the wheelbarrow to the terrace steps near the courtyard, where the walk began. As he started to unload bricks to the grass, Clarissa joined him. Emma, however, held back, still standing at the wall and gazing at the sword. He shook his head. There was no understanding her. He hefted out another armful of bricks, soiling the sleeve of his black morning coat.

"She has a great interest in your sword," Clarissa whispered as she brushed the dirt from his arm. His wife looked so sweet, giving her attention to his dishevelment and whispering as if they had some great secret. As she leaned closer, he wondered if they did. "And in your grandfather."

"She's heard the tales of his bravery in battle. But she thinks war is romantic, all knights and kings and gallantry. She has no idea what it's like."

"Yes," Clarissa said, her gaze darting between him and his daughter, "and you could capitalize on that. Use it to your advantage."

"How?"

"First, stop scowling when you look at her." Clarissa's sweet tone tempered the harshness of her words—words that needed to be said.

He'd done it again. Since she'd pointed it out, he could feel the tension in his face, the pull of his brows. Samuel turned his back to his daughter and took a deep breath, exhaling with a low growl, massaging his forehead and between his eyes. *God, help me...*

"What do I do?" He lowered his voice to a whisper. Could he ask Clarissa for her help, admit he had no idea how to reach his daughter? "She's my girl, and I love her, but I don't know how to talk to her, show her love... be her father."

"You do. Be kind and show interest in what she's doing."

"She's interested in nothing but that book of hers—and Beau."

Clarissa cocked her head toward Emma. "And the sword, and her great-grandfather. Find out why. Offer to teach her swordplay."

What? No. "Women don't swordfight, much less little girls. She probably couldn't lift it off the wall."

"She's not a little girl. She's nearly marrying age. And has fascinations all her own."

The tension started in his forehead again, and he rubbed it in the hope of smoothing the frown lines so he'd look less like an ogre and more like a father.

Leaving Clarissa to mind the bricks and little Prudy, he started toward his daughter, more unsure of himself than he'd ever been, either in battle or in the ministry. When he reached her, he sat on the low brick wall.

"Would you like me to teach you to use it?"

Emma looked him in the eye for the first time since he'd left her in Kentucky. "Just me?"

She wanted to be with him, just the two of them? He'd longed for it so long, he didn't know what to say, what would draw her nearer and what would drive her even further away. He paused. "If you like."

Her bright smile told him he'd said just the right thing. *Thank You, God.*

She touched the sword's hilt. "It would be even better if Clarissa would take lessons with me."

"Of course. Let's ask her. We can start tomorrow." But he knew Clarissa would. She'd do anything to bring him and Emma closer.

Today had been a small victory, but it was the most progress he'd made with Emma in years. He glanced heavenward and gave thanks for it, and for his wife who seemed somehow to know him better than he knew himself.

After a quick swordplay lesson with Emma and Clarissa, Samuel stashed his weapon in his room and came to breakfast, finding Harold Goss in his chair, next to Absalom. Remembering how Goss had looked at Clarissa the previous night, not to mention how he'd tried and failed to force Samuel into a courtship with his cousin in Memphis, Samuel felt no inkling of hospitality toward him. "What can we do for you so early this morning, Goss?"

"Just here to sample Miss Ophelia's good cooking and have a talk with Absalom. And enjoy the view."

The gentle smile Goss aimed at Clarissa, seated across from him, was the kind designed to bring back memories. Memories that didn't include Samuel.

"The view is mine, not yours, and you're in my chair."

Goss's laugh cut through Samuel like a saber. "Surely you can keep your eyes off her for one meal, preacher."

The man's irreverence reminded Samuel of his first encounter with Absalom. His initial instinct was to invite the dandy to leave this house and never return. But would such a confrontation glorify the Lord? Or should he turn the other cheek and risk looking like a coward to Harold and Clarissa?

Father, if You have a third way, I'm willing to hear it...

"A change of scenery is good from time to time." Clarissa picked up her plate and silverware and moved to the other end of the long table, near where Emma sat with the twins. "Today I think I'll sit here and enjoy the view from this window instead. Samuel, will you join me?"

He wanted to laugh but managed to hold it back. "Fine. I'll sit across from you and enjoy the same view I had yesterday."

Samuel thanked the Lord for sending His third way. And for a long dining table that put a good fifteen feet between them and Absalom and Goss. He leaned forward to murmur to Clarissa, "I'd prefer a solitary breakfast at church."

Her pretty pink cheeks were his reward. "As would I."

She would? "Perhaps, if we try again, we might make it through the meal without more orphans showing up."

"Or the deacons." Clarissa's laugh tinkled through the room as she took three cookies from a glass cake stand to her left and set them on his plate.

Applesauce cookies.

"You—made them for me?"

She nodded, her eyes sparkling emeralds in the early morning sunlight. "Last night before bed."

Something about the curve of her lips made him think of their kiss, made him relive it for a moment. He drew a deep breath. The kiss hadn't been far from the front of his mind since last night. "You must have stayed up until midnight."

Her face bloomed with a smile that could have stopped his heart. "I know it sounds silly, but my father always wanted his favorite cookies on the breakfast table. He has a terrible sweet tooth, and Mother indulged him. It was one way she showed her—showed him how much she cared."

Had Clarissa made breakfast cookies because of family tradition? Or could she possibly care for Samuel in some small way?

He picked up the largest of the three cookies and took a big bite. Delicious. Perhaps he should simply enjoy them instead of trying to discern her motive.

Then again, what was life without hope? Without risk?

Before he could stop himself, Samuel reached across the table and took her hand. Soft and strong, it captivated him for a moment—the dainty nails, the long, slender fingers of a piano player. He couldn't say how long he held it, but when Willie came plodding in with Honey in his arms, he took one look at them and turned back around.

"Eww. Lovey stuff. I'll eat in the kitchen."

"Willie, come back." Clarissa snatched away her hand, her pink face now flaming red, and swung around in her chair to peer into the hall after him. "It's not 'lovey stuff.' Samuel was just…was just…"

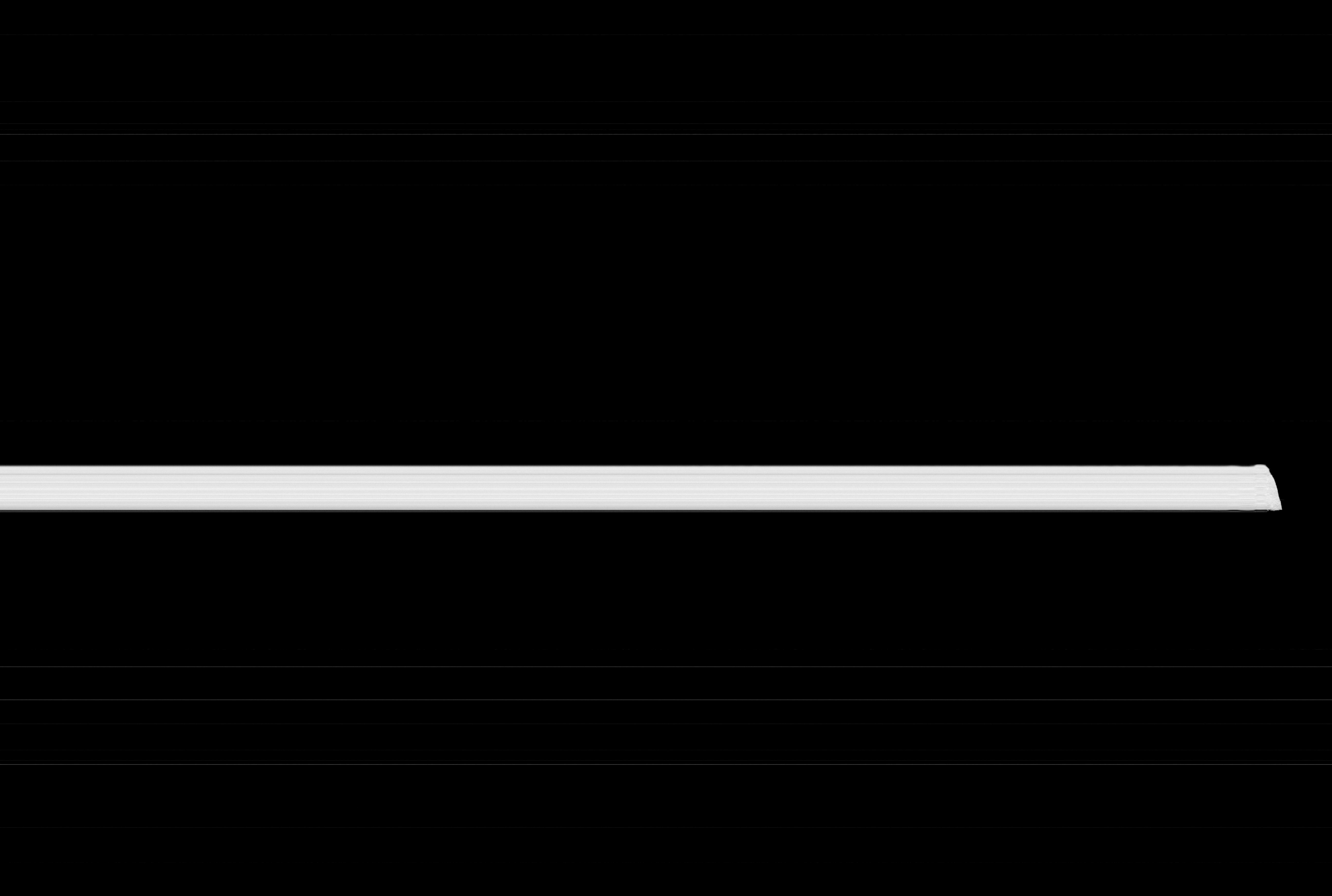

salom." Clarissa got up and the men all stood. "Samuel, Joseph, Emma and I need to get to choir practice."

Samuel stayed behind while Clarissa went upstairs to fetch her cloak and check on baby Lilliana in her crib. Paying no mind to Absalom's boasting and Goss's irritating comments about money, Samuel took a moment to reflect on Clarissa's detailed plans for fixing the grounds. They made good sense. She'd clearly given the restoration much thought. It seemed Samuel's most valuable asset, in ministry and at home, was his wife.

The thought warmed a part of him he'd once thought eternally frozen.

Joseph didn't listen to Absalom and Goss long before he finally stood. "I have no further interest in your conversation, Adams. And I don't want to be late for choir."

When he and Samuel reached the hall, Goss's voice rang out from the dining room. "Your tenor section was always weak. Can I stand in? What time is rehearsal?"

Samuel ignored him and stepped outside with Joseph. "Absalom and Goss are annoying enough by themselves, but together they're irritating as a tone-deaf soloist." And if Samuel needed to, he'd stretch his baritone voice into tenor and squeak out every note like a girl to keep Goss out of the choir.

Joseph whacked him on the shoulder, a hard slap for an octogenarian. "Don't let them get to you."

Well, they already had. He glanced behind him, where Clarissa had come downstairs. Goss detained her near the back door, regaling her with some inane story about having seen a wild turkey chasing a bobcat on Lookout Mountain—

Wait—wasn't that where Absalom said he'd been taken prisoner?

Had the two served together there?

Samuel hastened toward the door, fire in his gut. If they'd been together as soldiers and were captured together, had they escaped together too? And what had they been doing since they got out? Something profitable enough to earn Goss a Paris wardrobe and a whopping-big diamond tiepin. Enough for Absalom to buy President Davis's luxury carriage…

And now Absalom and Goss had shown up in Natchez three days apart.

There was more to this than Samuel knew, than Clarissa knew. It was time they found out.

Chapter Eleven

For the first time, Clarissa dismissed the choir fifteen minutes early. Joseph's gray-haired driver stepped down from his high seat outside the carriage and opened the door. Then Joseph helped her into his brougham to take her home, as was his custom after choir. He motioned for Emma to join them as well. The canny slant of his eye brought a flush to Clarissa's cheeks. Had he seen Samuel's tender look as he bid her good day? Hitting a sour note in a packed sanctuary would have embarrassed her less. That look had brought back every detail of their kiss—as if those details weren't always just under the surface of her consciousness.

She settled into the leather seat, Emma flouncing in beside her. "I shouldn't have cut practice short, but all I can think about is Camellia Pointe." Well, almost all. "I have hundreds of bricks to replace, not to mention the other work the grounds need. And I can't start until my voice students have gone home this afternoon."

"Choir sounded fine. We didn't need to sing the anthem again." Joseph lumbered up the steps, the carriage creaking and swaying with his weight. In the opposite seat, he grabbed his walking stick from the floor and rapped the ceiling, signaling his driver to take off. "You'll get the work done. I've never known you to fail."

"Mister Forbes has been helping a lot by making the children care for the grounds as part of their horticulture class. Except Beau. Absalom made him stop. Mister Forbes, Emma and Willie are painting the bridge and gazebo today. But we have so many distractions." Not the least of them being her memory of Samuel's kiss—feeling like a cherished wife, false though the notion was. She'd give Mother's best pearls if she could forget it.

Her face heated again, and a snort from Joseph made her glance up. That look was back.

"Joseph, you're mistaken about whatever you think you know about us."

His laughter shook his stocky frame. The man was impossible. "There's nothing wrong with having feelings for your husband."

"I admit he is extraordinarily handsome and a fine man. But this marriage was arranged for convenience." At Emma's cheeky giggle, she frowned. "If anyone knows that, it's the man who read my grandfather's will."

When they'd finally turned off East Melrose Street and had mercifully made it halfway up Camellia Pointe's drive, something white and billowy caught Clarissa's attention. Grandmother Euphemia sat in a rocker on the front gallery—in her nightgown? At eleven o'clock in the morning?

Grandmother never wore her gown outside her bedroom, let alone the house. Something had to be wrong. She was so overworked, she'd probably become ill, and it was Clarissa's fault for not looking out for her. But why was she outside in her nightclothes?

She turned to Joseph as his driver stopped the conveyance behind an unfamiliar shay and pony parked just beyond the door. "She must be sick. She stayed home from choir to take care of the children, and it must have been too much for her. I should have canceled rehearsal today. From now on, I need to stay home more."

"It's probably nothing—"

"She might have come out to see the pony." Emma leapt from the carriage as soon as the driver opened the door.

"Not dressed like that." Clarissa bounded out behind her and raced toward the house, where baby Lilliana slept in Grandmother's arms, and Prudy played at her feet. "Are you sick? Is the baby all right?"

"We're fine." She lifted her hand to her chest, her voice weaker than Clarissa had ever heard it. "I've merely been putting Lilliana to sleep. She was awake most of the night and, wouldn't you know, the privacy of the backyard doesn't suit her fine sensibilities."

Which meant Grandmother had been up all night too. The dark circles under her eyes and her disheveled hair proved it. "I didn't hear her cry last night."

"I brought her outside when she started to fuss. Poor little thing apparently likes the outdoors." She glanced in Joseph's direction as he alighted from his carriage. "Excuse me for my appearance, Joseph, but it seems we stand on convention less every day around here. It's hard telling how you'll find us from now on."

"But you can't sit on the porch with her every night," Clarissa said. "Lilliana will sleep with me from now on."

"No, she won't. Samuel has an important job and needs his sleep."

Stepping toward her, Clarissa reached for the baby. "So do you."

"Clarissa." The sharp hazel gaze pinned her to her place. "I'll not have it."

With a questioning glance at Joseph, now at her side, Clarissa let the matter drop, along with her empty hands.

"Your husband bought the shay and pony for you and had them delivered," Grandmother said, clearly changing the subject to her own advantage.

Shay? Clarissa turned toward the little carriage and gray pony she'd barely noticed in her concern for Grandmother.

"Mister Blaize from the livery said Samuel wanted a small, dependable conveyance and a gentle horse you or I can handle alone. I'm sure Joseph and Ophelia will be glad they won't have to carry us to town anymore." She started back into the house with the baby and little Prudy, calling over her shoulder as she pulled the door shut behind her. "The pony's name is Stonewall Jackson, of all things."

A pony. How long had it been since Clarissa had her own horse? She eased toward Stonewall and petted his nose. Thick-maned and with kind brown eyes, the pony was just what she needed, although she hadn't realized it until this moment.

"A perfect match." Joseph ran his hand over Stonewall's mane. "He's a gentle one, all right. Your parson has a good eye for horses."

And a good heart.

"Clarissa, your grandmother is right." Joseph's voice took on his fatherly tone as he took her elbow and led her a distance from Emma. "You shouldn't keep the baby in your room. Someone else needs to care for her at night."

"There's no one else. Emma is too young and has her studies."

Joseph ran his index finger and thumb over his magnificent moustache, as he always did when thinking through a dilemma. "How about Maisie Johnson? You know her—the freedwoman who used to work for your grandmother."

"The seamstress? I haven't seen her much lately. We've been making over our old clothes instead of buying new."

"She's now the former seamstress. Yesterday, Harold Goss bought all the Main Street property that wind and war hadn't already claimed. Maisie's little rented shop was one of them."

"But she lived above the shop."

"Last night she slept at Good Shepherd. She's in a tough spot. Her sewing machine belonged to her former landlord, so it'll be a while before she can save enough to start over. If she moved in here as governess, you could let her use your machine as part of her pay."

The solution seemed almost too simple.

"I'll talk to Maisie today," Joseph said, starting toward his brougham.

That afternoon, when Clarissa finished her weekly voice lessons with two of her students from town, she fed and diapered the baby and rocked her to sleep, leaving Grandmother to rest. Then she changed into her brown work dress, the one her mother had used as a gardening dress, and headed outside to her repair work. The frock's old-fashioned style and sweet modesty suited Clarissa today as a sense of calm and thankfulness settled upon her. Everything might work out after all. She had more hope for Camellia Pointe than she'd had since before the war. Even her grandmother's health might improve, now that they may soon have a governess.

As she descended a crumbling set of steps in the landscaping, she glanced around for the children. Knowing Willie, he was outside with Peter, exploring and investigating who-knew-what. She hastened to the gazebo, but

Emma wasn't there. Come to think of it, she hadn't seen the girl since she'd stopped to pet Stonewall.

Beau, however, gazed down at Clarissa from his perch on the upper gallery rocker. Clarissa paused and looked around again, but the lawn was empty of children playing and void of their giggles. When she turned toward the house again, Beau was gone.

Approaching the spot where Samuel had unloaded bricks for her, Clarissa stopped and breathed a prayer for them all, including Maisie Johnson. Camellia Pointe needed her—

Clarissa stopped at the sight before her. The wheelbarrow was missing and the bricks were gone from half the walk, their sand bed dug up. The bricks lay scattered about the lawn, along with the sand. Beau must have done this, to slow their progress.

And wouldn't you know—right in front of the little rise where the choirs would perform on Festival day.

She turned to check the garden path and brushed her fingers over the tip of the angel statue's wing as usual. But this time, the angel's right hand was missing.

Her short-lived peace vanished like mist over the bayou on a hot summer morning.

Footsteps sounded on the walk nearer the house. Clarissa glanced up as Samuel wove his way through the camellia bushes around the courtyard and headed toward her.

Home for his dinner. Was it one o'clock already?

His brows rose as he drew near enough to see the damage. Reaching her, he hesitated, then his mouth twitched into a crooked grin. "Absalom's not above stealing your inheritance, but I didn't expect him to do it brick by brick."

His quirky smile was adorable in its boyishness,

lighting on his ever-manly face, mischief in the always-serious, soft brown eyes. Somehow his lightheartedness lifted some of her gloom. If Samuel wasn't worried about the missing bricks, maybe she shouldn't be either. Perhaps she could trust his judgment this once.

"Although I can't imagine why anyone would dig up the dirt under the sand bed," he said.

"Or break one of our statues." She showed him the handless limb.

"I'm not sure what I can do about a marble statue." Samuel leaned over, sifted some fresh soil through his fingers, then dusted off his hands. "But I'll take care of the walks. Where can I get more sand?"

"At the sandbar, downriver from the waterfront. But you don't have time—"

At the sound of a whoop behind her, she turned to see Willie and Peter struggling to push the wheelbarrow, half full of bricks, across the lawn.

"What are you doing?" Samuel called to them while they were still fifty yards away.

"Helping." When they reached Samuel and Clarissa moments later, Willie collapsed on the grass, his chest heaving with exertion.

"By tearing up the part of the walk that didn't need to be fixed?"

"'Course not. We came out here to lay bricks and found it this way."

"Did you see anybody when you got here?" Samuel asked, kicking at the fresh dirt.

"Beau was heading inside when we were going out. It had to be him."

No doubt. Clarissa pointed to the marble angel near the steps. "Do you boys know anything about the broken statue?"

"Yeah, I was going to tell you about that..." Willie dropped his gaze to the ground. "Remember last Sunday, when Papa Samuel preached, 'And if thy right hand offend thee, cut it off'?"

At least Willie had been listening in church.

The sternness in Samuel's eye suggested he hadn't seen this bright side of the situation. "I mentioned the verse in passing, yes."

"Well, I was chasing Pete and I ran into the statue, and one of its fingers jabbed me in the chest. Since its hand offended me, I cut it off with my sword."

Samuel puffed out a breath. "Willie, that's not what that verse means. And it's not how we use our swords."

"Guess not. I didn't think it would break." The boy's remorse spoke loudly in his tone.

"Let's forget it this time," Clarissa said. "You can make up for it by helping to fix the sidewalks."

When the boys had unloaded their wheelbarrow and raced off toward the stable for more bricks, Samuel gestured for Clarissa to join him on the terrace wall. "I'll take the boys to the sandbar. We'll load up and be back before you know it."

Which would give Clarissa plenty of time to have a talk with Absalom.

"And leave Absalom to me. Since he seems to respect the Fighting Chaplain nonsense, I might be able to get more cooperation from him than you would."

There Samuel went again, somehow sensing exactly what she was thinking. How could he know her so well in such a short time? "He's trying to keep us from meeting our deadline, but I can deal with him. You need to give your attention to the church. Camellia Pointe is my concern."

So were Absalom and his family. Clarissa would need to watch them closer—

Unfamiliar voices in the camellia and rose garden interrupted her thoughts. The branches rustled as a dozen or so uninvited guests left the paths and trampled through the garden, crushing the snapdragons and pansies.

At the front of the crowd, a hulk of a former Confederate soldier pierced Samuel with his hard blue gaze. He wore tattered grays, his right sleeve pinned up at the shoulder and his left hand hovering over the pistol on his hip. "I'm here for the Fighting Chaplain."

The last time Samuel heard those words, he'd been obliged to relieve three drunken Yankee privates of their weapons, along with what dignity they'd had. Now he shoved down the memory and surveyed the group. A few well-dressed men, a woman in a fancy blue dress. A half dozen dirt-smudged drifters with the hopeless expressions Samuel had seen on hundreds of defeated Southerners since Lee's surrender.

No threat there.

Except for the former soldier with the reckless, nothing-to-lose attitude of a man tough enough to take out a platoon by himself, with only one arm.

Samuel took a step toward the man, sizing him up, looking for weaknesses but seeing none save the missing limb. Which somehow heightened his intimidating demeanor and made him seem even more dangerous than if he'd had the arm.

Clarissa clutched Samuel's hand and held tight, as if she saw him as a real man rather than a roughneck. As if she trusted him to keep her safe.

The thought nearly brought him to his knees while

stirring every protective instinct he'd ever had. He squeezed Clarissa's hand before pulling away. "Wait here."

She followed him up the garden slope anyway. For a moment, Samuel relished the thought that she was convinced he could take care of her. He strode toward the crowd, the old alertness coming back fast as he headed toward the man with sergeant's stripes. He averted his eyes from the thin, curved scar across the man's left cheek. "What do you want, soldier?"

"I said I want to see the Fighting Chaplain. You him?"

Samuel's spine stiffened as it did every time he heard the puffed-up-sounding name. "Some refer to me as such. I'm the Reverend Samuel Montgomery."

The soldier held out his hand. "Sergeant John Buchanan. I fought down the line from you the day you saved your platoon. And you prayed with me in the trench the next day and changed my life." His throat worked, hard, as if the man had been holding back his emotions about that battle and that prayer these three years. "When you prayed with me, they had just cut off my arm, and I was in so much pain, I didn't remember what you looked like. But I came here from Charleston, South Carolina, anyway, to shake your hand and to pray God's blessings on you, sir."

He'd traveled hundreds of miles just to see Samuel?

What other suffering had the man endured? Samuel reached out and clasped the thick, muscled hand. The tremble in their grasp could have come from either of them; Samuel didn't know which.

"Well, I'm not here to pray," the woman in blue said, the whine in her Yankee-accented voice breaking the moment and grating against Samuel's nerves.

"Then why did you come?" He dropped the sergeant's

hand and spoke with all the gentleness he could muster, which wasn't as much as it probably should have been.

"You say you're the Fighting Chaplain, but you're not wearing your sword." The Yankee woman turned on Samuel, her youthful face marred with peevishness. "The article said you always wear your sword."

"What article?"

She drew a newspaper clipping from her blue-beaded reticule and thrust it at Samuel like a bayonet. "It says you're the most dangerous man in the South, and no one has ever beaten you in a swordfight. I paid good money to see the Fighting Chaplain and his sword that killed twenty-one of our good men. All I see is some preacher dressed up like a dandy."

A dandy, in his black minister's suit?

He reached inside his jacket for his eyeglasses, but the pocket was empty. He handed the article to Clarissa.

She took the folded page. "'Meet the Fighting Chaplain and tour his palatial home on the outskirts of Natchez, Mississippi, the South's most beautiful city. See his grandfather's sword, with which he cut down a platoon of despicable Yankee soldiers at the Battle of Chickamauga. Sit in the sanctuary, a tiny chapel where the Fighting Chaplain now writes his inspiring sermons. Hear the legend of hidden gold and search for it yourself on the estate's thirty acres. Only ten cents per person for a one-hour tour, every day at 1 o'clock. Camellia Pointe, East Melrose Street and Franklin Avenue, Natchez.'" Clarissa folded the clipping and slipped it into her pocket. "This is a mistake. We don't give tours."

"We paid for a tour, so give it to us." The tallest of the shabbily dressed men started toward Samuel.

He held up one hand, stopping him. "My sword is not on display, and we're not giving tours."

"Yes, we are."

Absalom and Beau strode out of the garden and through the middle of the crowd as if they already owned the place. The long-haired renegade tipped his outrageously huge stovepipe hat to the woman in blue. "They each paid ten cents to tour the house and grounds, and to see the Fighting Chaplain in all his glory."

Tour the home? Had Absalom lost his mind? "Adams, you're a fool. I have no glory, and you're not taking a bunch of strangers through Clarissa's house."

"The blazes I'm not." Absalom closed the gap between them, his garlicky breath heavy in Samuel's nose. "I'm going to recoup the money I spent on repairs."

"You're not turning our grandparents' home into a circus," Clarissa said in a harsh whisper.

Despite the flash in her eyes, Absalom crooked his elbow at the Yankee woman, clearly planning to guide the tour himself. He steered her around Clarissa and toward the angel statue, his long salt-and-pepper hair blowing in the breeze. "We'll see the grounds first. My great-grandmother planted this camellia and rose garden from slips she brought with her from Virginia back in—"

"Send them away, Adams." Samuel stepped in front of him, his voice lowered to a growl.

The sergeant joined him, stopping a foot from Absalom's now pale face. "I'll throw them out for you, Chaplain—"

A whoop from Willie interrupted him. The boy raced across the lawn toward the garden steps, waving his sword.

The sight shot fear into Samuel's heart and twisted his gut. He sprinted toward the boy. "Willie, stop! Don't run with it unsheathed…"

The boy tripped on an uneven step, fell the rest of the way down and let out a shriek.

"Willie…" Samuel poured on the speed, each jagged breath a prayer. He slid to his knees at the boy's side, the sergeant a fraction of a second behind.

The sword lay with its point a good two inches from Willie's belly.

"Turned my fool ankle," he said, rolling to a sitting position.

Samuel's pulse began to slow when he saw the boy was safe, but the weakness washing over him would take a minute to abate. "You know better than to run with an unsheathed sword. You almost killed yourself."

Clarissa caught up to them and fanned her face with the hated news page. "How bad is your ankle?"

"It's nothing." Willie scrambled up and hopped on one foot a couple of times. "I had to do it. You gotta stop Absalom."

Samuel stood too and laid his hand on the little troublemaker's shoulder, his strength coming back. He glanced behind him. Absalom had led the crowd toward the sanctuary. "Stop him from what?"

"Absalom and Harold Goss got an agreement. They're looking for something hidden here at this house. They're not just doing these tours for money. Absalom gives them to distract you while that poor sap Harold Goss searches the property."

"What are they looking for?"

"Hidden gold. They're going to dig around until they find it."

"How do you know?"

"When me and Pete went for more bricks, we saw ol' Absalom and Harold Goss skulking around the sanctuary, so I sneaked over there to make sure they weren't causing trouble. They were talking about gold and pointing at a newspaper, and when they left, they crammed the paper inside the altar urn. Said they might need it later, when the tourists show up."

"And after they were gone, you fetched the paper out of the urn and read it," Samuel said, a snippet of amusement in his tone.

"I had to know what they were all het up about. If there's gold at Camellia Pointe, I don't want Absalom to find it."

Clarissa let out a huff. "Absalom needs to grow up. He always believed the old stories about our great-grandfather hiding valuables on the estate. They're not true."

"That doesn't explain why you were running with the sword."

Willie puffed out his chest. "I couldn't let him start the tours. The poor sap might find the treasure."

Clarissa glanced around the property. "I don't see Harold anywhere. I think you misunderstood."

"The article said there's hidden gold here."

"That still doesn't mean—"

"I can prove it," Willie said. "What newspaper is the ad in?"

She pulled the clipping from her sleeve and unfolded it. "The *Daily Memphis Avalanche*."

"Who owns it?" the boy asked in a cheeky tone.

She checked the clipping and then raised her gaze to Willie's, her eyes wider than Samuel had ever seen them. "'Publisher, Harold Goss.'"

Wait—the *Daily Memphis Avalanche*...not a local paper as Samuel had assumed? It couldn't be.

Willie snorted. "I heard him tell Absalom he was gonna use that paper to cause a Mississippi avalanche."

"This isn't the first time he's tried to snow me." Despite Willie's boyish reasoning and conclusions, Samuel wouldn't put anything past Goss. "Remember when I told you of Miss Emily St. John, the young woman from Memphis who tried to trap me into marriage?"

"The one you spoke of your first day here?"

He nodded. "The rumor started with a gossip column in the *Avalanche*. Harold Goss is Miss St. John's cousin, and he did all he could to forge a marriage between us."

Clarissa studied the clipping again. Then she let out a gasp that carried a pain-filled edge. "The sanctuary—Grandfather's private little place—on the front page."

Samuel looked over her shoulder and squinted at the picture. Stepping back a little, he could finally see the sanctuary's outline. "How did someone get that photograph without us knowing?"

Willie pointed at the clipping. "Ain't a photograph. It's a drawing."

Clarissa held the paper closer to her face then turned to Samuel. "He's right. And Drusilla must have made it. She spent all her time drawing until she left for Memphis."

No doubt. "Willie, please put your sword away with mine in my room."

The boy's shoulders drooped but he quickly pulled them back again and saluted. "Yes, sir."

Samuel started to reach into his coat pocket for his key but then stopped. "How did you get it? I keep my door locked."

"I used the key that hangs on the little tack above the door trim." At a more sedate pace than before, Willie headed for the house.

Samuel glanced at Clarissa for her reaction. "I didn't know a key was up there."

"Nor did I." Her gaze turned suspicious as she watched her cousin blathering in front of the sanctuary. She eased herself onto the stone bench beside the walk. "Perhaps I should check the spare-key ring in the kitchen. Absalom or Beau might have taken the spare and hung it there so they could search your room whenever they wanted."

Suddenly weary down to his marrow, Samuel sank to the bench, keeping a little distance from Clarissa. Perhaps he should offer his services as tour guide. Then he could keep an eye on the crowds—and Absalom.

He cast a glance at the sergeant, his gaze fixed on Samuel as if awaiting orders.

What if the tough-looking soldier would do that for him? Not be the guide but rather the estate watchman… "Sergeant, when must you return home?"

"Got no home to return to. Yankees burned everything, and my family is long gone."

"If my wife approves, I'd like to capitalize on this situation instead of shutting it down."

He chanced a glance at Clarissa but the reluctance he'd expected to see wasn't there. Rather, she leaned forward a bit, a light of interest in her eyes.

"The ad could bring us a lot of guests. I'd like you to stay with us and keep the estate secure." He drew a deep breath, knowing his wife might well object to the rest of his plan. "They're coming to see the Fighting Chaplain. What if we oblige them—turn this circus into a ministry opportunity? Every afternoon, I could deliver a gospel message in the sanctuary. Camellia Pointe would become a preaching point for the Gospel."

Judging from the way Clarissa's brows shot up and her eyes grew large as camellia blossoms, she didn't like it. Maybe it was a bad idea, but he felt it had come from the Lord. Now what should he—?

Her beautiful smile broke out like the sun emerging through the clouds. "Grandfather Hezekiah always said we should take every opportunity to preach the Gospel."

The prospect suddenly interested him even more than preaching in the church. And his amazing wife was behind him, his partner in the ministry. Something he'd dreamed of for years. "We'll have a lot of people trampling through here every day. You're sure that's what you want?"

"If Sergeant John can stay and help."

"I'm your man," the soldier said.

"You might as well get your sword and start now." The shine in her eyes, her clear confidence in Samuel, took his breath and confirmed what he'd been afraid to admit—even to himself.

He was in love with Clarissa. The realization sliced through him like that stupid sword, carving his heart into little pieces with its razor edge.

But he was a failure as a family man. So how could he trust himself not to let her down as he had Veronica? As he still did with Emma? He didn't deserve a happy marriage, a second chance at love, and he never would.

He turned abruptly from her and made for the house before she could see the truth in his eyes.

Chapter Twelve

Grandfather never would have dreamed of his sanctuary becoming a preaching point. But if he had, this is what he'd have wanted to see.

Clarissa stood off to the side, in case Samuel needed her, as he hovered his hand over the hilt of his grandfather's sword. Only she realized the depth of his disdain for the fuss and flurry that always surrounded the Fighting Chaplain. Yet today, as always, he submitted to the title's indignity for the sake of those gathered to listen.

And did it wholeheartedly.

Except for the moments before he took off at a run to the house, presumably to get his sword. In those seconds of hesitation, his eyes had burned with shame, almost regret.

Samuel drew the sword now and slashed it through the air, demonstrating the Bible story of the Apostle Peter cutting off the Roman soldier's ear in Gethsemane. "Big, strong fisherman Peter likely aimed for the soldier's head," he said, "hoping to split it down the middle rather than merely slicing off an ear. And Jesus, probably an equally big, strong carpenter, reached down with compassion and gently placed the ear back on the soldier's head, healing it."

Strength out of control, strength under control.

Clarissa was beginning to see the extent of her husband's strength—under control.

The faces of Samuel's audience—the disheartened soldiers, the Yankee woman, Sergeant John, the children and their tutor—assured her he was reaching their hearts with his message of forgiveness and second chances.

All but Absalom, who stood a safe distance from Samuel and his sword, and Harold Goss, who had appeared from who knew where when Samuel started preaching.

If only Clarissa could have a second chance—at life, at love. Entering into this marriage agreement, she'd known she'd never experience love, didn't want to experience it. Perhaps she'd been wrong to think so. She rubbed her bare wrist, the one Harold had once ornamented with a silver bangle. Why was she so inadequate? What did she lack? What intangible essence made other women capable of keeping their beaus, their husbands—their fathers?

"Missus Montgomery, will you sing 'Jesus Paid It All' as we close?"

She jerked up her head at Samuel's voice. So deep had been her musings, she hadn't realized he was closing the meeting.

Clarissa met his brown-eyed gaze, its intensity making her blink. She saw his intent: to give the Lord the opportunity to use his preaching voice and her singing voice together, as He had on Sunday, to reach this little crowd with the Gospel.

She drew a breath from deep within and started the song in breathy tones. The simple yet profound message warmed her, solidified her confidence in the One who'd made her. He would help her, would love her even though she'd never know the love of a man.

Of the good man, her fine husband, who stood watching and silently encouraging her.

When she'd drawn out the last notes, she slipped away, up the slope to the house.

"What's going on down there?" Grandmother said, Lilliana in her arms, when Clarissa entered her bedroom minutes later.

After Clarissa brought the older lady up to date on Absalom's nefarious activities and Samuel's redemption of them, Grandmother gave an unladylike grunt. "There's no treasure hidden at Camellia Pointe. When the Yankees left, your grandfather retrieved the few sentimental items stashed away here."

Well, all but one silver bangle.

Grandmother raised her voice over the sound of the baby's whimpering. "Samuel preached every bit as well down there as he did on Sunday."

"How do you know?"

"I opened the window and listened."

"You heard him from up here?" Clarissa took Lilliana and walked the fussy baby about the room. Had Grandmother gotten any rest this afternoon? Joseph had been right. They needed Maisie's help.

"Your grandfather used to say that if God hasn't equipped a man with a voice loud enough to carry to the back of the church, then He hasn't called him to preach. I could hear Samuel from my bedroom window." Grandmother sat at her dressing table, took out her hairpins and picked up the brush from her familiar amber vanity set. As she brushed her long, gray hair, she watched

Clarissa in the mirror. "I could hear you too. You have a special gift of helping Samuel in his ministry."

The rare, unexpected compliment brought a sting to Clarissa's eyes. "How can you tell?"

"I have fifty years of experience as a pastor's wife. When your grandfather started out in the ministry, he insisted I sing before he preached. He always got a peaceful look on his face. Samuel had the same look on Sunday."

"What does that mean?"

"For one thing, it means he's starting to trust you. To depend on you." She laid down her brush and turned around. "To develop feelings for you."

Feelings? "You're mistaken. Marriages of convenience don't end up happy."

"Why do you keep saying that? Mine was arranged and your grandfather and I couldn't have been happier." She returned to the mirror. "Unless Absalom and his father hadn't turned out so odd."

"Absalom's parents were never happy, and Grandfather arranged their marriage."

Grandmother parted her thick hair down the middle and twisted it into a chignon, speaking to Clarissa's image in the walnut-framed mirror. "I told you before, they were strange people. But I can't believe they're the reason you think all arranged marriages are unhappy."

How did Grandmother's steely gaze manage to slice open Clarissa's heart and look inside, even through a mirror? Why did she need to know the reason Clarissa didn't like arranged marriages? But the gray-haired lady wouldn't give up until Clarissa told her the whole truth. "Fine. If you have to know, I used to think the man of my dreams would show up one day and tell me he's been looking for me. For me, not just any woman who would agree to marry him. I want a man to want me, specifically."

"That's silly. He does want you, *specifically*."

"No, he wanted me because I could keep him at Christ Church. Any Natchez girl could have married him and made him eligible for this pastorate."

"He wouldn't have married any other girl but you." Grandmother's words burned through Clarissa, her eyes like fire. "What kind of man do you think he is, that he'd marry any girl who came along?"

No, Samuel did not choose her, because no man ever had. Not Father. Not Harold. She'd never been enough, never been adequate. "I'm just the convenient one. That's why they call it a marriage of convenience."

"No, you were in the place God intended you to be, at the time He intended it."

"Then what happened when Harold left? When my father left? Was I in the wrong place at the wrong time? I don't think so."

"That's not what I said."

"Papa always used the Delta plantations as his excuse for abandoning me. Then we said he neglected me because of his grief." Her tone sounded shrill in her ears, and she took a deep breath to lower it. "My love for my father could neither keep him here nor bring him back, any more than it could keep Harold."

"You read more into this than you should. Lots of people love you."

But Clarissa could no longer shove away the knowledge that her father had abandoned her long before he'd exited her life. And her mother's love, sweet as it had been, hadn't filled the gap he'd left.

Did anyone really want to be with her, to love her, to stay with her?

She set the now-sleeping baby in the middle of the bed and knelt at her grandmother's feet, her sudden tears blurring the older woman's face. "When my mother died and my father left, did you and Grandfather keep me out of love or duty?"

Grandmother Euphemia turned from the mirror and touched Clarissa's hair in a rare tender gesture. "Why did you take Lilliana? Why do you still have her?"

Not from duty. Duty without love would have taken her to the orphanage.

"We didn't have to keep you. We wanted you." Grandmother's voice turned nostalgic. "You were a sweet child, and now you're a sweet woman. Your father left because of his own failings, his own moral defects. Not yours."

If only it were true. She—not Father, not Harold Goss—was the flawed one. "He wasn't the only man who left me."

"Yes, Harold Goss—he has no more sense than Absalom does. You'd have been miserable with him."

Yes, but she'd also been miserable without him. "He made me feel special, as if I stood out from the other girls in town."

"You are special, and you still stand out. Harold was too greedy to understand what a treasure you are." Grandmother turned, secured pins in her hair, then stood and smoothed her skirt, breaking the warm mood. "I've never dressed this late in the day in my life."

To be sure, Grandmother was changing. Turning loose of time-honored traditions and habits no one would ever have thought she would abandon. Camellia Pointe was changing, as well.

But Samuel? She was certainly seeing new sides of him, and he was learning to laugh and relax a bit. But just an hour ago, he'd turned from a moment that might have become tender.

Grandmother was wrong. Samuel didn't love her and never would. Because Clarissa wasn't the kind of girl a man would love.

If only Clarissa could slow down time tonight.

An hour before dark, she slid open the pocket doors between the parlor and drawing room, making one big room for the household—all but Absalom and his family. And Sergeant John, who'd insisted on standing guard outside to prevent her cousin from wrecking any more of their work. With the grounds renovation completed, Joseph would arrive at any moment to inspect their efforts, and then he'd open his decades-old portmanteau. When he did, she'd hear her grandfather's last words to her.

She'd treasure those words, as she still cherished the memory of Mother's last touch, her last, precious breaths. And then they would be over, and she'd have no more communication from him until the day she would see him again in heaven. She held Lilliana a little tighter in her arms. God had a way of bringing comfort in the midst of sorrow, and the baby certainly brought comfort and joy to this home.

Funny how an infant could do that…

Lilliana affected even Samuel. Having her in their home and using Camellia Pointe for ministry clearly made it easier for him to live here. Tonight, for the first time since he'd come to this house, Samuel looked at home, relaxed, with his easy manner and quick smile. As Emma floated toward him in the drawing room, her creamy yellow hoopskirt swaying prettily, he smiled at her.

Actually smiled. The sight brought a mistiness to Clarissa's eyes.

His ease calmed the rest of the family in the cozy back room as well. Peter and Prudy sat on the rug with Willie and played quietly with the puppy for once. Even Lilliana had quieted a bit in Clarissa's arms, merely making little squawking sounds instead of crying her heart out as before.

If only Clarissa could compose herself as well. In a few more minutes, they would be one step closer to the end of the contest. Both she and Absalom had fulfilled their duties well and completed the second stipulation, but what was to come? She still believed her grandfather had intended to award her Camellia Pointe and Good Shepherd. But his first two letters had certainly held the unexpected. Who knew what he'd thought up for the third?

After a long afternoon of hard physical labor, the small crowd of workers looked as tired and sore as Clarissa felt. Willie, Peter and Prudy, Mister Forbes, Emma—even Grandmother had helped by minding Lilliana and Honey during the hectic afternoon.

She sat next to Samuel on the red velvet sofa. "A big part of me doesn't want to hear this last letter."

He arched his brows. "Whatever it says, it'll be the truth that will set you free from Absalom."

One way or the other.

Joseph's two-horse brougham pulled up, its unmistakable deep-toned bells ringing outside the parlor window. Samuel hastened to the hall as if he'd been greeting guests in this house all his life.

Nothing could have surprised Clarissa more than his obvious, sudden pleasure in Camellia Pointe. Then again, it shouldn't have, considering the way he'd preached in the little sanctuary this afternoon.

She shifted the baby in her arms in the hope of distracting the child, kissed her sweet little cheeks. She could hardly believe she'd married a man with a pastor's heart as big as her grandfather's. Her eyes stung a bit as she remembered Samuel's intensity, his fervency, as he'd preached the Gospel to the tourists in Grandfather's chapel.

As her pride in him grew, her longing grew as well—to be more than just ministry helper and applesauce-cookie baker and stepmother to his daughter. She nuzzled Lilliana's sweet-smelling neck, hoping to hide her own embarrassment and flushed face.

Because as sure as the sunrise, she was beginning to lose her heart to her husband.

"I brought a new governess and cook." Joseph's basso voice snatched Clarissa from her unruly thoughts as he and Samuel entered the big room.

Maisie.

Clarissa hastened to welcome the former seamstress, whose peach-colored, iridescent dress had one of the new elliptical skirts and a matching snood. High style for Natchez after the war. Clarissa tucked under the slightly frayed cuffs of her own made-over green-and-white gingham. "Maisie, we need you desperately. I simply don't know what I'm doing." About more issues than one.

"If there's anything I'm good at, it's taking care of children. I helped raise most of my nieces and nephews." Maisie held out her plump hands and took the complaining baby. Lilliana continued to fuss, but more quietly. Maisie simply patted her back and crooned a song so sweet and low, it calmed even Clarissa a bit.

Joseph had known exactly how to help them, as always.

As she instructed Emma and Willie on settling Maisie and the baby in their new room, the back door opened and then banged shut. A moment later, Absalom and Beau barged in. Absalom plopped himself into the gold fireside wing chair.

"Let's get this inspection over with." He glanced at Grandmother, who had raised her cane. "And don't start with that weapon of yours."

Seated next to him, Grandmother poked him in the shin anyway. "You needn't have sat down. We're heading straight outside for the grounds inspection before dark."

So soon? "Joseph, wouldn't you care for coffee first? It gets damp outside this time of evening."

The attorney hesitated, cocking his head at her. "Best to get it done, little girl."

Little girl. He hadn't called Clarissa by his pet name for her since she'd started wearing her hair up. He must know something she didn't…

When everyone had filed out and Clarissa followed Joseph into the hall, Honey growled, long and loud. Clarissa turned around to the drawing room again and found Beau making for the round walnut table in the center of the room and reaching for the portmanteau resting there.

The sneak. Staying quiet in the back of the room until they'd all forgotten about him. "Don't touch it."

Beau's wide-eyed stare might have looked innocent on a child half his age, who wasn't the son of a renegade like Absalom.

"You're coming with us, where I can see you." Joseph strode back into the drawing room, grabbed the handle of his aged leather bag with one hand and Beau's arm with the other. "March."

The young man stalked outside, his naive look gone.

Clarissa snatched up the puppy and gave it a gentle squeeze.

"You'd better watch them every minute," Joseph said, still the protector.

Twenty minutes later, they stopped at the sanctuary after a tour of the gardens and lawns. Joseph laid his hand on Clarissa's shoulder, a fatherly pride in his eye. "You've done well. In my opinion, you've met the criteria of the will."

"Of course she'll pass the inspection, since her husband has the final say." Absalom's voice turned spiteful. "But even with all the help she had, she didn't finish. The live oak behind the sanctuary needs trimming."

"Reverend Montgomery, what say you?" Joseph said.

Samuel didn't hesitate a moment. "According to Clarissa, the late Reverend Adams let the tree grow as it wished. Clarissa has fulfilled both the letter of her grandfather's request and the spirit thereof."

"Well spoken." Joseph turned toward the house and started up the slope.

Fifteen minutes later, with the house inspection complete, Absalom flopped into the gold wing back again, the frame groaning under his weight, and lit the fat cigar he'd pulled from his coat pocket. "Let's get this over with. I have an appointment."

Clarissa turned her face away, fussed with the seam on the side of her skirt. How could Absalom be so cold as to rush through this painful ceremony? Or was she the only one to mourn Grandfather, to realize they were about to hear the last words he had for them? Never again would he share his mind, his heart, with them. "Must we hurry through it so? Could we not take a moment and—and remember Grandfather, his kind ways, his love for us? Can we not—pray?"

"Prayer would be appropriate." Samuel hastened to his feet and began a prayer.

Clarissa drank in the tenderness and kindness in her husband's voice and breathed a wordless prayer of her own. Grandfather Hezekiah—kind and always gentle. Surely he meant this situation for her good. Surely he wanted her to have Camellia Pointe and Good Shepherd. Surely he meant Clarissa to win.

But she'd broken her grandfather's trust when she'd become engaged to Harold Goss that summer. For reasons she didn't understand then, Grandfather didn't like him. Almost hated him. Could he be testing her with this will?

Clarissa glanced over at Samuel again as he completed his prayer. She needed some of the control he had such a grip on.

Joseph opened his bag and drew out a bundle of papers tied with string. "As with the second letter, the reverend is to read it to Absalom and Clarissa together. Everyone else, please vacate the room."

Within moments, the four were alone, the divider doors pulled shut again, the drawing room door closed tight. Joseph handed an envelope to Samuel, who slid on his eyeglasses and opened the single page.

"'To meet the third stipulation of my will, my grandchildren will formulate and execute separate plans for the improvement of my properties. Absalom Adams will take charge of Good Shepherd Dining and Lodging. Clarissa Adams will do likewise for Camellia Pointe.'

"'To succeed in this third phase, one contestant will improve his property to make it the more useful, aesthetic and functional. Since this phase is a contest, attorney Joseph Duncan, the current minister of Christ Church of Natchez, and the deaconate of said church will determine which candidate has better achieved his objective. The winner will become heir of Camellia Pointe and Good Shepherd Dining and Lodging. Plans must be submitted in three days and completed in one year. Listen. "His compassions fail not. They are new every morning.'"

New every morning… Clarissa was going to need that. A stone sunk in her middle. Could her grandfather have made this contest any harder?

Lord, I need those new compassions now. I can't wait until morning...

"How much money did the old man give us for these improvements?" Absalom ashed his cigar on the parlor rug.

Clarissa bounded up from the sofa. "You never cared for our grandparents, only their money. Well, there isn't any left. What the Yankees didn't steal, the Confederates confiscated."

"Then explain those coin silver candlesticks on the piano. And Great-grandmother's garnets that you still wear. And the old man's silver traveling communion set—"

"How did you know the communion set was here?" Against her will, her voice rose an octave. "You've been snooping in Samuel's study. I checked the spare key ring in the kitchen, and the key to his study was missing. You took it, didn't you?"

"I'm still family, like it or not." He pounded his fist on the Hepplewhite side table. "I have a right to know!"

"Fine. It's none of your business, since Grandfather left the house's contents to me," Clarissa said. "But he hid the silver and garnets because they were irreplaceable. He was the fourth generation to use the communion set, and Grandmother's ancestors brought the candlesticks and garnets over on the *Mayflower*."

"What else did he hide?" Absalom lowered his voice to a menacing growl. "Confederate gold?"

That settled it—her cousin had gone crazy. "I know your scheme to keep us occupied with tourists so you and Harold can look for hidden treasure. I never heard of anything so childish."

"Time to go, Adams." Her husband stood and slowly strode to Absalom's side, sliding his eyeglasses into his inner coat pocket. "Keep in mind that anything you find belongs to Clarissa. And if you take anything, you're stealing."

When Absalom had stomped out and slammed the back door, Clarissa hastened to scan the hall and parlor. Upon returning to Samuel and Joseph, she closed and locked the drawing room door. "I don't trust him not to eavesdrop."

"And I don't trust him not to tear the house apart stone by stone, looking for treasure," Samuel said as Clarissa returned to the sofa.

She reached under the Hepplewhite table next to her and opened its drawer. Then she pulled out the newspaper advertisement and handed it to Joseph. "Do you know anything about the *Daily Memphis Avalanche*? Harold owns it and printed a picture Drusilla drew of our little sanctuary."

"I'll see what I can find out. Keep the sergeant around to secure the place. He's a tough one. He could scare grown men off the property with one glance." Joseph read the advertisement and handed it back. "I'll be here Sunday afternoon to hear your plans."

Plans completed in three days. Work finished in one

year. If Clarissa had wished to hold back the clock hands before, she'd slow them to a near stop now.

Or would she? "Will the first person to complete the work have a better chance at winning?"

Joseph nodded. "If the quality of the plan and work are similar, the first person finished would have an advantage."

"Then I'll make sure we're done first." Somehow.

When the attorney had taken his leave, Clarissa sighed and turned to Samuel in the hall. "I have a lot of work to do and not much time. I'll get a basic plan together, and we can meet tomorrow evening—"

A clattering sound in the formal dining room stopped her. Clarissa crept toward the noise and flung open the door.

In the waning light, Emma and Beau crouched near the door, obviously eavesdropping on Clarissa's private meeting with her attorney.

Clarissa opened her mouth to question them then hesitated. Emma's father needed to handle this. She raised her gaze heavenward for a moment and then put all her encouragement and confidence in him into a bright smile—at least, she hoped that was what it looked like.

Could he do it? She believed he could. *Dear God, please remind him not to frown at her.*

Looking back, Samuel couldn't have said where he'd suddenly gotten the idea to take Emma out to the sanctuary yesterday after catching her spying. Why he'd been able to have a fatherly talk with her instead of merely "scowling," as Willie called it, and then given up, not knowing what else to do. Or why Emma had agreed to go with him. But for the first time, he'd refused to let his past failure cripple him in the present.

One sweet smile from Clarissa had broken the habit—permanently, he hoped—as she showed him her faith in him.

Now, waiting on the back gallery for Clarissa as the sun began to set, he gave thanks that his daughter understood how wrong she'd been to eavesdrop with Beau. How they could lose Camellia Pointe if they all didn't do their best to save it.

Yes, things had begun to change in Emma…

The door swung open and Clarissa stepped onto the gallery. Her long, dark hair flowed loose, soft in the wind, down her back and to her waist, as if she'd just brushed it for the night.

The way she looked at him took his breath—as if she wanted to be there with him. Enjoyed his company. Chose to spend time with him. It made him want to memorize her beautiful face, her enormous green eyes and flawless, fair skin. Made him never want to look away.

A thousand times he'd wished he could become a different sort of man, unbroken, who could win the love of his wife rather than constantly disappoint her. Now, Clarissa's quick smile and sparkly eyes almost made him think he could.

"You—look lovely."

Was that the best he could come up with? He winced, wishing he could pull those limp words back into his mouth.

And on Valentine's Day yet. The envelope he'd slipped into his inner coat pocket rustled as he took a step nearer.

But she seemed not to care about his lack of flowery phrase or clever compliment, judging from the way her cheeks pinked and her hazel eyes darkened to a dewy green.

Then he noticed the leather-bound book in her hand, the size of a business ledger, its corners worn and its cover scratched.

Her business plan. Of course. For a moment, he'd forgotten the purpose of their meeting.

"Maybe we could take a stroll. I think better while I walk." She took the arm he extended to her, and they started across the courtyard. "The moon's full tonight, and the wind and clouds will make the moonrise spectacular. We could watch it later."

Wait—was this heart-poundingly beautiful woman, her hair blowing wild in the wind, suggesting a romantic evening? With him? He slowed their pace, took a deep breath, until his pulse slowed a bit. "Let's do that."

He could feel her smile as they took the newly tuck-pointed steps to the lower gardens.

"I love this time of year—the camellias and azaleas in bloom, the paperwhites and dogwoods and tulips. I smelled the first scents of spring this morning."

She turned her head toward the gardens in the gathering dusk, giving Samuel a whiff of her flowery perfume as it wafted from her hair. "I thought about Camellia Pointe's improvements all day and finally decided on a two-point strategy. First, we divide the third-floor attic into bedrooms, then fix up the old servants' cabins east of the house."

"What will we do with those areas when we're done?"

"I visited the city orphanage this afternoon. Miss Caldwell is beside herself. I'd like to bring home some of the children and put the girls in the attic and the boys in the cabins."

More orphans? "How many?"

"They have bedding for all but five."

With her beautiful eyes filled with her enthusiasm, her love for the orphans, she'd never looked prettier to Samuel. No woman had. But did she understand the sacrifice? "You're talking about turning Camellia Pointe into an orphanage. Are you sure that's what you want? Because Absalom could never come up with a better plan, so you'll win the contest, but our lives will never be the same."

"I had the idea last night, after I tucked the twins in bed and realized how quickly we formed a daily routine as a new family. Without the twins and Willie and Lilliana, this house would feel empty."

It would also feel empty without Clarissa. "I feel better about living at Camellia Pointe since we use it for ministry. But how could we could afford to feed and clothe five more children?"

"The will says I'm to take charge of Camellia Pointe, so I'll set a rental fee for Absalom and his family. That and the tour proceeds will pay for the renovations and the extra children."

It seemed his wife was as smart as she was beautiful.

They stopped at the cabins, where they discussed and listed the necessary repairs, including supplies needed to make one cabin into a schoolhouse.

An hour later, when Samuel extinguished the lamp in the future schoolhouse and they stepped outside, night had fallen. Clarissa stopped a moment to glance behind them. "Don't look to the east. I want you to get your first glimpse of the moon from the bridge."

Amid the roar of the wind in the woods, they set out for the moonrise show, his anticipation surprising him. All this for a moon? But in the waxing and waning light, when the clouds were no doubt concealing and then revealing the moon, he could imagine that frosty globe in her eyes.

When they reached the duck pond, she set her book on a flat rock near the bridge, turned and took his hand. “You can look when we reach the crest of the arch.”

Happy to oblige, he kept his focus on her stunning face as they ambled up the bridge’s incline.

Then she stopped, gazed into the eastern sky and caught her breath. “It’s magnificent tonight.”

The full moon illumined the sky around it with cold, white beauty, black clouds scudding by and veiling the silver orb, then flying on toward the north. Now the moon was completely obscured in a black night sky, now it beamed forth again, shining behind and amid the clouds until another black shroud raced before it.

A magnificent sight indeed.

And then the thin cool light reflected on the crisp white collar of Clarissa’s dress, the wind blowing her dark hair before it, obscuring it as the clouds had the moon. And her eyes, shimmering in the moonbeams, lovelier than the sight above…

She tilted her head, a hint of a smile on her pink lips. A smile of invitation.

It couldn’t be. She welcomed his touch—perhaps even his kiss?

“Clarissa, dearest…” She tightened her hold on his hand, just a fraction, until the memory of their kiss rose in his mind. She leaned a little closer, bringing her sweet, flowery scent with her.

Since that night, he’d made her as untouchable as the moon. Now she seemed to draw him toward her with some invisible pull, and he cupped his other hand behind her neck, her hair silky in his hand.

Her eyes slid shut and Samuel held her closer yet—

Until movement from a distance stopped him.

No.

In the gazebo, fifty feet from them, a silhouette. Two silhouettes, nearly as close together as he now held Clarissa. Then a muffled giggle.

Emma.

Out here with Beau.

Getting into trouble. Big trouble.

Samuel broke free from Clarissa and sprinted to the gazebo. “Emma Louise, come out here. Right now.”

His fourteen-year-old daughter, out after dark with this young man—again? His gut wrenched as if he’d just gulped a whole pot of Clarissa’s coffee. What was Samuel still doing wrong? What was he doing even more wrong than before?

When Emma slunk out of the gazebo, Beau beside her, he saw her as both the child he’d left behind in Kentucky and the woman she was trying to be.

If he could only sever the bond between her and Beau. Cut in two whatever kept her running toward this young man and away from him. Couldn’t Emma see that he wanted her affection, her attention, her love? Even if he could separate his daughter from Beau, it wouldn’t draw her heart to him, her father.

He lifted his hand, meaning to touch her hair, draw her to him and away from the young man at her side.

She flinched as if he meant to slap her.

The thought ripped through his heart as if she’d drawn the sword on him. “Emma, please don’t cower before me. You know I won’t strike you. I never have.”

Her downcast face in the moonlight said all he needed to know.

Her mother had struck her.

Why had Emma not told him her mother had mistreated her? Why had he left her so much alone with Veronica?

Why had he never seen the truth until now?

Then he noticed something glistening near her face in the moonlight. He hadn't seen it before, but her hair was up, like a grown woman's. A woman of marrying age, as Clarissa had said. And from Emma's earlobes dangled filigree earrings set with sapphires.

The earrings that had mysteriously shown up on Veronica's ears the evening after she'd betrayed him.

He'd always known his rival had sent them. And now his daughter wore them to a tryst with the son of his current wife's enemy.

"Go to your room." Of all he wanted to say, wanted to beg, wanted to demand, this was all he could manage around the tightness of his throat. And although he would rather have fled, he followed his daughter into the house and up the stairs.

She slammed her door behind her. He made for his own lonely room, shut the door and locked himself in, an even bigger failure than he'd been when he'd come to this town.

Chapter Thirteen

Clarissa flew across the bridge toward the family cemetery the next evening, running to beat the impending storm despite sore muscles from her swordplay lesson that morning. But had she made the right decision? Was her motivation pure? Perhaps not. But after last night, when Samuel had been only a breath away from kissing her—really kissing her—she had to carry out her task. Couldn't wait to do it.

Across the pond now, carrying a fresh bouquet of camellias, she hastened down the dirt path to the woods' edge where the stones stood. Absalom had been right about one thing: something of modest value was hidden at Camellia Pointe.

Clarissa slowed her pace as she approached Great-grandfather's marker. She laid her flowers on the ground and brushed her fingers over the scripture verse Grandfather had etched into his own father's stone: *His compassions fail not. They are new every morning.* Then she twisted the urn-shaped finial atop her ancestor's headstone until it revealed the secret compartment inside the obelisk. The spot where Grandfather had hidden her garnet necklace the day the Yankees occupied Natchez.

She looked inside. After five years, the blue-velvet bag was still there.

When she had retrieved the bag and slid the finial back into place, she opened the drawstring and pulled out the silver bangle bracelet, engraved with blossoms and vines.

Time to get rid of it.

Clarissa had carried the pain and memory of this bracelet long enough. When Harold had given it to her all those years ago, she'd believed him when he'd said he loved her and wanted to marry her and wipe away all the tears of her past. If only she'd known he'd buy another, identical bracelet only a month later—and Belinda Grimes would wear it on their wedding day.

And on that day, Clarissa had hidden hers here, where she would never need to see it again. Until now, when bringing it out of the tombstone felt like starting a new life.

When the time was right, she'd give this bracelet to Emma. The girl needed a tangible sign of Clarissa's love. Perhaps a woman more at peace with her past would sell the bracelet and use the money to buy a new gift for her stepdaughter. But somehow she needed to do this, needed to see that bracelet on the wrist of a girl not much younger than Clarissa had been when she'd accepted it. The finality felt right. She'd carry out her plan as soon as she could.

Having scattered most of the flowers on her mother's and grandfather's graves, she started back toward the house and her room.

When she had hidden the bracelet in her jewelry box and arranged the remaining camellias in Samuel's vase, footsteps sounded on the stairs and hall, and then a knock at her door.

Samuel's knock.

Clarissa hurried to let him in and close the door, her first glimpse of him taking her breath. How did he manage to grow more handsome every day?

"I stopped by Colonel Talbot's house and he caught me up on some news." Samuel moved a bit closer as if wishing to shield her. "He was at the docks this morning, checking on a cotton shipment, and he saw your cousin in an alley with a liquor wholesaler. Colonel Talbot sneaked into the alley to listen, and it seems Absalom has plans to build a large room onto the inn and turn it into a drinking parlor after the contest is over and he has won."

"That doesn't surprise me, but how can we prove it? What can we do to stop him?"

"Since it isn't a drinking parlor now, we can't do anything except make sure we win."

Samuel's mood shifted, his expression turning sheepish. He strode to the window and gazed out, as if he'd come here for another purpose but wasn't sure how to carry it out.

Oh, Samuel. If only he knew how capable he was, how powerful his way with words. She moved closer, standing between him and the door. The way he fidgeted in front of the window, he might try to bolt. "Do you need my help with something?"

His dark curls gleamed in the waning sunlight as he turned to her. He reached into his coat and handed her an envelope with her name inscribed on the front, written in his bold, steady script.

She lifted the flap and drew out a card with a drawing of a young boy and girl in a flower garden, holding a big red heart between them.

"We can pretend it's a camellia garden," he said, his voice low and a boyish grin on his face.

She opened the card. *Fondly, Samuel.*

It made her smile. She'd grown fond of him as well. Quite fond.

"I had it with me last night and would have given it to you on Valentine's Day had my daughter not required my attention."

She touched his arm. "You're a good man, Samuel."

Not only good, but solid, dependable. One she could count on, could love. Could trust with Camellia Pointe, with her broken family. Even with her heart.

The realization washed over her like the wake of a steamboat on the riverbank. She was in love with Samuel.

More surprising, the knowledge didn't send her into a panic as she'd always thought falling in love would do.

As he took her hand, a cloud passed across his face. She'd seen that look before, the day he'd proposed an inconvenient marriage, when he'd asked if she preferred another man to him. A sense of vulnerability, of opening his heart to her with no guarantee that she would accept what he had to say.

But this day, her answer would come from her heart rather than her head.

He lowered his gaze to the floor. "I…have something to tell you…"

Say it!

"I…well, I care for you a great deal, Clarissa."

She saw through his hesitation to his fear. He merely needed a little help. "Samuel, do you mean you *love* me?"

Samuel's head shot up, his eyes wide but not with pleasure. "What…what did you say?"

His sudden look of horror ripped through her heart. Had he not meant to profess his love?

He held up one hand, his head slowly shaking.

No. No, he had not. Not at all—

Sudden movement outside the window caught her attention. Grandmother, running across the lawn, her hands gesturing wildly above her head.

Absalom in the camellia garden, waving a gun at her.

Harold off to one side, holding Absalom's coat.

"Oh, no—"

Clarissa turned and shot out of the room and down the stairs, letting the little valentine slip to the floor.

Do you mean you love *me?*

Samuel rubbed both hands over his face, trying to discern whether Clarissa's words had been real. He could not have just heard them for the second time, from his second wife. From the second woman he'd fallen in love with.

He stood there silent in her room, numbness washing over him as it had when Veronica had spoken those exact words. But this time the numbness wore off as soon as it came, letting him feel every sliced nerve ending, every severed vein to his heart. Because this time he'd thought he had a chance at love.

As he reached for his discarded valentine, the back door squeaked open. He forced himself to look out the window, to see what Clarissa had seen before she'd shattered what had remained of his heart.

His pulse stalled.

Harold Goss stood in the camellia garden, smiling at Clarissa as she ran toward him—just as Veronica had raced to the man she loved after Samuel had confessed his love for her.

How had this happened twice? He didn't know, but this time he wouldn't linger while the two ridiculed him. He'd move out first.

He stormed into his study, that pathetic bachelor bedroom, and threw his clothing and books into his smaller trunk. Hefting it onto his shoulder, he fled the room. Within minutes he had his horse and carriage in the drive, and he'd loaded his trunk. The church study would be his new home.

He took one last trip upstairs, snatched his father's portrait from the mantel and stashed it in the large trunk next to Grandmother's lavaliere. He locked the trunk and slipped the key into his pocket. He couldn't exactly heave the chest into the Mississippi River as he wished, but he could at least throw away the key.

He grabbed his carpetbag, filled it with his remaining clothes and toiletries. Moving fast, giving himself no opportunity to reconsider, he stalked out of the room and up the hall to the front gallery. He pitched the bag over the railing and beside his carriage.

How could he have been such a fool as to have believed Clarissa loved him? She'd been kind, gentle and cheerful with him as she was with everybody. Even Honey. Samuel should have known better.

He wouldn't make this mistake again.

"Absalom, have you lost your mind?" Clarissa raced to the camellia garden, where she had seen her cousin from the window. Where had he gone and where was Grandmother? Only Harold stood alone in the garden, grinning like the fool he was.

Absalom emerged from behind the stand of myrtles at the courtyard's edge. Staggering a bit and waving his gun again, he turned his questionable focus toward Clarissa. "Are you going to try to throw me out too?"

If only she could.

His slurred speech verified his condition as he took a clumsy step toward her.

"Absalom Adams, you're drunk. What's wrong with you?"

He wagged the pistol in front of her face. "Don't get sassy with me."

She strode to him and held out her hand. "Give me that gun. You don't even know how to use it when you're sober."

He shook his head like a petulant child.

"Give it to me or I'll ask Samuel to get his sword."

At the mention of the sword, Absalom's hand began to shake. Clarissa snatched the weapon from it and grasped his elbow, hard, leading him toward the house. "Get in your room and sleep this off. You're a disgrace."

Grandmother slunk around the corner of the kitchen and toward them. "I'm going to get a gun of my own."

As Clarissa passed her grandmother in the courtyard, she gave her Absalom's pistol. "No need. You can have this one. Or give it to Samuel if you like."

"Gladly, but where is he?"

Clarissa glanced around the courtyard and through the open door to the center hall. "I thought he was right behind me."

But he wasn't. Clarissa deposited her cousin on his bed and returned to the courtyard, certain Samuel would have arrived to make sure she and Grandmother were unharmed.

Instead, Grandmother stood alone, still holding Absalom's weapon. "Harold Goss has gone home. He was as drunk as Absalom."

Clarissa gave silent thanks for that small favor. But Grandmother had that look in her eye. "Did you encourage him to leave?"

Grandmother ran one finger down the barrel, those hazel eyes turning stormy in the falling dusk. "From now on, I'll throw out or shoot any man who dares become intoxicated on these premises."

At the sound of heavy footsteps on the stairs, Clarissa dashed into the house. Samuel hit the bottom step like thunder. She backed away. If Grandmother had a stormy expression, Samuel's was a cyclone.

He brushed by her without slowing down or looking at her, his Bible and portmanteau in his grip.

"What's the matter? I thought you'd—"

By now Samuel was out the front door. She followed him at a fast clip but stood aside when he stalked back in and up the stairs.

"Samuel, wait..." Clarissa lifted her skirts and climbed the steps behind him, barely able to keep up.

In the second-floor hall, she reached his door just as he exited, his pillow and a blanket in his arms. He headed for the front gallery, pitched the items over the rail, and started back toward the stairs.

Clarissa planted herself in front of the steps. When he approached and she saw him up close, she realized she'd mistaken his emotions. He wasn't angry, as she'd thought. Deep pain clouded his eyes, softened his mouth. "Samuel, I'm sorry. I shouldn't have said that earlier."

"No. No, you shouldn't have."

"I didn't understand how you felt. I shouldn't have assumed—"

"I can't stay here anymore. It was a mistake from the beginning. The deacons have rented the manse, so I'm moving into my study at the church. The sergeant and

Mister Forbes will still be here, so you and your grandmother and the children will be safe."

This was it? He was leaving her—just as she'd fallen in love with him? Just as she'd let herself trust him?

Just as she'd begun to think maybe she wasn't inadequate after all…

He nodded toward the stairs. She moved aside.

Samuel took the steps at a sprint. Within moments, the back door opened.

But his carriage was in the front. Clarissa dashed to her bedroom window in time to see Samuel racing toward the duck pond. He ran up the bridge and stopped at the apex, where he had nearly kissed her. He drew a small object from his coat pocket and hurled it into the middle of the pond. Small but heavy, judging from the size of the ripples.

Whatever else he'd just tossed aside, he'd also thrown away their chance for love, their chance to be a family. Last night he had to have realized how happy they could be, had admitted he cared.

Fight for me, Fighting Chaplain...

Samuel stood there until the ripples subsided then strode toward the path to the drive.

She turned from the window, unwilling to watch him go.

Chapter Fourteen

Having Clarissa in the room next to his every night had been one of Samuel's few comforts. If only he'd realized it while he'd still lived with her.

Some evenings, she hummed a hymn or an old-fashioned little tune at bedtime. And in the mornings he'd heard her bustling about and imagined her tidying her room and readying for the day. Always cheerful, always a bright encouragement to him in his lonely room.

Always his beautiful, faithful wife.

And now he would have that small comfort no more.

He stood and gazed out the study window. Who'd have thought he'd find so many travelers camping in the churchyard last night? Here to see the Fighting Chaplain and hear him preach, they'd all said as he'd trudged from tent to tent in the rain, his coat and trousers sopping wet and his hair matted to his head.

But what could Samuel give them, since he wasn't the man they thought he was? The words of 1 Timothy 3:5 rang in his head now as they had since his first marriage. *For if a man know not how to rule his own house, how shall he take care of the church of God?*

And Samuel knew not how. His marriage to Veronica

proved it. His failed relationship with Emma proved it. And now Clarissa…

Samuel didn't suspect her of impropriety with Goss. On the contrary. Samuel had merely been a fool to think she'd fall in love with him, a roughneck preacher who couldn't even manage his own house.

Yet he'd hoped to win her heart.

At his desk, wind and rain hitting the window behind him, he drew his little valentine from between the pages of his Bible for at least the fifteenth time since he'd left Camellia Pointe. His failings notwithstanding, he'd not imagined the light he'd seen in her eyes when she'd opened it. And he'd give his grandfather's sword if he could see it again.

He glanced around the study, at the chair where she'd sat a week ago, the hearth where she'd set her pail of caustic coffee. He'd drink the whole quart and another if it would change things.

The wall clock chimed its mournful tune, then announced the eighth hour. Only three hours until the service. Until his congregation and all of Natchez would somehow sense his charade, would know he was not the man he preached a husband should be.

Worse, all those misguided people camping in the churchyard would know. Men and women who had driven from all over Mississippi and Louisiana to hear Samuel preach would now be disappointed, could not receive the help they'd come to find.

As thunder shook the church, a throbbing pain slammed into the back of his head, and he rubbed the scar there. He lay his head on the desk, on top of his sermon notes. "'It is of the Lord's mercies that we are not consumed, because his compassions fail not. They are new every morning. Great is thy faithfulness…'"

* * *

"Reverend Montgomery!"

Samuel jerked his head up from his desk as the door flung open and crashed against the wall. "What? What's wrong?"

The deaconate burst into the study, their panic as evident in their faces as in their voices. "This isn't what we wanted," Deacon Bradley said in a tone somewhere between a moan and a wail.

Samuel cleared his dry throat and rubbed his eyes. He must have dozed off in the midst of his prayer and meditation. *Never did that before...at least not on a Sunday morning.* He glanced at the clock. Nine forty-five. "What isn't?"

"The crowd. Don't you hear it?" Deacon Bradley set his palms on the desk and leaned toward Samuel. "They're in the street, the churchyard, the neighbors' yards—all up and down Pearl Street, and State, and Commerce, and Main. People here to see the Fighting Chaplain. And we don't like it."

Samuel felt that scowl coming on. "But when you called me, you knew who I was. You thought my military honors would be good for Natchez."

"We knew it would bring in more locals," Deacon Bradley said. "Last Sunday was the highest attendance we've had since before the war. But now with the newspaper ad, and your tours of Camellia Pointe, people have been flocking into town since yesterday afternoon."

Deacon Holmes's eyes seemed to droop even more than usual. "It's not yet ten o'clock, but they've filled the sanctuary, including the galleries, and they're sitting on the floor and in the windowsills. They're noisy and unruly, and they tracked mud all over the carpet."

"That's nothing. There's horses in the churchyard. In

the churchyard!" Deacon Morris lifted his foot as high as his ample belly would let him. "And when I went over there to ask them to move, I stepped in something."

Samuel tilted his head and gazed at the sole of the deacon's shoe, catching a pungent whiff. Sure enough, a bit of "something" remained underneath, against the heel. He handed the deacon his handkerchief.

"What are you going to do?" Deacon Bradley asked, still hovering over Samuel's desk.

"What do you want me to do?" Samuel stood so the lanky deacon would straighten while he still could, and he looked him dead in the eye. "Chase them out? Make sure they don't hear the Gospel this morning?"

The deacon shifted what weight he had. "Not exactly..."

"Then here's the plan. Go to Camellia Pointe and get Sergeant John. He'll take charge and bring order to this mess. Meanwhile, I'll preach to the crowd that's here now. We'll have our eleven o'clock service as usual and forget about the mud—" he glanced at Deacon Morris's shoe again "—and other things until afterward."

"But you won't have music," Morris said. "And you can't preach with people sitting on the floor and in the windows."

"Would you rather send them outside to stand in the rain again, when they could have a few hours here where it's dry? Be reasonable. In fact, go and make sure no one's still outside. If so, bring them in and find a place for them." When the deacon hesitated, gaping at him, Samuel pointed to the door. "Go!"

Deacon Morris hastened toward the hall, staring over his shoulder, mouth still open, as if Samuel had asked him to bring in the horses too.

"Fine, but remember what I told you last week. We

don't want any more trouble in this church," Deacon Bradley said as he and Deacon Holmes edged toward the door. "And where is Missus Montgomery? We thought she'd come early again today."

The words, carelessly spoken, stabbed his heart, mocked his failure, his loneliness. She wouldn't come early on Sunday mornings anymore, bringing breakfast and coffee, helping him with his duties and cheering him with her beautiful smile and gentle laugh. The realization nearly brought him to his knees.

He muttered something about the children needing her, which was surely true. But trouble? The deacons had no idea how much trouble rumbled through his heart like thunder.

Trouble he could neither understand nor keep at bay.

Driving up Franklin Street in the blowing rain, Clarissa urged Stonewall to a faster clip and checked her timepiece. Quarter of ten. Of all mornings to have a coughing, feverish baby. Today she should have been at church earlier than before, to show Samuel she would continue to carry out her duties, despite her embarrassment. Despite her heartache.

As she turned onto Commerce Street, the sounds of horses and voices made her slow Stonewall to a more sedate pace. The streets were full on a Sunday morning, an hour and a quarter before service time?

The closer she got to Christ Church, the more chaotic the streets. And there—

She squinted at the sight of horses tethered to the churchyard trees. And men pitching tents in the pouring rain. And children dancing in puddles.

What did it all mean? It wasn't this disorderly even when the Yankees came.

Then a flash of understanding hit her. They were here to see the Fighting Chaplain.

No, no, no...

Samuel was going to hate this.

She breathed a quick prayer for him and then stopped. No, he wouldn't hate this new development. Rather, he would see it as an opportunity, as he had the invasion of tourists at Camellia Pointe. And he was going to need help.

Catching sight of Deacon Morris, she waved him over and brought Stonewall to a stop in the middle of the street. "I have to get inside to help Reverend Montgomery."

"Go on. I'll find a place to park." Rushing to the shay, he held out his hand. "Watch where you step."

She let him help her from the carriage, then snatched her basket and coffee pail and waved her thanks as she took to the sidewalk at a run. The wind whipped her bonnet, mercifully tied tightly under her chin, and the rain soaked her pink-and-white-sprigged muslin skirts before she made it to the back door.

Dripping water on the wood floors, she dashed down the hall to the study. The door opened as she approached, and Samuel stepped out.

"Clarissa..." His eyes spoke something tender, something soft, for an instant. Then a cloud passed over them and hovered like a wall between her and Samuel.

She hesitated as her words rushed back to her and squeezed the breath from her lungs. *Do you mean you love me?* How had she been so stupid?

The silence turned painful and she considered her next words carefully. It was better to think before speaking or acting, and she would never again blurt out the first thing that came to mind. Never again make any move without careful thought. "All those people outside—they're here to see the Fighting Chaplain, aren't they?"

He raised his familiar, strong hand and rubbed the back of his head.

The hand that had held hers on the bridge, in the study when he'd introduced her to Willie, in the church parlor when he'd suggested marriage. The hand she would likely never hold again.

"They're here to see a legend. A giant of a man. A hero." His tone turned bitter. He pushed past her, plowed down the hallway toward the sanctuary. "They think that man is me."

What could he mean? "Of course, you're that man…"

Clarissa took off at a near-run, following him, calling to him to wait. He pushed on toward the pulpit, toward the crowd. At the sanctuary door, he stopped, turned to her, his dark curls falling boyishly over his forehead. The agony in his beautiful brown eyes wrung the same emotion from her heart.

"Please don't try to console me." He looked away, as if he couldn't allow her to see the anguish seeping out of his soul and into those eyes. "I can bear anything but that from you."

"Samuel." Clarissa clasped his wrist, her own eyes filling now. "Why do you not think you're a hero? You're the Fighting Chaplain. Everyone admires you."

His bark of a laugh held more sarcasm than she'd have thought possible. "Everyone except the ones who matter most."

"Give yourself time. Emma will come around."

"Perhaps. Perhaps not. Even if she did, the Fighting Chaplain myth is just that—a myth."

What did he mean? "You didn't fight a platoon of Yankees?"

"I did, but it wasn't what everybody thinks."

"What was it, then?"

He tried to tug his arm away, but Clarissa held firm. "Tell me. What happened in that fight?"

Perhaps he sensed she wasn't going to let him go until he told her, or perhaps he finally recognized the need to speak of it. He drew a deep breath and gazed heavenward for a moment. "The fight itself happened the way the newspapers described it. But it wasn't gallantry and glory. I didn't fight for the sake of the Confederacy."

"Then why?"

"Because they were about to slaughter my men who were out of ammo—helpless. They wouldn't have had a chance." His sigh seemed to emerge from his bones. "My men were like my own sons. I ate with them, slept beside them, prayed with them, for them. They were my life those four years." He paused, his brown eyes taking on a rough edge. "I gave up everything in order to answer the call of God to shepherd them, be a father to them."

"You gave up—" a flash of understanding made Clarissa take a step back as she gasped "—Emma."

The weariness in his eyes told her she was right.

"And since I gave up everything for them, they were all the more precious to me."

Of course.

"Federal troops had exploded a mine that blew a gap in our defenses. Our men were forced back into a valley beneath a cliff. I ran to help the injured but as I crept through the underbrush, our men gradually stopped firing until they all were out of ammo. I watched enemy soldiers gun down five defenseless soldiers whom they could have taken prisoner instead." Samuel rubbed the back of his head, hard. "By no means could I let them slaughter any more of the men I'd come to love like family. So, under cover of the brush, I crept up behind the Yankees, one by one, and—"

He paused, the agony of remembrance in his eyes. "It was their men or mine. I had to make a fast decision, and I don't regret it. I knew those men, and many of them had resisted the Lord, refusing His mercy and forgiveness."

His expression was so pained, it kindled more love for him than she'd known she had. "You had no choice—"

"You don't know everything yet." He looked at her straight-on. "Willie was in the valley."

Willie.

No wonder the boy all but worshiped Samuel.

"See? I'm not a Confederate hero at all. I'm just a man who used the sword skills his grandfather taught him, trying to save men and a boy, not a nation. Not a cause." He took another step toward the sanctuary. "I'm an imposter, a play-actor in more ways than you know."

His words were frosty, colder than river wind.

And he meant them.

The depths of his agony, his guilt, spiked into her heart. How had she ever thought she could comfort him, could win his heart? He'd probably hoped she, as the granddaughter of one of the greatest preachers Mississippi had ever seen, would be the kind of woman he could fall in love with. And perhaps he'd tried, with the near kiss on the bridge, the valentine. But it hadn't worked. He didn't love her—couldn't love her, because she wasn't worthy of him.

A man like Samuel could never fall in love with a woman as lacking as she.

He turned from her. With the most broken demeanor

she'd ever seen, he opened the door and stepped into the sanctuary, closing it behind him.

Closing her out.

Closing the door to her last shred of hope.

Chapter Fifteen

As the case clock chimed two that night, Clarissa stirred from her fitful sleep and sat up, listening. Some sound had awakened her. In the silence that followed, she struggled to remember the noise but recalled only a vague sense of foreboding. Had it been dream or reality?

Dream, apparently. And how she wished to hear something, anything, from the other side of the suite door. The sound of Samuel rising in the night, the muted scrape of his desk chair against the floor. The rustle of the leaves of a book. His muffled prayers, his voice low in a hymn of praise…

How could she have known how precious those sounds would become in her memory?

Today Samuel had come home for Sunday dinner and attended her meeting with Joseph as both she and Absalom revealed their plans for the two properties. At midnight, after listening to Absalom drone on about his supposed plan to build more sleeping rooms and another dining room onto Good Shepherd, Samuel had gone back to church to stay the night. With him gone, the house felt empty, void of life, even with ten other people there. And would from now on, so Clarissa just had to get used to—

The sound of horse's hooves on the drive made her scramble to sit up. Then she remembered. The noise she'd heard in her sleep was the popping of the floor-board outside Emma's room.

Emma...

Clarissa flung back her blankets and made for the front gallery, her white muslin nightgown billowing, her bare feet hot against the cool floor. At the sidelight, she caught sight of Beau's runabout as it careened down the drive.

The board popped again as she rushed into Emma's room. Coals smoldered in the hearth. The full moon shone through the east window, illuminating the empty bed with its quilt still spread and a note on the pillow.

Clarissa snatched the sheet of paper, her breath fast and her heart pounding to keep up with the fear shooting from her stomach to her chest, her throat. She hastened to the window and squinted in the dim light, barely able to make out the words.

> If my father doesn't love me enough to stay, I'm not staying either. When you read this, I'll be in Vicksburg and I will be Emma Louise Montgomery Adams.

Adams?

Clarissa looked out the window as Beau's runabout turned onto Melrose Street.

With no time to think, she dashed toward her room, clutching the letter as if it could somehow change things. She had to stop them before Emma was ruined. And Samuel…

This would bleed his heart dry.

"Missus Montgomery!" Sergeant John's voice growled up the stairs like a grizzly as booted feet charged up the steps.

She rushed to her room to slide on her wrapper. Holding it together at the waist, she met him in the hall. "Emma is gone. She's off to marry Beau—"

"I heard the runabout and got outside in time to see her climb in. Throw on some clothes while I get your shay. We're going after her."

She hesitated. The shay—a buggy for two…

"We'll pick up the chaplain at the church."

Her face heated like the coals in Emma's room. The sergeant knew their secret.

She hastened to dress, then met him downstairs at the front door and climbed into the shay, whispering a quick prayer for Emma, Samuel and the rest of their household. Did Absalom know Beau was gone? Did everyone at Camellia Pointe except the children know Samuel wasn't there?

After a five-minute drive that felt like fifteen, they screeched to a halt in front of the church. Carriages and wagons still filled the streets, leaving nowhere to park except the middle of State Street. The sergeant handed Clarissa the reins and swung to the ground.

Within minutes Samuel raced out the church's side door, clambered in and sped along the still-muddy streets. His silence punctuating their problems, he kept his focus forward and his demeanor guarded.

Finally they rounded the corner and found Beau's runabout at the steamboat office. Samuel barely had the shay stopped before he hit the ground. Clarissa hastened down as well, the bright moon and burning gaslights of the surrounding businesses lighting her way.

"Emma Louise, get out of the carriage." Samuel kept his voice low and controlled, as if holding back from giving Beau the thrashing of his life.

Beau leapt from the runabout and faced Samuel, fists balled at his sides. "She doesn't have to do anything you say."

Before Samuel could reply, Absalom's landau pulled up next to them. Immediately he leaped from the carriage and into the row.

Amid the obscenities Absalom and Beau fired at Samuel, Clarissa hastened to Emma's side. "Let's wait in the shay—"

"I'm not going." Emma folded her arms across her middle like a child. "Beau is taking me to Vicksburg. We're getting married and living with my grandparents."

"No, you're not." Samuel's voice held both authority and a gravity Clarissa had never heard from him. "You're coming home."

"What home? You abandoned me, just like you did when you went to war. And then again when you took me to that Kentucky school. Why should I live at Camellia Pointe when you won't?"

Samuel jerked back as if he'd been shot.

"She's right," Absalom said, puffing out his chest. "She has no reason to stay in Natchez. Especially with a fraud of a preacher for a father."

"Emma, I never abandoned you…" Samuel's voice cracked, all sternness gone, his impossibly handsome face drawn.

His brokenness, his desperation, cried out to Clarissa to go to him, to comfort him, to make all this right somehow.

But how could she, given the finality of his spurning?

"I don't care what your little brat does, but Beau is coming with me." Absalom gave his stepson a shove toward the runabout. "I have bigger plans for him than marrying a penniless preacher's daughter."

Clarissa held out her hands. "Come home, Emma."

The girl turned to Beau. "Let's go. Forget the steamboat and drive me to Vicksburg."

Beau glanced at Absalom, who gave him a quick nod. "Nah, I'm going back. Pa's right. I got no use for a choir girl, after all."

"But you said…" She dropped her gaze, the reality of Beau's betrayal clearly sinking deeper every moment.

And Clarissa knew how that felt. With Emma's anguish burning inside her as if it were her own, Clarissa snatched the girl's hands and gave them a tug. "Your father didn't abandon you, dear. But Beau just did, so let's leave him here with his snake of a father. Come home with me, where people love you and want you."

Emma leapt down from the runabout, fire in her beautiful brown eyes. "At least *someone* does."

Beau watched until he caught Emma's eye, then he winked.

Winked? After all but abandoning her on the wharf?

And that nod from Absalom…

They'd set up this entire event—Beau gaining Emma's confidence, learning of her dream to live in Vicksburg, then offering marriage. Driving to the landing in an expensive runabout with a fine horse no young man would leave behind. Absalom knowing exactly when to catch them at the steamboat office.

Beau had planned to drive the carriage home all along.

And then they'd use the impropriety to blackmail Clarissa into forfeiting her inheritance.

"You might turn a young girl's head with your wink, Beau, but you don't fool me," Clarissa said. "You never had any intention of marrying her, and you still don't."

Then Emma's wide-eyed trust in the young man brought another flash of clarity. Beau would always be a bad influence in the girl's life.

As long as they all still lived together.

The realization burned into her, scorched her soul. With Beau there, Camellia Pointe would ruin Emma.

With a flourish, Beau snapped his reins and took off at a gallop.

"Emma, Clarissa, please get in the shay." Samuel squeezed out the words as if a boulder were lodged in his throat. "We're going home."

"Which home, Parson? Camellia Pointe or the church study—where you sleep these days?" Absalom swung up into his landau, clearly missing the irony of his comment, given his own wife's absence from Camellia Pointe.

As her cousin took off, an ache started in Clarissa's chest and seemed to intensify with every heartbeat, as if her heart wept within her.

She had to leave Camellia Pointe.

And when she did, she'd also leave behind her hope of reconciling with Father in their beloved home during the Festival. However, Emma couldn't stay there with Beau. And by no means would Clarissa allow her to be sent away again. The girl would likely never recover from a wound so deep.

She slipped her arm around Emma's quivering shoulders and drew her toward the shay, crowding close to fit the three of them.

Within moments they started back to the home that wasn't a home with Samuel gone. But perhaps, just for tonight, Clarissa could fall asleep and forget for a few hours how she'd failed everyone in her life—and Camellia Pointe itself.

The next morning Samuel awakened to a sense of comfort in his bachelor bedroom. The sweet soprano voice in the next room, the aroma of bacon wafting under the door, the fresh camellias in his little vase all melded into an image of home.

A false image. One he didn't deserve.

The bacon and singing made sense. They would be there even if he wasn't. But the camellias? Why would Clarissa continue to grace his room with them when she hadn't known he was coming home? It didn't add up.

He'd come back last night to discourage Absalom from telling the deacons that Samuel no longer slept in this house. But to be honest, he couldn't have stayed away, even without Absalom's interference.

Emma clearly needed him here, and he also had to be near Clarissa, to hear her voice, to smell her sweet perfume. As much as he wished it wasn't so, Samuel loved his wife, couldn't stay away from her. Even if it meant sleeping in this bachelor bedroom.

He rose and stood at the window. Maisie passed by below, taking the four youngest children for a walk. He'd missed the sunrise, having slept through it after his talk with Emma that had lasted until four in the morning, for all the good it did. Apparently, Clarissa had overslept too, since her morning sounds still drifted from her room.

Samuel washed and dressed hastily, unsure of the reason for his rush. Did he want to sneak out before Clarissa made it to the dining room? Or was he trying to get downstairs quickly so he could spend as much time with her as possible?

He had to be the sorriest excuse for a husband in the South, unable to live with his wife but unable to stay away. For the hundredth time he replayed the night on the bridge, and for the hundredth time he called himself a fool. Clarissa knew his failures as well as he did. If she'd begun to care for him that night, she'd come to her senses the next day, as she should. He'd already ruined Veronica's and Emma's lives. No need to destroy a third.

He slid his Bible into his portmanteau and sat on the bed to pull on his boots.

To his surprise, Clarissa knocked on his door as he was about to sneak out. Dark circles under her eyes gave her a wistful look that only accented her otherwise perfect skin, her gray dress clearly reflecting her mood. Her smile faltered a bit and she bit her bottom lip. "Can we talk before breakfast?"

His heart stalled as her words rolled about in his mind. Was she weary of the constant tension? Whatever it was, it would change everything. That much he could discern.

After an unsettling, silent walk to the pergola, they sat in rush-bottomed chairs Mister Forbes had put there for the children's horticulture studies. "We've a decision to make," Clarissa said as she arranged her gray skirts around her. "I don't think Camellia Pointe is good for Emma. Keeping her here with Beau for a year would lead to even more trouble."

A lightning bolt of disappointment shot through him at her words, and he dropped his gaze to the open structure's brick floor. He'd have thought Clarissa would fight to the death for Emma to stay with them. "I've been thinking the same thing all night but have no solution.

I should probably send her away to school, as you say, but then she'd become even more rebellious."

"I didn't say to send her away."

He raised his gaze to her wearied eyes.

"We need to move, Samuel."

Move? "We can't. We have to stay a year—"

Then it hit him. She wanted to sacrifice her home for Emma. "No. We're not giving up Camellia Pointe. Give me some time and I'll think of something."

"There's nothing to think of. Emma is more important than this house. I don't put anything past Beau, let alone Absalom. I'm certain those two staged the incident with Emma, trying to force us out of this home, and they could do something worse next time."

"But if we leave Camellia Pointe, you'll lose your grandfather's legacy, and your grandmother will move away. We can't go with her because I'm committed to the church. Besides, the move would affect everyone here. The children, Maisie, Sergeant John, Mister Forbes. I couldn't afford a house big enough to hold us all—and we're a family now." He stood and gazed at the little white cabins that would house more orphans. "I won't let you lose this home."

Samuel's sudden desire to stay surprised him more than her willingness to go. When had this place begun to feel like home? Of a sudden, he understood her love for Camellia Pointe. Something about it, perhaps the years a man of God spent bathing it in prayer, now made it the most precious place on earth to him.

Or was it simply because his heart was so entangled with the woman who'd loved it first?

As they continued to debate to no avail, Willie ambled up to them, Honey nipping at his heels and his sword at his hip. Apparently he'd escaped Maisie's watchful eye. "Wha'cha talking about? I never heard you argue before."

"We're not arguing," Clarissa said, not looking at him.

"Sounded like it to me."

"No, we have a decision to make, and we don't like either of our options. We're merely discussing the possibilities."

"Then do this." Willie crammed his hand into his pocket and pulled out a coin. "Heads, we do what Miss Clarissa says. Tails, we do what Papa Samuel says." He set it onto his bent thumb, poised to toss.

"Willie, we make important decisions through prayer and fasting and listening for God's voice in our hearts. Not by tossing—"

But Willie had already flicked the coin in the air. It flew high, glimmering in the brightening sun, fell to the brick walk, bounced and wedged into a crack—standing on its edge.

Samuel blinked, moved closer. "How do you like that?"

"Now what do we do? It's not heads, and it's not tails either," Willie said, his eyes wide.

What, indeed? Then Samuel recalled the morning he'd asked God for a third way… "It means God has another solution. A third way."

Clarissa's fatigue intensified in her face. "Neither move out nor stay? We have to do one or the other."

Willie bent over and retrieved the coin, held it up and examined it as if it held the answer. It wasn't a copper Indian head penny as Samuel had thought. He moved closer and stretched out his hand. "I've never seen a coin like this. It's gold…"

"Real gold?" Willie shouted as he surrendered the coin.

Samuel turned it over and then gave a long, low whistle. "Confederate gold. See here, where it says CSA?"

"Willie, where did you get that?" Clarissa said, peering at the coin Samuel placed back into the boy's grimy palm.

"Absalom."

Clarissa frowned. "When? Absalom never gave anything away in his life, let alone Confederate gold."

"About an hour ago. I was fishing and I saw him and Harold Goss out in the cemetery. They had the lid off one of the old tombstones, and ol' Absalom was messing with a blue sack. Then he said a piece of the roof blew off the sanctuary, and I could have the coin if I'd bring him a ladder so him and Harold Goss could fix it."

"They're too lazy to patch a roof. I think they're going to trim that tree, just to spite me." Clarissa shaded her eyes with her hand and looked toward the chapel.

Maisie came near then with the younger children. "Willie, you were supposed to stick close to me. It's almost breakfast time."

"First I gotta think of a hiding place for my money. Hey, how much is it worth?"

"Twenty dollars," Samuel said.

Drawing closer and examining the coin, Maisie lifted her brows. "How'd you get one of those French coins, Willie?"

"French? It's Confederate," Samuel said.

"Mister Loubet was from France, wasn't he?"

"Grandfather's friend from Paris?" Clarissa asked. "How do you know him?"

"I was here fitting you and your grandma for new dresses when he visited, right after Mississippi left the Union. He was showing the reverend these coins and boasting as how this would be the Confederate money."

Clarissa somehow found a smile for the memory. "I didn't know about that, but Grandfather so enjoyed Monsieur Loubet's company. He always had the cook, Essie, prepare her Southern version of coq au vin for him. And she never made it the same way twice. Grandfather always said Essie's cooking was like the mercies of God—new every morning."

Samuel rubbed his chin. Confederate gold… France… "I've heard about these coins. The French minted them for the Confederacy, to be used in trade with them. Clarissa, Loubet must have come here to sell them to your grandfather."

"And that rat Absalom found them." Willie crammed the coin back into his pocket.

"But why would he give Willie twenty dollars just for carrying a ladder?" Samuel said.

"New every morning…" Clarissa hesitated then drew in a quick, audible breath. "Grandfather's favorite verse. 'It is of the Lord's mercies that we are not consumed, because his compassions fail not. They are new every morning. Great is thy faithfulness.'"

"And in the letter he said, '*Listen.* "His compassions fail not."' The word *listen* isn't in the verse." Why hadn't Samuel thought of this before? He glanced over at the sanctuary. "He was giving us a clue. The stone he etched with the Bible reference must be loose, and he hid the gold there."

"And he must have hidden some in my great-grandfather's tombstone as well. The verse is engraved on it too." Clarissa stood, her hands trembling. She clasped them together, held them to her mouth. "Absalom was right about treasure at Camellia Pointe."

Samuel leapt to his feet. "Let's go. Absalom might still be there—"

He shot across the lawn, Clarissa and Willie running behind him. As he passed the bridge, someone let out a yell and then a string of curses.

Samuel rounded the corner of the sanctuary. A toppled ladder and a stone and chisel lay on the ground near the structure's foundation.

Absalom dangled from the untrimmed oak tree, his long, curly hair caught in the branches, his feet kicking at the air three feet from the ground. A dozen or so gold coins littered the grass beneath him.

"Get me down!" Absalom grabbed the branch with both hands and squirmed as if trying to ease the pulling on his scalp.

Willie dashed around the corner. With a flourish, he drew his sword. *"En garde!"*

"You don't fight a man who's hung up in a tree by his hair." Still breathing fast from his hard run across the lawn, Samuel moved closer to Absalom and his snarled hair.

"That's not in the rules." Willie made as if to run the man through. "He deserves it. He was trying to steal Miss Clarissa's gold."

"It's still bad sportsmanship. Just guard him."

The boy puffed up, adding an inch to his height.

Clarissa reached them then, panting with her exertion. She skidded to a stop at the sight of her cousin in the tree. "Absalom! Have you been drinking again?"

The foul words he shot down from the tree should have made its leaves wither.

"Get that sword out of here!" Absalom's voice shook like the leaves all around him as he kicked the air.

Samuel picked up the ladder and propped it against the building. "Support yourself on this until we can get you out of the tree."

When Absalom had managed to position his feet on the rungs, Samuel turned to Willie. "Can you climb the tree and shimmy out to Absalom on the branch?"

"Sure. Do I get to cut his hair?"

"I'm not sure the branch would hold me, so, yes."

"Cut my hair?" Absalom's scream turned his face red. "Nobody's cutting my hair. Just get it untangled."

Willie waved his sword. "This'll cut it just fine."

"I'll get my sewing scissors," Clarissa said, turning toward the house.

When she'd gone, Samuel moved a little closer to Absalom, careful the man wouldn't kick him in the head, and picked up the gold from the ground around him. He put it in his pocket and then stretched to stick his hand in the hole in the sanctuary wall. "I can't reach all the way in there. Is that where the rest of the gold is, Absalom?"

His foul-mouthed response did nothing to answer Samuel's question.

Within minutes Clarissa hastened back, scissors in her hands. Sergeant John, the three deacons and a sheriff strode across the lawn with her. "Sergeant John figured out what was going on and fetched Sheriff Joshua Tillman," she said.

Miss Phemie followed at a slower pace, one hand tucked in the crook of Joseph's elbow and the other clutching her cane. "My word, Absalom's stuck in the tree like a long-tailed kite!"

Absalom flinched, whether at Miss Phemie's high-pitched voice or her apt comparison, Samuel didn't know.

"The Fighting Chaplain. It's an honor." Sheriff Tillman stepped forward, his voice cracking a bit as he took in the weapon. "That sword saved my brother's life."

"We'll sit down for a long talk soon. I want to hear all about him."

Tillman swallowed hard and nodded. "What kind of animal did you catch in this trap?"

"Gold thief," Willie hollered.

"Are you Willie?" At the boy's nod, Sheriff Tillman pulled an empty blue-velvet bag from his coat pocket and pointed to Absalom. "Did you see that man holding this bag in the cemetery?"

Willie peered at it. "Yep."

"Cut him down," the sheriff said. "Absalom Adams, you're under arrest for theft of your cousin's gold."

"You can't arrest me. I'm entitled to my grandfather's property—"

"Then why did you sneak into the cemetery at dawn to take it? You know all the contents of the house and grounds were left to Clarissa. You're a disgrace to the Confederacy," Sergeant John said as Willie scrambled up the tree, took the scissors from Samuel and cut the first of Absalom's long locks of thick hair. "He carried out the gold that was hidden inside the tombstone. I saw him and Goss headed that way, and Willie following them, so I wanted to make sure everything was all right. Since it wasn't, I went to the sheriff."

"John also helped me search Callaway House for the gold and lock it in the jail's safe. Then we arrested Harold Goss as Absalom's accomplice. I'm trying to talk the sergeant into becoming my deputy." Tillman paused, watching Willie cut the sides of Absalom's hair. "This capture must be sweet for you, Parson."

"How so?" Samuel said.

The sheriff rubbed the shadow of stubble on his chin. "You haven't been searching for him?"

"Why would I?"

"If I were you, I'd be on the lookout for the man who

defied your order to get reinforcements for your platoon."

Wait—Adams was that man? The stranger from another platoon, who'd cowered behind a boulder, watching Samuel fight alone instead of running for help? He hadn't gotten a good look at the weakling, occupied as he'd been with saving his platoon. But now that he thought about it, that man could easily have been Absalom. "Adams, you could have saved some of those Yankees' lives if you'd gone for reinforcements," he said through clenched teeth.

As Absalom climbed down the ladder, his now-short hair sticking out in all directions, his hands trembled as they often had when he'd seen or even heard mention of the sword.

Of a sudden, Samuel saw only a man he'd failed.

Samuel's jaw relaxed a fraction, his anger no longer mattering in light of Absalom's silent, unconscious accusation. Why hadn't Samuel attempted to reach the man with love, with the Gospel? Sure, it probably would have done no good, but the fact was, he hadn't tried. He turned from the eyes that unknowingly shot shame into his soul.

Clarissa, Veronica, Emma—his regret for his failure there had torn three separate holes in his heart. But this time, remorse nipped at him the way Honey nipped at his heels. Not as painful as his damaged heart, but there nonetheless, constantly reminding him of its presence. He hadn't paid enough attention to Absalom, hadn't been concerned enough about his soul. Now he'd have to find a way to make up for it.

Absalom's ever-louder cursing pulled Samuel from his thoughts. Sheriff Tillman had searched Absalom's coat and found a few coins in one pocket and a crinkled sheet of paper, folded in fourths, in the other. He passed it to Clarissa.

She read silently for a moment and then looked up, gaping at her cousin. "It's a receipt from Monsieur Loubet for twenty thousand dollars in gold coin. Where did you get this?"

When her cousin refused to answer, Samuel did it for him. "That's what you were looking for in my study, wasn't it?"

Miss Phemie inched toward her grandson, swallowing hard and blinking fast. "I knew you wouldn't beat us, Absalom, and I thought I would get satisfaction from saying I told you so. But I can't do it."

Absalom stood still, quiet for once.

"I wish this had gone differently, and we could all live here as a loving family." She laid her hand on his cheek. "Somehow Hezekiah and I weren't able to reach you when you were young. And I'm sorry about that."

Samuel could do nothing but stare at Miss Phemie, at her transformation. Judging from the silence, neither could anyone else. It drove his own shame all the deeper.

When she stepped away and started toward the house, Tillman pulled Absalom's hands behind his back and snapped cuffs onto his wrists. "Reverend, I wish you hadn't had this kind of embarrassment so soon after moving to Natchez."

The man meant well, but he couldn't know Samuel's biggest embarrassment was of himself.

Absalom in jail, Beau on the steamer for Memphis, enough gold to provide for their family and the orphans, Grandmother looking better than she had since the day their worlds changed. All was right in Clarissa's world, except the one thing that had become the most important.

She let her gaze rest on her husband, reclined in his favorite Hepplewhite parlor chair. Would he move in with them again? Or would he continue his midnight journeys to the church, refusing to sleep in the room next to hers? She'd never before dreaded nightfall, but now she wished it would never come.

If only things could have been different. No, if only she could have been different…

Her entire household gathered in the opened parlor to hear the final decision. Within minutes, Joseph, Samuel and the deaconate would surely declare Camellia Pointe hers. But the victory seemed slim, her dream trivial. What did a house matter without love inside? That one special love, the one that gave the trials meaning…

"Absalom was in trouble before this," Samuel said, pulling her from her thoughts. "Sheriff Tillman found out that Absalom and Goss are both wanted for bribery and fraud in Tennessee. They're cell mates now, and it's not the first time. They were in prison camp together as well."

Clarissa refilled Samuel's cup with the apple-mint tea she'd brewed earlier and handed him a plate of applesauce cookies. As she refreshed the other cups in the room, he reached for the biggest cookie and took a bite.

"I still don't understand why Absalom gave a coin to Willie," Grandmother said, sitting next to Samuel. "As far as I know, the only thing he's ever given anybody is dyspepsia."

Willie looked up from the floor, where he played with Honey. "To get rid of me when I got too close. He got scared I'd see the stone and figure out he was stealing the gold."

"Absalom will get a sure conviction. But if we need any more evidence, we can always use his bad haircut against him. Willie, don't ever become a barber." Joseph reached down and ruffled the boy's hair, then opened his portmanteau. "Let's put this inheritance business to rest. Clearly, Absalom Adams will not fulfill the second term of the will—residing at Camellia Pointe for one year. I suggest we award the inheritance to Clarissa Adams Montgomery."

"I'm giving the gold to Grandmother. She deserves some consolation for having a grandson who would steal from us." And wave a gun at her, and turn Good Shepherd into a drinking parlor.

"As many mouths as we have to feed around here, I suggest you hold on to it, missy," Grandmother said, a new strength in her voice. No, it was her old strength returned to her, since Absalom was gone. The vigor she'd lost on that first day, when Samuel raced into Christ Church and disrupted all their lives.

"We can't simply give the inheritance to her. The will says the deacons get to vote." Deacon Bradley sounded much like a little boy who'd been cheated out of a piece of candy. "This whole affair has been highly irregular, just like everything else since Reverend Montgomery arrived. We've had a hasty marriage, an orphan drummer, tents and horses in the churchyard, now Confederate gold and who knows what else. You have to let us vote. It's the law."

Joseph glanced at the deacons and then at Samuel. "Very well. All agreed to awarding the inheritance to Missus Montgomery, please signify by raising your right hand."

Joseph raised his hand, as did Samuel. For a moment, Clarissa dared not look at the deaconate. Without their votes in her favor, she still would not win…

Chapter Sixteen

The deacons sat like statues, but unlike the one in the garden, they each had two good hands to raise.

And if they didn't raise them in the next two seconds, Samuel would march over to the sofa and jostle the deaconate into action.

Except he couldn't, because the will had given them the right to vote.

"Gentlemen," Joseph said, an edge to his voice, "it's time to cast your votes."

Deacon Morris wiggled his fingers, then he glanced at Deacon Bradley and stopped.

Do it! Be a man.

Bradley kept his fragile-looking folded hands in his lap. "I vote no."

What? Was he being obstinate to spite Samuel for opposing him on Sunday? "Why?"

"Absalom hasn't yet been declared guilty. We should wait until after the trial."

"He can't meet the terms of the will." Joseph rose and stood over the deacon, his eyes turned cold. "He's in jail."

"For now. We don't know the outcome of the trial. It's too soon to decide."

"I've been in law for sixty years. Trust me, he'll be in jail just as long." Joseph returned to his chair and turned his glare to Deacon Holmes. "What do you say?"

Holmes looked at Bradley and cleared his throat. "I say we wait."

How could this happen? It should have been easy. Samuel turned to Clarissa, seated to his left, to Miss Phemie on the right. The apprehension in their eyes drove him to a silent petition, a wordless groaning of a prayer.

"Morris?" Joseph said. "The reverend and I voted for Clarissa receiving the inheritance now. The other deacons voted against. Your vote will decide."

Deacon Morris hesitated, turned wide eyes to Bradley. Raised his trembling hand a few scant inches above his belly. "I vote yes."

Yes.

An hour later, Samuel sat alone with his wife and daughter in Clarissa's drawing room—in the home she now owned.

"Emma, I know Beau hurt you." She moved to sit on the hassock at Emma's feet and handed her the jewelry box she held. "Just this week, I decided to give you this bracelet when the time was right. I'd like you to have it now and always remember how much I love you."

His daughter reached slowly for the box, a glistening of tears in her eyes. "You're sending me away?"

Clarissa paused, confusion clouding her eyes. "Of course not."

Emma turned to Samuel. "You're leaving then?"

"What are you talking about? Nobody's leaving. We just won the contest so Clarissa could keep this place."

"I saw you pack and leave Saturday night, and you

don't sleep here anymore." Her tears turned her voice tight. "I can't stand you leaving me again."

Emma didn't want him to leave? "I won't go anymore if you don't want me to. I'll stay here."

She laid her head in Clarissa's lap and sobbed as if her heart would break.

Samuel sat helpless, because what were you supposed to do with a crying female? Then Clarissa caught his glance and tilted her head toward Emma.

What, she wanted him to come over there?

But Clarissa had been right about everything concerning his daughter so far. With more angst than he'd ever had at war, he came to Emma and squatted at her side, laid his hand on her head.

"You're the Fighting Chaplain. You fill churches with people who want to hear what you have to say," Clarissa whispered. "In army camps and in pulpits, you sway hearts with your words. Now you have to hear from God and speak to your daughter."

She was right. He bowed his head and listened for the voice of the Spirit in his heart.

"Emma," he choked out through the lump in his throat, "I've failed you as a father. I failed your mother too. I was wrong to send you to Kentucky, and if I'd thought for a moment that the war would come so far north, I'd have come for you and brought you home—walked there if I'd had to."

He drew a shuddering breath against the pain shattering his heart. "I know I've hurt you and left you feeling abandoned. But believe me, you were on my mind every day during the war. Your mother and I didn't have a good marriage, and you're right—I was relieved when God called me to war. But I never wanted to leave you. Never."

Emma lifted her head and wiped her tears. "Do you want to leave now?"

"No, I don't want to leave you."

"But you want to leave Clarissa."

He felt as well as heard Clarissa's sharp intake of breath. She straightened in an instant and, of a sudden, the air felt charged with her emotion—whatever it was.

His daughter kept her gaze on him, waiting for his answer, and he had to be honest before her and God. "Things aren't what they seem between Clarissa and me."

"I know. I heard everything on Valentine's Day."

"You were eavesdropping?"

"How will I know what's happening if I don't? How will I know what to do, how to be safe?"

She'd started the bad habit in Kentucky. Perhaps she told the truth, thought it was the only way she could stay safe, as she had during the war. "We're not at war any-more. I want you to stop."

"I'll stop if you'll let me tell Clarissa something."

His sigh came from his toes. "Go ahead."

"When I was eight, I heard him try to tell my mother he loved her."

What? "Emma Louise…"

She turned to him. "I heard what you said and what she said, and I saw what she did afterward. I hated her for that. I know I acted like it was your fault. But I felt safe with you. I never felt safe with her."

Emma, how you suffered... "I should have been there for you—"

She turned to Clarissa. "When my father tried to tell you he loved you, you said the same exact words my mother did. But she said it in a mocking way, not out of love, like you did. That made him think you didn't love him either. But I know you do." She opened the jewelry box and slipped the bangle over her wrist. "I know about this bracelet too. I heard Harold Goss tell Absalom about it. Since you're giving it to me now, you must not be in love with Harold anymore."

"You're right. I'm not."

She sounded certain, as if she'd known it for a long time.

"Please make my father happy." Emma took the little jewelry box and made for the door, then stopped and turned to Samuel. "You're a good father, and I'm sorry for what I did."

As Emma's footsteps sounded on the stairs, Samuel realized his eyes were closed. A good father? And Clarissa loved him—at least, his daughter thought so. Could it all be true?

And when Clarissa asked if he loved her, she hadn't meant to refuse him?

He dared not open his eyes, see what was in Clarissa's, in case Emma was wrong. But at her gentle touch on his arm, he had to open them, had to see if his world had suddenly changed from bleak to sun-drenched, from solitary to full.

And when he did, he saw not only color and sunshine but also love. "Is she right, Clarissa? Do I have hope?"

Her sweet lips curved upward into a perfect smile that infused more joy into him than he'd known in—forever. "I promise, if you tell me you love me, I won't reject you."

"Could you love me, just a little? Because I've loved you ever since you brought me the pail of coffee at church."

"And you drank it even though it nearly ate a hole in your stomach."

"How did you know?"

"I visited Ellie Talbot yesterday, and Graham told me how the strong army coffee made you sick."

Samuel stood, took her hand, lifted her to her feet. Slid one arm around her waist and pulled her close. "I love the way you cover my mistakes, the way you love my daughter, the way your eyes shimmer in the moonlight…"

"I do love you, Samuel. And I love how you kiss me."

As Clarissa wrapped her arms around his neck, Samuel realized he'd come home. Home to love, to family. And when he kissed her, tasted the fruity sweetness of the tea and breathed in her flower perfume, his past turned loose of the hold it had on his heart for more years than he could remember.

Turned loose so he could love again.

When she kissed him back, he felt her change as well, her fears dissolving as she held him closer. He could become the man Clarissa needed—he could sense it.

One thing yet remained. He pulled away and gazed into those smiling hazel eyes of hers with their gleaming gilded flecks. "You became my wife—and Emma's mother—out of necessity. But could we start over now? Would you become my true wife—my chosen bride? Because you're the woman I've always been looking for."

He hesitated, in case he was moving too fast. "You know I've always been a man of action. Do you need time to think it over?"

"Not a single minute. I have a feeling my thinking-things-through days are over." Her smile widened, then she laughed her tinkling laugh that always brought more happiness than he had a right to feel.

For the first time he could remember, he didn't feel

like a failed father, a failed family man. The sparkle in Clarissa's eyes proved quite the contrary.

Perhaps it was time to take a hatchet to the trunk that held Grandmother's lavaliere…

Three weeks later, after a birthday breakfast prepared by Samuel and the children, Clarissa stepped out the back door, tranquility restored to Camellia Pointe. She allowed herself a moment to enjoy the peace before surveying the grounds one last time before all of Natchez would arrive for the Spring Festival.

And what a festival it would be. Croquet was set up for the first time since the war, to be removed before Samuel and Willie's late-afternoon swordplay demonstration. Refreshment tables and chairs waited in the pergola. A podium stood before a rise in the gardens from which the choirs would sing, and Sergeant John had found a little rowboat for romantic rides in the duck pond.

And the camellias bloomed as they hadn't in years.

Today would be nearly perfect.

Samuel, having gone to the sanctuary for prayer, now ambled her way, Honey nipping his heels. She smiled at his easy pace, his relaxed countenance. Was this the man who'd burst into Christ Church at a run a mere month ago, demanding action and demanding it now? Clarissa closed her eyes for a moment and thanked God for Samuel's newfound sense of peace, of calmness, unhurriedness. Camellia Pointe had been good for him.

Late in the afternoon, the Natchez Community Choir sang to a crowd that packed the grounds, the last choir in the contest. When the final tones faded away, they filed from the makeshift stage, but Samuel remained at the podium. Within moments, the judges handed an envelope to him, and he held it in the air.

"According to Mississippi Community Choir Association tradition, the host choirmaster announces the winner of the annual contest. However, this year, we have a special guest to do the honors. Please welcome the founder of the Association—Mister Barnabas Hezekiah Adams."

Clarissa's breath caught in her throat as she watched her father cross the lawn from the pergola. She clutched Emma's arm beside her for a moment, then ran toward him, the details of his face blurred by sudden tears in her eyes. Her father, home again, with her once more…

"Papa—"

At her shout, he turned in time to catch her in his arms.

After a moment, she released him and stood back to look at him. Still straight, still handsome, although gray at the temples and with crinkles around his eyes.

Papa kissed her cheek and whispered over the murmur of the crowd, "Little girl, you're as beautiful as your mother."

With a wink, he bounded up the slope and clasped Samuel's hand, then snatched the envelope from him. "The winner of the annual Mississippi Community Choir Association Contest is—" he ripped open the seal "—Natchez Community Choir, led by Choirmaster Montgomery with a duet by Missus Reverend Samuel Montgomery and Miss Emma Louise Montgomery."

Emma raced to Samuel's side and smothered him with a hug as Clarissa took the makeshift stage with her own father. Vaguely aware of Samuel's words of thanks and the treble-clef-shaped trophy he accepted, Clarissa kept her gaze upon her father, her attention on his voice.

"I should have come sooner." He ran his hand over her hair, just as he had when she was a girl. "The first year after your mother left us, I lived in a fog. The only place I could get any peace was at the Delta. Then, after so much time had gone by, I wanted to come back but didn't know how. I didn't know if you'd want me."

"I wanted you," Clarissa whispered.

"Then last week, when I got your letter and realized I'd missed your wedding, something broke in me. And you took on all the work of hosting the Festival just so you could see me. I knew then that I could come back, could ask you to allow me in your life again."

If something broke in her father, then it shattered to shards in her. He hadn't stayed away all these years because she hadn't been enough for him. "Will you stay?"

"For a while. The Delta will always be my home. But I'll be back. You can count on it."

That evening, when Samuel and Willie's swordplay demonstration was over and the crowd had dispersed, the entire household, along with Joseph, retreated to the drawing room. Seated between her father and Samuel on the velvet sofa, Clarissa told Papa of the events since Samuel had come to town, of the wedding, the will and the treasure.

"I can see Absalom figuring out that the gold was in the sanctuary, the same way you did." Papa leaned back against the cushion and patted Clarissa's hand, comforting her as he always had in the old days. "But how did he know Grandfather had hidden half the gold in the cemetery?"

"He must have followed me out there the day I took my bracelet from the secret compartment."

"But you didn't find the gold that day."

She shook her head. "I didn't know the stone had another, much larger, compartment underneath."

"Speaking of stones, I never understood why your father inscribed the sanctuary stone with only Lamentations 3:22, since his verse encompasses verse 23 as well," Samuel said.

"He was a stickler for scriptural accuracy," Papa said. "You must have missed it."

Willie leapt up from the windowsill, where he'd played with Honey. "I'll go look."

At least it gave the boy something to do.

"I'm disappointed to hear Absalom turned out the way he did. He lived like his namesake in the Bible, and his wild hair brought his demise as it did for the biblical Absalom," Papa said as Willie slammed the back door on his way out, Honey scrambling to keep up. "I'd hoped he'd turn out better than his father had, than any of the rest of the Poes, for that matter."

"The Poes? What have they to do with Absalom?" An image of the family of horse thieves and drunkards passed across Clarissa's mind. "Come to think of it, they have a lot in common."

"More than you think," Grandmother muttered under her breath, resting her hand on her chest.

Clarissa went to her side and knelt by her chair. "What is it, Grandmother? Are you well?"

"Better than you will be when I tell you about the Poes." She waved Clarissa away, so she returned to the sofa. "I heard what your father said to you about something having broken in him when Samuel told him of our problems here. And it broke me too."

She paused, drawing her handkerchief from her lacy sleeve and dabbing the corners of her eyes. "It's time you knew the truth. Nobody outside the family knows this, because my pride kept it hidden all these years. But Absalom's father, Ben, was not our son. He was a Poe."

A Poe. Not their son. Absalom was not her blood relation.

As the truth began to feel real, she glanced at Samuel, who winced, his eyes half closed as if the news hurt him.

"Ben's mother was dead and his father in prison, and we took him in. Your grandfather always hoped Absalom would repent of his sins and give his life to Jesus, and he prayed for him daily. But in case he didn't, he wanted the estate to go to you, since Absalom would waste it. He knew that, if Absalom had changed, you would share it with him. And God may yet answer our prayers for him."

"Go on, Euphemia," Joseph said. "Tell the rest."

Grandmother frowned at him a moment then stared straight ahead, looking at no one. "Clarissa, you asked why I said Absalom left us for dead during the epidemic that took your dear mother. Your grandfather, parents and I were still sick, along with more than half the town. But the doctors had run out of medicine. Absalom stole our calomel, sold it to the wealthiest families in town for hundreds of dollars, and ran off. Thus he left us for dead. It's a wonder any of us lived without our medicine. None of us saw him again until he barged into church."

Clarissa had no words.

"Emma," Grandmother said, "run to my room and bring me the small gold box on the top shelf of my wardrobe."

Emma shot out the back door to Grandmother's suite, now fumigated and reclaimed from Absalom.

"It's a relief to have all the family secrets out in the open, Grandmother." Now that their secrets and regrets lay behind them, they could all move on to a better life, a bigger life.

"That's not all of them," Grandmother said. "Samuel, the day you came to Natchez, you asked why I called you to this church when I didn't care for your grandfather. Well, that isn't entirely true."

He shot his gaze to her, frowned. "What isn't?"

"That I didn't care for Jonas Montgomery."

Emma came back in and gave the box to Grandmother Euphemia.

"Your grandfather and I courted for two years."

After a few seconds of sudden silence in the room, Clarissa realized her mouth was open, and she shut it. Courted—with Samuel's grandfather?

"I haven't opened this box in sixty-four years." She lifted the hinged lid and gazed at its contents. "Jonas shattered my heart when he broke our engagement and married my stepcousin, Esther, instead. It was Christmastime, and I had bought these cufflinks for him. Plain black onyx, appropriate for a minister of the Gospel."

Samuel coughed, shook his head. "I don't know what to say. I had no idea my grandfather would do such a thing."

"Don't let it tarnish your memory of him. He was a fine man, and we were young. I married well afterward and fell in love with my Hezekiah before our first month was out. Much as my granddaughter has done, but not as fast." She held out the box to Emma. "Give this to your father, sugar. They'll go well with his new Sunday suit."

Samuel accepted the gift, rose and kissed the elderly woman's cheek. "I'll wear them proudly."

After a moment, the back door opened and banged shut, breaking the mood.

"Miss Clarissa, look at this!" Willie dashed in, waving an envelope. He thrust it at her like a sword. "There was another loose stone, and this one had XXIII on it. It was so faint, I had to squint to see it. I climbed the tree and pulled out the stone, and this was in there."

Clarissa turned over the envelope. Her name was written on the front, in her grandfather's hand. She pulled out a hairpin, broke the seal and found a single sheet of paper and a lock of dark hair tied with a thin blue ribbon.

Her mother's, she was sure. Her fingers trembled as she ran them over the long strands of soft hair. Then she laid it on the arm of the sofa and opened the page.

Dearest Clarissa,

I'm sure your grandmother has explained why I insisted you and your cousin compete for my estate. I have every confidence in you and know you'll someday read this in my home, which you have won. But I also want you to know why I insisted you marry before inheriting.

I know how hard you took Harold Goss's betrayal. But he isn't worthy of you. I know things about him that you do not. Seeing you after his marriage, I feared you would harden your heart against men, against love. I wanted you to marry so you could learn to love a man. This is what happened to your grandmother as well, when her betrothed betrayed her. We have a happy marriage and I wish the same for you.

Your loving grandfather,
Hezekiah Daniel Adams

"Well, Father has done it again," Papa said, a catch in his voice. "Proven he is the wisest man in the family."

Later, upstairs in their suite, Samuel beckoned Clarissa to join him on the settee by the west window, the early evening sun shining in a thin light. "I found this in my coat pocket yesterday," he said, handing her an envelope. "It's your valentine."

She reached for it, couldn't help the smile blooming on her face. "You signed it, 'Fondly, Samuel.'"

"Foolish, I know. But what I wanted to write was, 'Yours forever, and yours alone.' That evening didn't go the way I'd hoped."

"I'm glad we had a second chance."

He drifted his arm about her shoulders in the darkening room. "Your father invited Miss Phemie and Emma to the Delta for the rest of the spring, before the summer heat. Can you let your grandmother go?"

She glanced around the room, the place where they had nearly lost each other. Now the place of her second chance. "I can. I will."

"No need to think it through first?"

"No need."

Samuel slid something from beneath the cushion and held it out to her. A green velvet box. "My grandmother asked me to give it to the woman who would fall in love with me."

Clarissa hastened to accept the box and open it. The emeralds inside gleamed in the last rays of the sun.

He lifted the lavaliere from the box. When he'd fastened it around her neck, he cradled her face in his hands, kissed her—the woman who'd fallen in love with him. He drew her closer, his past rolling away, the future beckoning from a place nearer than he'd have thought.

She finally pulled away, touching the green stones

that matched her eyes. Eyes that held a hint of a smile. “For a man of action, you took a long time to give this to me.”

“Not so long.” He gazed into the beautiful face of the woman who’d taught him how to wait, how to love. “Sometimes it takes a while to discover a second chance.”

* * * * *

If you liked this story,
pick up this other heartwarming book
from Christina Miller:

COUNTERFEIT COURTSHIP

Available now from Love Inspired Historical!

Find more great reads at www.LoveInspired.com

Dear Reader,

Thank you for reading my second Natchez story! Since my first visit there many years ago, Natchez has been an inspiration to me. The wealthiest city in the country before the War, Natchez has since struggled to survive. But its citizens decided to give it a second chance, working hard to restore the grand old homes there. Their Garden Club Spring Pilgrimage—the inspiration for Camellia Pointe's Spring Festival—draws droves of history lovers each year as the town opens their antebellum mansions for tours.

God offers us all a second chance—for eternal life, for love, for peace—as we place our trust in Jesus. My prayer is for you to discover that second chance as Samuel and Clarissa did, and to rest in God's love, knowing you are restored to Him.

I'd love to hear from you! Please contact me through Love Inspired, at https://www.facebook.com/christinalinstrotmiller or at @CLMauthor.

Christina Miller

COMING NEXT MONTH FROM
Love Inspired® Historical

Available March 6, 2018

FRONTIER MATCHMAKER BRIDE
Frontier Bachelors • by Regina Scott

When the most influential women in Seattle ask successful matchmaker Beth Wallin to find a wife for Deputy Sheriff Hart McCormick, she can't turn them down...even if the handsome lawman once refused her love. But when she realizes *she's* his best match, will she be able to convince him?

THE AMISH NANNY'S SWEETHEART
Amish Country Brides • by Jan Drexler

After moving in with her sister to act as nanny for her nieces and nephew, Judith Lapp doesn't expect to teach Pennsylvania Dutch to the *Englischer* across the road...or to fall for him. But will he put his past aside to embrace Amish life—and their love?

ACCIDENTAL FAMILY
The Bachelors of Aspen Valley • by Lisa Bingham

After newborn twins are left on his doorstep—along with a note begging him to protect them—Pastor Charles Wanlass marries mail-order bride Willow Granger to keep the babies safe. But can their temporary arrangement blossom into the forever family they both hope for?

HUSBAND BY ARRANGEMENT
by Angel Moore

Pregnant and abandoned by the man who promised to marry her, Rena Livingston must enter a marriage of convenience with Sheriff Scott Braden to save her reputation. The more time they spend together, though, the more she wishes theirs could be a true marriage...

SPECIAL EXCERPT FROM

Love Inspired® HISTORICAL

When the most influential women in Seattle ask successful matchmaker Beth Wallin to find a wife for deputy sheriff Hart McCormick, she can't turn them down...even if the handsome lawman once refused her love. But when she realizes she's his best match, will she be able to convince him?

Read on for a sneak preview of FRONTIER MATCHMAKER BRIDE by Regina Scott, *the next heartwarming book in the* ***FRONTIER BACHELORS*** *series, available March 2018 from Love Inspired Historical!*

"Beth, stay away from the docks. There are some rough sorts down there."

The two workers hadn't seemed all that rough to her. "You forget. I have five brothers."

"Your brothers are gentlemen. Some of those workers aren't."

She really shouldn't take Hart's statements as anything more than his duty as a lawman. "Very well. I'll be careful."

His gaze moved to the wharves, as if he saw a gang of marauding pirates rather than busy longshoremen. "Good. I wouldn't want anything to happen to you."

Beth stared at him.

"I'd hate to have to explain to your brothers," he added.

Well! She was about to tell him exactly what she thought of the idea when she noticed a light in his eyes. Was that a twinkle in the gray?

Beth tossed her head. "Oh, they'll take your side. You

LIHEXP0218

know they will. They always say I have more enthusiasm than sense."

He shrugged. "I know a few women who match that description."

Beth grinned. "But none as pretty as me."

"That's the truth." His gaze warmed, and she caught her breath. Hart McCormick, flirting with her? It couldn't be!

Fingers fumbling, she untied the horses and hurried for the bench. "I should go. Lots to do before two. See you at the Emporium."

He followed her around. Before she knew what he was about, he'd placed his hands on her waist. For one moment, she stood in his embrace. Her stomach fluttered.

He lifted her easily onto the bench and stepped back, face impassive as if he hadn't been affected in the slightest. "Until two, Miss Wallin."

Her heart didn't slow until she'd rounded the corner.

Silly! Why did she keep reacting that way? He wasn't interested in her. He'd told her so himself.

She was not about to offer him her heart. There was no reason to behave like a giddy schoolgirl on her first infatuation.

Even if he had been her schoolgirl infatuation.

She was a woman now, with opportunities, plans, dreams for a future. And she wasn't about to allow herself to take a chance on love again, especially not with Hart McCormick.

For now, the important thing was to find the perfect woman for him, and she knew just where to look.

Don't miss
FRONTIER MATCHMAKER BRIDE by Regina Scott,
available March 2018 wherever
Love Inspired® Historical books and ebooks are sold.

www.LoveInspired.com

LIHEXP0218